At HQN Books, we're dr

Of balmy breezes...endle... ... ... lounging on the sand.

But no summer vacation is complete without the perfect beach read. HQN is proud to offer six sizzling options from six *New York Times* bestselling authors. We hope you'll enjoy these excerpts from some of the many original titles we'll be publishing in summer 2008.

So join Gena Showalter on an incredible journey as six cursed immortal warriors—and the women who change their lives—travel the world on an ancient quest.

Follow Carly Phillips's small-town publicist as a new job at The Hot Zone shakes up her professional life...not to mention her personal one.

Watch Susan Mallery's sheltered concert pianist discover that the only sound more satisfying than music is a little *Sweet Talk*.

Cheer as Susan Andersen's uptight museum curator finally learns to cut loose—with a little help from one ridiculously sexy man.

Accompany Brenda Joyce's modern-day heroine on a riveting voyage through time to ancient Scotland, where a most unusual warrior waits.

Enjoy the best of both worlds as Christina Skye's newest navy SEAL hero embarks on a mission that leads him to Draycott Abbey...and to one unforgettable woman.

From darkly sensuous paranormal adventures to thrilling romantic suspense and breathtaking contemporary romance, HQN Books is delighted to offer something for every reader. So pull up a beach chair, break out the sunscreen and escape today with these six sexy reads—sure to keep the heat on all summer long!

Happy reading,

The Editors, HQN Books
www.HQNBooks.com

CONTENTS

H

NEW YORK TIMES BESTSELLING AUTHOR

Gena Showalter

Lords of the Underworld

THE DARKEST KISS

*He is ultimate darkness
and all-consuming desire...*

Dear Reader,

I'm thrilled to present my brand-new paranormal trilogy, LORDS OF THE UNDERWORLD, which began with *The Darkest Night* and continues with *The Darkest Kiss*. In a remote fortress in Budapest, six immortal warriors—each more dangerously seductive than the last—are bound by an ancient curse none has been able to break. When a powerful enemy returns, they will travel the world in search of a sacred relic of the gods—one that threatens to destroy them all.

Join me on a journey through this darkly sensual world, where the line between good and evil blurs and true love is put to the ultimate test.

Wishing you all the best,

Gena Showalter

PROLOGUE

HE WAS KNOWN AS THE Dark One. Malach ha-Maet. Yama. Azreal. Shadow Walker. Mairya. King of the Dead. He was all of those things and more, for he was a Lord of the Underworld.

Long ago he had opened *dimOuniak,* a powerful box made from the bones of a goddess, unleashing a horde of demons upon the earth. As punishment, he and the warriors who aided him were forced to house those demons inside themselves, melding light and darkness, order and chaos, until they were barely able to retain any tether on the disciplined warriors they'd once been.

Because he was the one to open the box, he had been given the demon of Death. A fair exchange, he supposed, for his action had nearly caused the demise of the world.

Now he was charged with the responsibility of collecting human souls and escorting them to their final resting place. Even if he opposed the idea. He did not like taking innocents from their families, found no joy in delivering the wicked to their damnation, but he did both without question or hesitation. Resistance, he'd soon learned, brought something far worse than death to his door. Resistance brought an agony so complete, so inexorable, even the gods trembled at the thought.

Did his obedience mean he was gentle? Caring? Nurturing? No. Oh, no. He could not afford softer emotion. Love, compassion and mercy were enemies to his plight.

Anger, though? Rage? *Those* he sometimes embraced.

Woe to anyone who pushed him too far, for man would become fully demon. A beast. A sinister entity who would not hesitate to curl his fingers around a human heart and squeeze. Squeeze so tightly that human would lose his breath and beg for the sweet kiss of eternal sleep only he could offer.

Oh, yes. Man had a very short leash on demon. And if you weren't careful, they would come for you....

CHAPTER ONE

ANYA, GODDESS OF ANARCHY, daughter of Lawlessness, and dealer of disorder, stood on the edge of a crowded dance floor. All of the dancers were human females, beautiful and nearly naked, chosen specifically by the Lords of the Underworld to provide the night's entertainment. Both vertical and horizontal.

Wisps of smoke cast a dream-fog around them, and pinpricks of starlight rained from the swirling strobe, illuminating everything inside the darkened nightclub in slow, sweeping circles. From the corner of her eye, she caught a scintillating glimpse of a taut immortal ass pounding forward, back, forward, into an ecstatic female.

My kind of party, she thought with a wicked grin. Not that she'd been invited.

Like anything could have stopped me from coming, though.

The Lords of the Underworld were delectable immortal warriors who were possessed by the demon spirits that had once resided inside Pandora's box. And now, with a few rounds of hard liquor and even harder sex, they were saying goodbye to Budapest, the city they'd called home for hundreds of years.

Anya wanted in on the action. With one warrior in particular.

"Part," she whispered, fighting her intrinsic compulsion to shout "Fire" instead and watch as the humans raced away in a panic, screaming hysterically. *Let the good times roll.*

An erratic pulse of rock music that matched the erratic beat of her heart blasted from the speakers, making it impossible for anyone to hear her. They obeyed, anyway, compelled on a level they probably didn't understand.

A path cleared, slowly…so slowly….

Finally the object of her fascination came into view. Heated breath caught in her lungs, and she shivered. Lucien. Deliciously scarred, irresistibly stoic and possessed by the spirit of Death. Right now he sat at a table in back, expression blank as he stared up at Reyes, his friend and fellow immortal.

What were they saying? If Lucien wanted the keeper of Pain to procure one of those mortal women for him, a false declaration of "fire" would be the least of their worries. Teeth grinding together, Anya tilted her head to the side, zoned in on them while discarding all surrounding noise, and listened.

"—she was right. I checked the satellite photos on Torin's computer. Those temples *are* rising from the sea." Reyes knocked back the contents of the silver flask he held. "One is in Greece and one is in Rome, and if they continue to rise at such a swift rate, they'll be high enough to explore sometime tomorrow."

"Why do humans not know about them?" Lucien scrubbed his jaw with two strong fingers, a habit of his. "Paris has watched the news stations and there has been nothing. Not even speculation."

Silly boy, she thought, relieved sex was not the night's topic. *You know about them only because I wanted you to know.* No one else would—or could—see them. She had made sure of that with a sweet little thing called chaos, her strongest source of power, hiding the temples with storms to keep humans away, while at the same time feeding the Lords enough information to draw them the hell out of Buda.

She wanted Lucien out of Buda and off his game. Just for a little while. A disconcerted man was easier to control.

Reyes sighed. "Perhaps the new gods are responsible. Most days I am sure they hate us and long to destroy us, simply for being half-demon."

Lucien's expression remained blank. "Does not matter who is responsible. We will travel in the morning as planned. My hands itch to search one of those temples."

Reyes tossed the now-empty flask onto the table. His fingers curled around the top of one of the chairs, his knuckles slowly bleaching of color. "If we're lucky, we'll find that damned box while we're there."

Anya ran her tongue over her teeth. Damned box, aka *dimOuniak*, aka Pandora's box. Constructed from the bones of the goddess of Oppression, the box was powerful enough to contain demons so vile even hell had not been able to hold them. It was also powerful enough to suck those same demons out of the Lords, their once unwilling hosts. Now these wonderfully aggressive warriors were dependent on the beasts for their survival, and needless to say, they wanted the box for themselves.

Again, Lucien nodded. "Do not think about that now; there'll be time enough for that tomorrow. Go and enjoy the rest of your evening. Do not waste another moment in my boring presence."

Boring? Ha! Anya had never met anyone who excited her more.

Reyes hesitated before ambling off, leaving Lucien alone. None of the human women approached him. Looked at him, yes. Cringed when they saw his scars, sure. But none of them wanted anything to do with him—and that saved their lives.

He's taken, biyatches.

"Notice me," Anya commanded softly.

A moment passed. He didn't obey.

Several humans glanced in her direction, heeding her demand, but Lucien's gaze latched on to the empty flask in front of him and remained, becoming a wee bit wistful. Much to her consternation, immortals were immune to her commands. A *courtesy* of the gods.

"Bastards," she muttered. Any restrictions they could place on her, they did. "Anything to screw with lowly Anarchy."

Anya hadn't been favored during her days on Mount Olympus. The goddesses had never liked her because they assumed she was a replica of her "whore of a mother" and would jump their husbands. Likewise, the gods had never respected her, again because of her mother. The guys *had* wanted her, though. Well, until she'd killed their precious Captain of the Guard and they'd deemed her too feral.

Idiots. The captain had deserved what she'd done to him. Hell, he'd deserved worse. The little shit had tried to rape her. If he had left her alone, she would have left *him* alone. But *noooo*. She didn't regret cutting the black heart out of his chest, didn't regret placing said heart on a pike in front of Aphrodite's temple. Not even a tiny bit. Freedom of choice was precious, and anyone who tried to take hers away would feel the sting of her daggers.

Choice. The word rang inside her mind, bringing her back to the present. What the hell would it take to convince Lucien to choose her?

"Notice me, Lucien. Please."

Once again, he ignored her.

She stomped her foot. For weeks she'd cloaked herself in invisibility, following Lucien, watching, studying. And yes, lusting. He'd had no idea she lurked nearby, even as she willed him to do all sorts of naughty things: strip, pleasure himself… smile. Okay, so the last wasn't naughty. But she'd wanted to see his beautifully flawed face light in humor just as much as she'd wanted to see his naked body glisten with arousal.

Had he granted even that benign request, though? No!

A part of her wished she'd never seen him, that she hadn't allowed Cronus, the new king of the gods, to intrigue her with stories about the Lords a few months ago. *Maybe* I'm *the idiot.*

Cronus had just escaped Tartarus, a prison for immortals and a place she knew intimately. He'd imprisoned Zeus and his cohorts there, as well as Anya's parents. When Anya returned for them, Cronus had been waiting for her. He had demanded Anya's greatest treasure. She'd declined—duh—so he'd tried to scare her.

Give me what I want or I'll send the Lords of the Underworld after you. They are demon-possessed, as blood-hungry as starving animals, and they will not hesitate to peel the lovely flesh from your bones. Blah, blah, blah. Whatever.

Far from frightening her, his words had caused excitement to bloom. She'd ended up seeking out the warriors on her own. She'd thought to defeat them and laugh in Cronus's face, a sort of look-what-I-did-to-your-big-scary-demons kind of thing.

One glance at Lucien, though, and she'd become

instantly obsessed. She'd forgotten her reasons for being there and had even *aided* the supposedly malevolent warriors.

It was just that contradictions tantalized her, and Lucien had so very many. He was scarred but not broken, kind but unbending. He was a calm, by-the-book immortal, not blood-hungry as Cronus had claimed. He was possessed by an evil spirit, yet he never deviated from his own personal code of honor. He dealt with death every day, every night, yet he fought to live.

Fascinating.

As if that wasn't enough to prick her interest, his flowery fragrance filled her with decadent, wicked thoughts every time she neared him. Why? Any other man who smelled like roses would have made her laugh. With Lucien, her mouth watered for a taste of him and her skin prickled with white-hot awareness, desperate for his touch.

Even now, simply looking at him and imagining that scent wafting to her nose, she had to rub her arms to rid herself of goose bumps. But then she thought about *him* rubbing her, and the delicious shivers refused to go away.

Gods, he was sexy. He had the freakiest eyes she'd ever seen. One was blue, the other brown, and both swirled with the essence of man and demon. And his scars... All she could think of, dream about, *crave,* was licking them. They were beautiful, a testament to all the pain and suffering he'd survived.

"Hey, gorgeous. Dance with me," one of the warriors suddenly said at her side.

Paris, she realized, recognizing the promise of sensuality in his voice. He must have finished screwing that human against the wall and was now looking for another bimbo to sate himself on. He'd just have to keep looking. "Go away."

Unaffected by her lack of interest, he grabbed her waist. "You'll like it, I swear."

She brushed him aside with a flick of her wrist. Possessed by Promiscuity, Paris was blessed with pale, almost glittery skin, electric-blue eyes, and a face the angels probably sang hallelujahs over, but he wasn't Lucien and he did nothing for her.

"Keep your hands to yourself," she muttered, "before I cut them off."

He laughed as if she were joking, unaware she'd do that and more. She might deal in petty disorder, but she never uttered a threat she didn't plan to see through. To do so smacked of weakness, and Anya had vowed long ago never to show a single hint of weakness.

Her enemies would love nothing more than to exploit it.

Thankfully, Paris didn't reach for her again. "For a kiss," he said huskily, "I'll let you do anything you want to my hands."

"In that case, I'll cut off your cock, too." She

didn't like having her ogling interrupted, especially since she rarely had time to indulge. Nowadays, she spent most of her waking hours dodging Cronus. "How's that?"

Paris's laughter intensified and managed to snag Lucien's attention. Lucien's gaze lifted, first landing on Paris, then locking on Anya. Her knees almost buckled. Oh, sweet heaven. Paris was forgotten as she fought to breathe. Did she imagine the fire that suddenly sparked in Lucien's mismatched eyes? Did she imagine the way his nostrils flared in awareness?

Now or never. Licking her lips, never removing her gaze from him, she eased into a sensual bump and grind and made her way toward his table. Halfway, she stopped and motioned for him to join her with a crook of her finger. He stood in front of her a moment later, as if he'd been pulled by an invisible chain, unable to resist.

Up close, he was six-feet-six of muscle and danger. Pure temptation.

Her lips edged into a slow smile. "We meet at last, Flowers."

Anya didn't give him time to respond. She ground her left hipbone against the hard juncture between his legs, turning erotically and presenting him with a view of her back. Her ice-blue corset was held together by nothing more than thin ribbons, and she knew her skirt hung so low on her waist that it failed to cover the bands of her thong. Oopsie.

Men, mortal or otherwise, usually melted when they caught a glimpse of something they shouldn't.

Lucien hissed in a breath.

Her smile widened. Ah, sweet progress.

Her unhurried movements were completely at odds with the fast-pounding rock, but she never ceased the slow gyrations of her body as she raised her hands over her head then leisurely ran them through the thick mass of her snow-white hair, down her arms, stroking her own skin but imagining his hands instead. Her nipples hardened.

"Why did you summon me, woman?" His voice was low, yet as disciplined as the warrior himself.

Listening to him speak was more arousing than being touched by another man, and her stomach clenched. "I wanted to dance with you," she said over her shoulder. Bump, bump, slllooow grind. "Is that a crime?"

He didn't hesitate with his answer. "Yes."

"Good. I've always enjoyed breaking the law."

A confused pause. Then, "How much did Paris pay you to do this?"

"I get paid? Oh, goodie!" Stepping back, grinning, she brushed her ass against him, arching and swinging as sensually as she was able. Hello, erection. The heat of him nearly liquefied her bones. "What's the currency? Orgasms?"

In her dreams, he always grabbed her and meshed the hard length of his cock into her at this point. In reality, he jumped backward as if she were a bomb about to detonate, creating more hated distance between them.

A sense of loss immediately blanketed her.

"No touching," he said. He'd probably done his best to sound calm, but he had sounded on edge. Strained. More tense than arousing.

Her eyes narrowed. All around, people watched their interaction and his rejection of her. *This isn't prime time,* she projected at them with a scowl. *Turn the fuck around.*

One by one, the humans obeyed. However, the rest of the Lords closed in on her, staring intently, no doubt curious as to who she was and what she was doing here.

They had to be careful, and she understood that. They were still pursued by Hunters, humans who foolishly believed they could create a utopia of peace and harmony by ridding the world of the Lords and the demons they carried inside them.

Ignore them. You're running out of time, chica. She returned her attention to Lucien by twisting her head to face him without actually turning all the way around. "Where were we?" she asked huskily. She ran a fingertip over the top band of her thong, not stopping until she drew the hot focus of his gaze to the glittery angel wings in the center.

"I was just about to walk away," he choked out.

At his words, her nails elongated into little claws. He still thought to deny her? Seriously?

She'd shown herself to him, even knowing that the gods would be able to pinpoint her exact location—something it was best to avoid since they planned to snuff her out like a mangy animal. She would *not* leave this club without a reward.

Determination intensifying, she swung around with another roll of her hips, the length of her pale hair caressing his chest. As she nibbled on her bottom lip, she plumped her breasts. "But I don't want you to leave," she said with a practiced pout.

He backed up another step.

"What's wrong, sweetness?" Merciless, she moved forward. "Afraid of a little girl?"

His lips thinned, but he didn't reply. Thankfully, he didn't move farther away, either.

"Are you?"

"You have no idea at what game you play, woman."

"Oh, but I think I do." Her gaze swept over him, and she stilled in renewed amazement. He was utterly magnificent. Rainbow-colored strobe lights rained down his face and body, a body so finely sculpted it could have been chiseled from stone. He wore a black tee and stone-washed jeans, and both hugged rope after rope of hand-over-your-panties muscle. *Mine.*

"I said no touching," he barked.

Her gaze snapped back to his and she held up her hands, palms out. "I'm not touching you, sweet-cakes." *But I want to…I plan to…I will.*

"Your gaze suggests otherwise," he said tightly.

"That's because—"

"I'll dance with you," another warrior said, cutting her off. Paris again.

"No." Anya didn't switch her attention. She wanted Lucien and only Lucien. No one else would do.

"Could be Bait," a different Lord piped in, probably eyeing her with suspicion. She recognized the deep timbre of his voice. Sabin, keeper of Doubt.

Please. Bait? As if she would try to lure anyone anywhere for reasons that weren't completely selfish. Bait, stupid girls that they were, were all about self-sacrifice; their job was to seduce a Lord to distraction so Hunters could sneak in and slay him. And really, what kind of moron wanted to kill the Lords rather than make out with them a little?

"I doubt Hunters were able to assemble so quickly after the plague," Reyes said.

Oh, yes. The plague. One of the Lords was possessed by the demon of Disease. If he touched any mortal skin-to-skin, he infected that person with a terrible sickness that spread and killed with amazing swiftness.

Knowing this, Torin always wore gloves and rarely left the fortress, willingly keeping to himself to protect humans from his curse. Not his fault a group of Hunters had sneaked inside the fortress a few weeks ago and cut his throat.

Torin had survived; the Hunters had not.

Unfortunately, there were many, many more

Hunters out there. Seriously, they were like flies. Swat one away, and two more soon took its place. Even now, they were out there somewhere, waiting for a chance to strike. The Lords had to remain cautious.

"Besides, there's no way they could have figured out a way to bypass our security," Reyes added, his harsh voice drawing Anya from her thoughts.

"Just like there's no way they could get into the fortress and nearly behead Torin?" Sabin replied.

"Damn this! Paris, stay here and watch her while I check the perimeter." Footsteps, muttered curses.

Well, shit. If the warriors found any trace of Hunters out there, there'd be no convincing them of her innocence. Of that crime, at least. Lucien would never trust her, never relax around her. Never touch her except in anger.

She didn't allow her trepidation to play over her face. "Maybe I saw the crowd and snuck in," she told Paris and another Lord who was studying her, adding tightly, "And maybe the big guy and I can go the next few minutes without an interruption. In private."

They might have gotten the hint, but they didn't leave.

Fine. She'd work around them.

As she began to once again rock softly to the beat, she kept her gaze on Lucien and caressed her fingers down the planes of her stomach. *Replace my hands with yours,* she projected.

Of course, he didn't. But his nostrils did that delicious flare as his eyes followed every movement of her palms. He swallowed.

"Dance with me." This time, she said the words aloud, hoping he would not so easily ignore her. She licked her lips, moistening them.

"No." Hoarse, barely audible.

"Pretty please, with a cherry on top of me."

His eyes flickered with fiery provocation. Not her imagination, she realized. Hope flooded her. But when several seconds ticked by and he failed to reach out for her, that hope turned to frustration. Time really was her enemy. The longer she stayed here, the greater her chance of being caught.

"Do you not find me desirable, Flowers?"

A muscle ticked below his eye. "That is not my name."

"Fine, then. Do you not find me desirable, muffin?"

The ticking spread to his jaw. "What I find you matters little."

"That doesn't really answer my question," she said, close to pouting again.

"Nor was it meant to."

Grrr! What an infuriating man. *Try something else. Something blatant.*

As if I haven't been blatant already.

Alrightie, then. She turned and bent down to the floor. Her skirt rode up her thighs and gave him another, better, glimpse of her blue thong and the wings stretching from the center. As she pushed to a stand, mimicking the motions of sex as she did so, she slowly circled, offering a lingering full-body shot.

He sucked in a breath, every muscle in his powerful body tense. "You smell like strawberries and cream." As he spoke, he looked like a predator about to pounce.

Please, please, please, she thought. "Bet I taste like it, too," she said, batting her lashes despite the fact that he'd made the fragrance seem like a horrendous affront.

He growled low in his throat and took a menacing step toward her. He raised his hand to—grab her? Hit her? Whoa, what was *that* about?—before stopping himself and fisting his fingers. Before remarking on her scent, he'd been distant but maybe-kinda-sorta interested. Now he only seemed interested in throttling her.

"You're lucky I do not strike you down here and now," he said, proving her thoughts. Still, his hand lowered to his side.

Anya ceased moving, staring up at him in openmouthed astonishment. Because she smelled like fruit, he wanted to hurt her? That was—that was supremely…disappointing. Her mind had tried to supply the word *devastating,* but she'd cut it off. She barely knew the man; he couldn't devastate her.

Wasn't like she'd expected him to fall at her feet, but she *had* expected him to respond favorably. At least a little.

Men liked women who threw themselves at them.

Right? She'd observed mortals for too many years to count, and that had always seemed to be the case. *Key word, chica—mortals.* Lucien wasn't, and had never been, mortal.

Why doesn't he want me?

In all the days she'd watched him, he hadn't favored a single woman. Ashlyn, his friend's lover, he treated with kindness and respect. Cameo, the only female warrior in residence here, he treated with gentleness and almost parental concern. Not desire.

He didn't prefer men. His gaze didn't linger on males with hunger or any hint of softer emotion. Was he in love with a specific woman, then, and no other would do? If so, the bitch was going down!

Anya ran her tongue over her teeth, and her hands clenched at her sides. Smoke continued to billow through the building, hazy, dreamlike. The human females began to crowd the dance floor again, trying to lure the Lords back to their sides. But the warriors continued to observe Anya, waiting for the final verdict of just who and what she was.

Lucien hadn't moved an inch; it was as if his entire body were rooted in place. She should give up, walk away, cut her losses before Cronus found her. *Only the weak give up.* True. Determined, she raised her chin. With only a thought, she changed the song blasting through the speakers. The beat instantly slowed, softened.

Forcing her expression to follow suit, she sauntered the rest of the way to him, closing that hated distance between them. She trekked her fingers up his strong, hard chest and shivered. No touching—ha! He would learn. Anarchy was hardly an obedient lapdog.

He didn't pull away, at least.

"You're going to dance with me," she purred. "That's the only way to get rid of me." Just to taunt him further, she stood on her tiptoes and gently bit his earlobe.

There was a rumble in his throat as his arms finally wrapped around her. At first she thought he meant to push her away. Then he jerked her deeper into the curve of his body, flattening her breasts against his torso and forcing her legs to straddle his left thigh. That quickly, she was wet.

"You want to dance, then we will dance." Slowly, decadently, he swayed her side to side, their bodies staying meshed together, her core rubbing just above his knee. Spears of pleasure ignited, traveling through her bloodstream and leaving no part of her unaffected.

Gods in heaven, this was better than she'd imagined. Her eyes closed in surrender. He was big. Everywhere. His shoulders were so wide they dwarfed her; his upper body so muscled it enveloped her. And all the while, his warm exhalations caressed her cheek like an attentive lover. Trembling, she moved her hands up his back and tangled them in his dark, silky hair. *Yes. More.*

Slow down, girlie. Even if he wanted her the way she wanted him, she couldn't have him. Not fully. In that respect, she was as cursed as he. But she could still enjoy the moment. Oh, could she enjoy it. Finally, he was responding to her!

His nose nuzzled her jawline. "Every man in this building wants you," he said softly, yet his words were so sharp they could have cut like a knife. "Why me?"

"Just because," she said, inhaling his heady rose perfume.

"That answers nothing."

"Nor was it meant to," she said, parroting his earlier words. Her nipples were still hard, so hard, and rubbing against her corset, enhancing her desire. Her skin was wonderfully sensitive, her mind hyperaware of Lucien's every move. Had anything ever felt so erotic? So… right?

Lucien gripped her hair tightly, almost pulling some of the strands from her scalp. "Do you find it amusing to tease the ugliest man here?"

"Ugliest?" When he appealed to her as no one else ever had? "But I'm nowhere near Paris, sugarpop."

That gave him pause. He frowned and released her. Then he shook his head, as if trying to clear it. "I know what I am," he growled with the faintest trace of bitterness. "Ugly is being kind."

She stilled, peering into his seductive bi-colored eyes. Did he truly have no idea of his attractiveness?

He radiated strength and vitality. He exuded savage masculinity. Everything about him enthralled her.

"If you know what you are, sweetness, then you know you're sexy and deliciously menacing." And she needed more of him. Another of those shivers raked her spine, vibrating into her limbs. *Touch me again.*

He glared down at her. "Menacing? Does that mean you want me to hurt you?"

Slowly she grinned. "Only if it involves spanking."

His nostrils flared again. "I suppose my scars do not bother you," he said, completely devoid of emotion now.

"Bother me?" Those scars didn't ruin him. They made him irresistible.

Closer…closer… Yes, contact. Oh, great gods! She glided her hands over his chest, luxuriating in the feel of his nipples as they reached for her, savoring the ropes of strength that greeted her. "They turn me on."

"Liar," he said.

"Sometimes," she admitted, "but not about this." She studied his face. However he'd gotten the scars could not have been pleasant. He'd suffered. A lot. The knowledge suddenly angered her as much as it entranced her. Who had hurt him and why? A jealous lover?

Looked like someone had taken a blade and carved Lucien up like a melon, then tried to put him back together with the pieces out of order. Still, most immortals healed quickly, leaving no evidence of their injuries. So even if he had been carved up, Lucien should have healed.

Did he have similar scars on the rest of his body? Her knees weakened as a new tide of arousal flooded her. She'd watched him for weeks, but she hadn't gotten a single peek at his delectable form. Somehow, he'd always managed to bathe and change after she left.

Had he sensed her and kept himself hidden?

"If I didn't know better, I would think you were Bait, as my men do," he said tightly.

"And what makes you know better?"

He arched a brow. "Are you?"

Had to venture down that road, did you? If she assured him she wasn't Bait, she would seem to be admitting that she knew what Bait was. She thought she knew him well enough to know that, in his eyes, the acknowledgment would negate the claim that she wasn't. He would then feel obligated to kill her. If she claimed that she *was* Bait, well, he would still feel obligated to kill her.

Total lose-lose.

"Do you want me to be?" she said in her most seductive tone. "'Cause I'll be anything you want, lover."

"Stop," he growled, that ever-calm mask loosening its hold on his features for the briefest of moments and revealing a stunningly intense fire. Oh, to be burned. "I do not like this game you are playing."

"No game, Flowers. I promise you."

"What do you want from me? And do not dare lie."

Now, there was a loaded question. She wanted all of his masculinity focused on her. She wanted hours to strip and explore him. She wanted him to strip and explore her. She wanted him to smile at her. She wanted his tongue in her mouth.

At this point, only the last seemed achievable. And only by playing unfairly. Good thing Devious was her middle name.

"I'll take a kiss," she said, gazing at his soft, pink mouth. "Actually, I insist on a kiss."

"I didn't find any Hunters nearby," Reyes said, suddenly standing beside Lucien.

"That doesn't mean anything," Sabin replied.

"She's not a Hunter and she is not working with them." Lucien's attention never wavered from her as he waved his friends back. "I need a moment alone with her."

His assurance stunned her. And he wanted to be alone with her? Yes! Except his friends stayed put. Jerks.

"We are strangers," Lucien told her, continuing their conversation as if it had never ceased.

"So? Strangers hook up all the time." She arched her back, pressing the core of her into his erection. Mmm, erection. He hadn't lost it, was still aroused. "There's no harm in a little bittie kiss, is there?"

His fingers sank into the curve of her waist, holding her still. "You will leave? After?"

His words should have offended her, but she was too caught up in the tide of pleasure that simple embrace elicited to care. All of her pulse points began a wild dance. A strange, luscious warmth fluttered inside her stomach.

"Yes." That's all she could have from him, anyway, no matter how much she desired more. And she'd take it any way she could get it: coercion, force, trickery. She was tired of imagining his kiss and craved the reality of it. *Had* to have the reality of it. Finally. Surely he would not taste as amazing as she dreamed.

"I do not understand this," he muttered, eyes closing to half-mast. Dark lashes cast shadows over his jagged cheeks, making him appear more danger-ous than ever.

"That's okay. I don't, either."

He leaned into her, hot, floral-scented breath scorch-ing her skin. "What will a single kiss accomplish?"

Everything. Anticipation beating through her, she traced the tip of her tongue along the seam of her lips. "Are you always this talkative?"

"No."

"Kiss her, Lucien, before I do. Bait or not," Paris called with a laugh. Good-natured as the laugh was, it was still edged with steel.

Lucien continued to resist. She could feel his heart beating against his ribs. Was he embarrassed by their audience? Too bad. She'd risked everything for this, and she wasn't about to let him back out now.

"This is futile," he said.

"So what. Futile can be fun. Now, no more stalling. Only doing." Anya jerked his head down to hers and smashed her lips against his. His mouth instantly opened, and their tongues met in a deep, wet thrust. There was an intense rush of heat through her as the addictive flavor of roses and mint bombarded her.

She pressed deeper, needing more of him. All of him. Plumes of fire infused her entire body. She rubbed against his cock, unable to stop herself. He fisted her hair, taking complete control of her mouth. Just like that, she was caught in a whirlwind of passion and thirst only Lucien could quench. She'd entered the gates of heaven without taking a single step.

Someone cheered. Someone whistled.

For a moment, she felt as if her feet were swept off the ground and she was without any kind of anchor. A moment later, her back was shoved against a cold wall. The cheers had somehow suddenly died. Frigid air nipped at her skin.

Outside? she wondered. Then she was moaning, unconcerned, and winding her legs around Lucien's waist as his tongue conquered hers. One of his hands crushed her hip in a bruising grip—gods, she loved it—and the other tunneled through her hair, fingers once again curling tightly around the thick mass and angling her head to the side for deeper contact.

"You are—you are—" he whispered fiercely.

"Desperate. No talking. More kissing."

His control vanished. His tongue thrust back inside her mouth, their teeth banging together. Passion and arousal were a hot blaze between them, a raging inferno. Truly, she was on fire. Frantic. Achy. He was all over her, already a part of her.

She never wanted it to end.

"More," he said roughly, palming her breast.

"Yes." Her nipples tightened, throbbing for his touch. "More, more, more."

"So good."

"Amazing."

"Touch me," he growled.

"Am."

"No. *Me*."

Understanding dawned, and with it an intensification of her desire. Maybe he did want her. After all, he yearned to have her hands on his skin, which meant he longed for more than just a kiss.

"My pleasure." With one hand, she gripped the hem of his shirt and lifted. With the other, she caressed the ropes of his stomach. Scars. She felt scars and shivered, the jagged tissue wonderfully hot.

His muscles clenched against each stroke, and he bit her bottom lip. "Yes, like that."

She almost came, his reaction like fuel to an already blazing fire. She did moan.

Her fingers traced the circle of his nipples before

dabbling at the tips. Each time she grazed them, her clitoris throbbed as if she were touching herself. "I love the feel of you."

Lucien licked his way down the column of her throat, his tongue leaving a trail of sensual lightning. Her eyelids cracked open, and she nearly gasped when she realized they were indeed outside, leaning against the club's exterior in a shadowed corner. He must have flashed them there, the naughty boy.

He was the only Lord capable of transporting himself from one location to another with only a thought. A skill she possessed, as well. She only wished he'd flashed them to a bedroom.

No, she forced herself to add, fighting a wave of despair. Bedroom bad. Bad, bad, bad. Bad Anya for thinking otherwise, even for a second. Other women could enjoy the electric press of skin against skin and naked bodies straining for release, but not Anya. Never Anya.

"I want you," he bit out roughly.

"About time," she whispered.

He raised his darkly haloed head, blue and brown irises intense, before pinning her with another scorching kiss. On and on it continued, until she was willingly, blissfully drowning in him. Branded to her very soul, where she was no longer Anya but Lucien's woman. Lucien's slave. She might never get enough of him, would have allowed him to penetrate her then and there if she'd been able. Gods, reality was so much better than fantasy.

"I need to feel more of you. I need your hands on me." She dropped her legs from him, standing, and was just reaching for his fly, wanting to free his cock and wrap her fingers around its swollen thickness, when she heard a nearby echo of footsteps.

Lucien must have heard them, too. He stiffened and jerked away from her.

He was panting. So was she. Her knees almost buckled as their gazes locked together, time momentarily suspended. Passion-lightning still sparked between them; never would she have guessed a kiss could be that combustible.

"Right your clothing," he commanded.

"But…but…" She wasn't ready to stop, audience or not. If he'd just give her a moment, she could flash them someplace else.

"Do it. Now."

No, there would be no flashing, she realized with disappointment. His hard expression proclaimed he was done. With the kiss, with her.

Tearing her gaze from him, she looked down at herself. Her top had been anchored underneath her breasts. She wasn't wearing a bra, so the hardened pink tips of her nipples were visible, two little beacons in the night. Her skirt was around her waist, showing off the front of that barely-there thong.

She smoothed her outfit, blushing for the first

time in hundreds of years. *Why now? Does it matter?*
Her hands were shaking, an embarrassing weakness.
She tried to will them to stop, but the only command
her body wanted to hear was to jump back into
Lucien's arms.

Several of the Lords rounded the corner, each
glaring and sullen.

"I love it when you disappear like that," the one
called Gideon said, his irritated tone making it clear
he didn't love it at all. He was possessed by the spirit
of Lies, Anya knew, so he wasn't capable of uttering
a single truth.

"Shut up," Reyes snapped. Poor, tortured Reyes,
keeper of Pain. He liked to cut himself. Once, she'd
even seen him jump from the top of the warriors'
fortress and luxuriate in the feel of his broken
bones. "She might appear innocent, Lucien, but you
failed to check her for weapons before you swallowed her tongue."

"I'm practically naked," she pointed out, exasper-
ated. Not that anyone paid her any heed. "What
weapon could I possibly be hiding?" Okay, so she *was*
hiding a few. Big deal. A girl had to protect herself.

"I had everything under control," Lucien said in
that unaffected voice of his. "I think I can handle one
lone female, armed or not."

Anya had always been fascinated by his calmness.
Until now. Where was his lingering passion? Wasn't
fair that he'd recovered so quickly while she still

struggled for breath. Her limbs hadn't even stopped trembling. Worse, her heart pounded like a war drum in her chest.

"So who is she?" Reyes asked.

"She might not be Bait, but she's something," Paris said. "You flashed her, but she isn't screaming."

That's when all of their narrowed gazes finally shifted to Anya. She'd never felt more raw, more vulnerable, in all the centuries of her life. Kissing Lucien had been worth the risk of capture, but that didn't mean she had to endure an interrogation. "All of you can just shut it. I'm not telling you a damn thing."

"I didn't invite you, and Reyes told me no one here claims you as a friend," Paris said. "Why did you attempt to seduce Lucien?"

Because no one would *freely* consort with the scarred warrior, his tone proclaimed. That irritated her, even though she knew he hadn't meant it to be rude or hurtful, was probably just stating what all of them considered fact.

"What's up with the third degree?" One by one, she glared at them. Everyone but Lucien. Him, she avoided. She might crumble if his features were still cold and emotionless. "I saw him, he appealed to me, so I went after him. Big deal. End of story."

Each of the Lords crossed their arms over their chests, a yeah-right action. They'd formed a semicircle around her, she realized then, though she'd never seen them move. She barely managed to stop herself from rolling her eyes.

"You don't really want him," Reyes said. "We all know that. So tell us what you do want before we *force* you to tell us."

Force her? Please. She, too, crossed her arms. A short while ago, they'd cheered for Lucien to kiss her. Hadn't they? Maybe she had cheered for herself. But now they wanted a play-by-play of her thought process? Now they acted as if Lucien could not tempt a blind woman? "I wanted his cock inside me. You get it now, asshole?"

There was a shocked pause.

Lucien stepped in front of her, blocking her from the men. Was he...protecting her? How utterly sweet. Unnecessary, but sweet. Some of her anger evaporated. She wanted to hug him.

"Leave her alone," Lucien said. "She doesn't matter. She's unimportant."

Anya's happy buzz evaporated, too. Doesn't matter? Unimportant? He'd just held her breast in his hand and rubbed his erection between her legs. How dare he say something like that?

A red haze winked over her vision. *This must be how my mother always felt.* Nearly all the men Dysnomia had taken to bed had hurled insults at the woman when their pleasure had been sated. *Easy,* they'd said. *Not good for anything else.*

Anya knew her mother well, knew Dysnomia had

been slave to her lawless nature, as well as simply looking for love. Mated gods, single gods, it hadn't mattered. If they had desired her, she had given herself to them. Probably because for those few hours in her lovers' arms, she had been accepted, cherished, her darker urges sated.

Which made the betrayal afterward all the more painful, Anya thought, eyeing Lucien. Of all the things she'd expected and yearned for him to say, *unimportant* hadn't been close. *She's mine,* maybe. *I need her,* perhaps. *Don't touch my property,* definitely.

She hadn't wanted the same life as her mother, much as she loved her, and had vowed long ago never to let herself be used. *But look at me now. I begged and pleaded for Lucien's kiss, and he never saw me as anything more than* unimportant.

Growling, channeling all of her considerable strength, fury and hurt, she shoved him. He propelled forward like a bullet from a gun and slammed into Paris. Both men *hmphed* before ricocheting apart.

When Lucien righted himself, he whipped around to face her. "There will be none of that."

"Actually, there's going to be a lot more of that." She stalked toward him, fist raised. Soon he would be swallowing his perfect white teeth.

"Anya," he said, her name a husky entreaty. "Stop."

She froze, shock thickening every drop of blood in her veins. "You know who I am." A statement, not a question. "How?" They'd spoken once, weeks ago, but he'd never seen her before today. She'd made sure of it.

"You have been following me. I recognized your scent."

Strawberries and cream, he'd said earlier, accusation in his voice. Her eyes widened. Pleasure and mortification blended, spearing her all the way to the bone. All along, he'd known she was watching him.

"Why did I get the third degree if you knew who I was? And why, if you knew I was following you, didn't you ask me to show myself?" The questions lashed from her with stinging force.

"One," he said, "I did not realize who you were until after the discussion about Hunters had taken place. Two, I did not wish to scare you away until I learned your purpose." He paused, waited for her to speak. When she didn't, he added, "What is your purpose?"

"I—you—" Damn it! What should she tell him? "You owe me a favor! I saved your friend, freed you from his curse." There. Rational and true and hopefully would move the conversation away from her motives.

"Ah." He nodded, his shoulders stiffening. "Everything makes sense now. You've come for payment."

"Well, no." Much as it would have saved her pride, she suddenly realized she didn't want him thinking she gave her kisses away so easily. "Not yet."

His brow furrowed. "But you just said—"

"I know what I said."

"Why have you come, then? Why stalk my every waking moment?"

She pressed her tongue to the roof of her mouth, her frustration renewed. There was no time to reply, however, as Reyes, Paris and Gideon closed in on her. All three were scowling. Did they think to grab her and keep her still?

Rather than answer Lucien, she snapped at the men, "What? I don't recall inviting you into the conversation."

"You are Anya?" Reyes eyed her up and down, his revulsion clear.

Revulsion? He should be grateful! Hadn't she liberated him from the curse that had forced him to stab his BFF every night? Yes, damn it. She had. But his look was one she knew well, and one that never failed to raise her hackles. Because of her mother's amorous past and the widespread expectation that she, with her free-spirited ways, would follow suit, every Greek god in Olympus had projected that same sort of revulsion at her at one time or another.

At first, Anya had been hurt by their smug disdain. And for several hundred years, she'd tried the good-girl thing: dressing like a freaking nun, speaking only when spoken to, keeping her gaze downcast. Somehow she'd even squelched her desperate need for disaster. All to earn the respect of beings who would never see her as anything more than a whore.

One fateful day, when she'd come home from

stupid goddess training, crying because she'd smiled at Ares and that bitch Artemis had called her *ta ma de*, Dysnomia had pulled her aside. *Whatever you do, however you act, they are going to judge you harshly,* the goddess had said. *But we all must be true to our own nature. Acting as anyone other than yourself merely brings* you *pain and makes you appear ashamed of who and what you are. Others will feed off that shame, and soon it will be all that you are. You are a wonderful being, Anya. Be proud of who you are. I am.*

From then on, Anya had dressed as sexily as she pleased, talked whenever and however she wanted and refused to look at her feet for any reason other than admiring her strappy stilettos. No longer had she denied her need for disorder. An offhand way of saying "fuck you" to the ones who rejected her, yes, but more importantly, she *liked* who she was.

She would never be ashamed again.

"It is…interesting to see you in the flesh after all the research I've done on you lately. You are the daughter of Dysnomia," Reyes continued. "You are the minor goddess of Anarchy."

"There's nothing minor about me." Minor meant unimportant, and she was just as important as the other, "higher" beings, damn it. But because no one knew who her father was—well, she did, *now*—she had been relegated as such. "But yeah. I am a goddess." She raised her chin, showing him no emotion.

"The night you made yourself known to us and saved Ashlyn's life, you told us that you were not," Lucien said. "You told us you were merely an immortal."

She shrugged. She hated gods so much she rarely used that title. "I lied. I often do. It's part of my charm, don't you think?"

No one replied. Figured.

"We were once warriors for the gods and lived in the heavens, as I'm sure you know," Reyes said as if she hadn't spoken. "I do not remember you."

"Maybe I wasn't born yet, smartie."

Irritation flickered in his dark eyes, but he continued calmly. "As I told you, since your appearance weeks ago I have been researching you, learning everything I can. Long ago, you were imprisoned for murdering an innocent man. Then, a hundred years or so after your confinement, the gods finally agreed on the proper punishment for you. Before they could carry out the verdict, however, you did something no other immortal had ever managed to do. You escaped."

She didn't try to deny it. "Your research is correct." For the most part.

"Legend claims you infected the keeper of Tartarus with some kind of disease, for immediately after your escape he weakened and lost his memory. Guards were placed in every corner to fortify security, as the gods feared the strength of the prison depended on the strength of its keeper. Over time the walls *did* begin to crumble and crack, which eventually led to the escape of the Titans."

Gonna blame that on her, was he? Her eyes narrowed. "The thing about legends," she said flatly, "is that the truth is often distorted to explain the things that mortals cannot understand. Funny that you, the subject of so many legends, don't know that."

"You hid here, among humans," Reyes said, ignoring her. Again. "But you weren't content to live in peace even then. You started wars, stole weapons and even ships. You caused major fires and other disasters, which in turn led to mass panic and rioting among the humans, and hundreds of people being imprisoned."

Warmth suffused her face. Yes, she'd done those things. When she'd first come to earth, she hadn't known how to control her rebellious nature. Gods had been able to protect themselves from it, humans hadn't. Besides that, she'd been almost…feral from her years in prison. A simple comment from her— you aren't going to let your brother talk to you like that, are you?—and bloody feuds erupted between clans. An appearance at court—perhaps laughing at the rulers and their policies—and loyal knights attempted to assassinate their king.

As for the fires, well, something inside her had compelled her to "accidentally" drop torches and watch the flames dance. And the stealing…she'd been unable to fight the voice in her head that whispered, *Take it. No one will know.*

Eventually she'd learned that if she fed her need for disorder with little things—petty theft, white lies and the occasional street fight—huge disasters could be averted.

"I did my homework on you, too," she said softly. "Did you not once destroy cities and kill innocents?"

Now Reyes blushed.

"You are not the same man you used to be, just as I am not—" Before she'd completed the sentence, a sudden wind blustered around them, whistling and harsh. Anya blinked against it, confused for only a moment. "Damn it!" she spat, knowing what would come next.

Sure enough, the warriors froze in place as time ceased to exist for them, a power greater than themselves taking hold of the world around them. Even Lucien, who'd been carefully watching her exchange with Reyes, turned to living stone.

Hell, she did, too.

Oh, no, no, no, she thought, and with the words, the invisible prison bars fell away from her like leaves from a winter tree. Nothing and no one could hold her prisoner. Not anymore. Her father had made sure of that.

Anya walked to Lucien to try to free him—why, she didn't know, after the things he'd said of her—but the wind ceased as suddenly as it had appeared. Her mouth dried, and her heart began an unsteady tango in her chest. Cronus, who had taken over the heavenly throne mere months ago, bringing new rules, new desires and new punishments, was about to arrive.

He'd found her.

Freaking great. As a bright blue light appeared in front of her, chasing away the darkness and humming with unimaginable power, she flashed away. With a sense of regret she had no business feeling, she left Lucien behind—taking the taste and memory of their kiss with her.

CHAPTER TWO

A BLACK FOG HAD DESCENDED over Lucien, locking his mind on a single thought: *Anya.*

He'd been in the middle of a conversation with her, trying to forget how perfectly she had fit against him, how razor-sharp his desire for her had been, and how, in the too-short minutes she'd been in his arms, he would have betrayed everyone he knew for a little more time with her.

Never had a kiss affected him more. His demon had actually purred inside his head. Purred. Like a tamed housecat. Such a thing had never happened before, and he did not understand why it had tonight.

Something must be wrong with him.

Why else would saying Anya meant nothing, *was* nothing, have nearly killed him? But he'd had to say it. For her benefit, and for his own. Such need was dangerous. And to admit to it, lethal to his infamous control.

Control. He would have snorted if he'd been capable of movement. Clearly he'd had no control with that woman.

Why had she pretended to want him? Why had she kissed him as if she'd die without his tongue? Women simply did not crave him like that. Not anymore. He knew that better than anyone. Yet Anya had practically begged him for more.

And now he could not remove her image from his head. She was tall, the perfect height, with a perfect pixie face and perfect sun-kissed-and-cream skin, smooth and shimmering, mouthwateringly erotic. He imagined laving every inch with his tongue.

Her breasts had nearly spilled from the cerulean half corset she'd worn, and mile after mile of delectable thigh had been visible thanks to her black miniskirt and high-heeled black boots.

Her hair was so pale it was like a snowstorm as it tumbled in waves down her back. Her eyes were wide and the same cerulean shade as her top. Uptilted nose. Full and red, made-for-sucking lips. Straight white teeth. She'd radiated wickedness and pleasure, every male fantasy come to glittery life.

Actually, he had not been able to remove her from his head since she'd entered their lives weeks ago and saved Ashlyn. She had not revealed her luscious beauty then, but her strawberry scent had branded him all the way to the bone.

Now, having tasted her, Lucien felt his heart pound in his chest and breath burn in his throat, blistering, sizzling. He experienced the same sensation when he glimpsed his friends Maddox and Ashlyn together, cooing, snuggling close, almost as if they were afraid to let go of each other.

Unexpectedly the fog lifted, at last freeing his mind and body, and he saw that he was still outside. Anya was gone, and his friends were seemingly frozen around him. His eyes narrowed as he reached up and wrapped his fingers around one of the daggers sheathed at his back. What was going on?

"Reyes?" No response. Not even the flicker of an eyelid. "Gideon? Paris?"

Nothing.

There was a movement in the shadows. Lucien withdrew the weapon slowly, waiting...prepared to do what was necessary...even as a thought slid into his mind. Anya could have taken his blades and used them on him, and he wouldn't have known. Wouldn't have cared. He'd been too consumed by her. But she hadn't taken them. Which meant she truly hadn't wanted to harm him.

Why had she approached him? he wondered again.

"Hello, Death," a grave-sounding male said. No one appeared, but the weapon was jerked from Lucien's grip and sent flying to the ground. "Do you know who I am?"

Though Lucien gave no outward reaction, dread slithered through him, devouring everything in its path. He had not heard the voice before, but he knew who it belonged to. Deep down, he knew. "Lord Titan," he said. Not so long ago Lucien would have welcomed acknowledgment from this god. Now he knew better.

Aeron, keeper of Wrath, had received such acknowledgment a month ago. He'd been ordered to kill four human women. Why, the Titans refused to reveal. Aeron had declined the assignment and was now the unwilling guest of the Lords' dungeon, a menace to himself and the world. Bloodlust consumed the warrior every minute of every day.

Lucien hated seeing his friend reduced to such an animal state. Worse, he hated the growing sense of helplessness inside himself, knowing that, as strong as he was, there was nothing he could do. All because of the being materializing before him now.

"To what do I owe this…honor?" he asked.

Fluid as water, Cronus stepped into a beam of amber moonlight. He had thick silver hair and a matching beard. A long linen chimation swathed his tall, thin body, so well-woven it could have been silk. His eyes were dark, fathomless pools.

In his left hand he held the black Scythe of Death, a weapon Lucien would have loved to seize and use on the cruel god, for it could cleave the head from an immortal in only an instant. As Death incarnate, the Scythe should have belonged to him, anyway, but it had disappeared when Cronus was imprisoned. Lucien wondered how Cronus had managed to find it—and if he could find Pandora's box so easily.

"I do not like your tone," the king finally replied, deceptively calm. A timbre Lucien knew well, for he used it himself while trying to keep his emotions under control.

"My apologies." Bastard. Despite the weapon, Cronus did not look powerful enough to have broken free from Tartarus and overthrown the former king, Zeus. But he had. With brutality and cunning, proving beyond any doubt that he was not someone to antagonize.

"You met the wild and elusive Anya." Whisper-soft now, the god's voice drifted through the night, yet it was a lance of power so strong it could have felled an entire army.

Lucien's dread increased a hundredfold. "Yes. I met her."

"You kissed her."

His hands clenched—in headiness at the memory, in fury that the passionate moment had been watched by this hated being. *Calm.* "Yes."

Cronus glided toward him, as silent as the night. "Somehow she's managed to evade me for many weeks. You, however, she seeks out. Why is that, do you think?"

"I honestly do not know." And he didn't. Her attention to him still made no sense. The ardor of her kiss had been faked, surely. And yet, she'd managed to burn him, body, soul and demon.

"No matter." The god reached him, paused to stare

deeply into his eyes. Cronus even smelled of power.
"Now you will kill her."

At the proclamation, Death rattled the cage of
Lucien's mind, but for once Lucien wasn't sure
whether the demon did so in eagerness or resent-
ment. "Kill her?"

"You sound surprised." Finally releasing Lucien's
gaze, the god brushed past him as though the conversation was over.

Though it was only the barest of touches, Lucien
was knocked backward as if he'd been hit by a car,
muscles clenching, lungs flattening. When he righted
himself, trying to catch his breath, he wheeled
around. Cronus was walking into the darkness, soon
to disappear.

"If it pleases you," he called, "may I ask why you
want her…dead?"

The god did not turn as he said, "She is Anarchy,
trouble to all who encounter her. That should be
reason enough. You should thank me for this honor."

Thank him? Lucien popped his jaw to quiet the
words longing to burst from his lips. Now, more than
before, he wanted to cleave the god's head from his
body. He remained in place, though, knowing just
how brutal the gods' retribution could be. He, Reyes
and Maddox had only just been released from an
ancient curse where Reyes had been forced to stab
Maddox every night and Lucien had been compelled
to escort the fallen warrior's soul to hell.

The death-curse had been heaped upon them by the Greeks after Maddox had inadvertently killed Pandora. How much worse would the Titans' punishment be if Lucien assassinated their king?

While Lucien did not care what they would do to him, he did fear for his friends. Already they had endured more torment than anyone should know in a hundred lifetimes.

Still, he found himself saying, "I do not wish to do this deed." *I will not.* Destroying the beautiful Anya would be a curse all its own, he suspected.

He never saw Cronus move, but the god was in his face a heartbeat later. Those bright, otherworldly eyes pierced Lucien like a sword as his arm extended, the Scythe hovering before Reyes's neck. "However long it takes, warrior, whatever you have to do, you *will* bring me her dead body. Fail to heed my command, and you and all those you love will suffer."

The god disappeared in a blinding azure light, gone as quickly as he'd appeared, and the world kicked back into motion as if it had never stopped. Lucien could not catch his breath. One flick of Cronus's wrist and he could have—would have—taken Reyes's head.

"What the hell?" Reyes growled, looking around. "Where did she go?"

"She was just here." Paris spun in a circle, scanning the area and clutching his dagger.

You and all those you love will suffer, the king had

said. Not a boast. Absolute truth. Lucien fisted his hands and swallowed a surge of bile. "Let us go back inside and enjoy the rest of the evening," he managed to get out. He needed time to think.

"Hey, wait a sec," Paris began.

"No," Lucien said with a shake of his head. "We will speak of this no longer."

They stared at him for a long, silent moment. Eventually, each of them nodded. He didn't mention the god's visit or Anya's disappearance as he strode past them. He didn't mention Cronus or Anya as they entered the club. Still he didn't mention them as the men scattered in different directions, their gazes lingering on him in puzzlement.

When Reyes tried to move past him, however, he held out a restraining hand.

Reyes stopped short and glanced at him in confusion.

Lucien motioned to the table in back, the one he had previously occupied, with a tilt of his chin. Reyes nodded in understanding, and they strode to it and sat.

"Spill," Reyes said, reclining in his seat and staring out at the dance floor as casually as if they were merely discussing the weather.

"You researched Anya. Who did she kill to earn imprisonment? Why did she kill him?"

The music was a pounding, mocking tempo in the background. Strobe lights played over Reyes's bronze skin and dark-as-night eyes. He shrugged.

"The scrolls I read gave no mention of why, only who. Aias."

"I remember him." Lucien had never liked the arrogant bastard. "He probably deserved it."

"When she killed him, he was Captain of the Immortal Guard. My guess is Anya caused some sort of disaster, Aias meant to arrest her, and they fought."

Lucien blinked in surprise. Smug, self-serving Aias had taken his place? Before opening Pandora's box, *Lucien* had been captain, keeper of the peace and protector of the god king. Once the demon had been placed inside him, however, he'd no longer been suitable and the duty had been stripped from him. Then he and the warriors who helped him steal the box had been banished from the heavens altogether.

"I wonder if she means to strike at you next," Reyes said offhandedly.

Perhaps, though she'd had the opportunity to do so tonight and hadn't taken it. *He* would have deserved it, though, no doubt about it. When they'd first come to earth, he and his friends had caused nothing but darkness and destruction, pain and misery. They'd had no control over their demons and had killed indiscriminately, destroyed homes and families, brought famine and disease.

By the time he'd learned to suppress his more menacing half, it had been too late. Hunters had already risen and begun fighting them. At the time, he hadn't blamed them, had even felt deserving of their ire. Then those Hunters killed Baden, keeper of Distrust as well as Lucien's brother-by-circumstance. The loss had devastated him, shaking him to the core.

Understanding the Hunters' reasoning had no longer mattered, and he'd helped decimate those responsible. Afterward, though, he'd wanted peace. Sweet peace. Some of the warriors had not. They'd desired the destruction of *all* Hunters.

So Lucien and five other warriors had moved to Budapest, where they had lived without war for hundreds of years. A few weeks ago, the remaining six Lords had arrived in town, hot on the heels of Hunters who had been determined to wipe Lucien and his men from the world once and for all. Just like that, the blood feud reignited. There would be no escaping it this time. Part of him no longer wanted to escape it. Until the Hunters were eliminated completely, there could be no peace.

"What else did you learn about Anya?" he asked Reyes.

The warrior shrugged. "As I mentioned outside, she is the only daughter of Dysnomia."

"Dysnomia?" He worried two fingers over his jaw. "I do not remember her."

"She is the goddess of Lawlessness and the most reviled immortal among the Greeks. She slept with everything male, no matter if he was wed or not. No one even knows who Anya's father is."

"No suspicions?"

"How could there be when the mother in question had several different lovers each and every day?"

The thought of Anya following her mother's path and taking multiple men to her bed infuriated Lucien. He hadn't wanted to want her, but want her—desperately—he had. *Did.* Truly, he'd tried to resist her. And would have, until he'd realized who she was and rationalized that she was immortal. He'd thought, *She cannot die. Unlike a mortal, she cannot be taken from me if I indulge in her. I will never have to take her soul.*

What a fool he'd been. He should have known better. He was Death. Anyone could be taken. Himself, his friends. A goddess. He saw more loss in a single day than most endured in a lifetime.

"Surprised me," Reyes said, "that such a woman could produce a daughter who looks so much like an angel. Hard to believe pretty Anya is actually wicked."

Her kiss *had* been sinful. Delightfully so. But the woman he'd held in his arms had not seemed evil. Sweet, yes. Amusing, absolutely. And, shockingly enough, vulnerable and wonderfully needy. Of him.

Why had she kissed him? he wondered yet again. The question and its lack of answer plagued him. Why had she even danced for him? With him? Had she wanted something from him? Or had he merely been a challenge to her? Someone to seduce and enslave, then abandon for someone more attractive, laughing at the ugly man's gullibility all the while?

Lucien's blood chilled at the very idea. *Do not*

think like that. You'll only torture yourself. What was he supposed to think about, then? Her death? Gods, he wasn't sure he could do it.

Because she had aided him all those weeks ago, he now owed her a favor. How could he kill a woman he was indebted to? How could he kill a woman he'd tasted? *Again?* He gripped his knees, squeezing, trying to subdue the sudden rush of darkness flowing through him.

"What else do you know of her? Surely there is something more."

Reyes gave another of those negligent shrugs. "Anya is cursed in some way, but there was no hint as to what kind of curse."

Cursed? The revelation shocked and angered him. Did she suffer because of it? And why did he care? "Any mention of who was responsible for cursing her?"

"Themis, the goddess of Justice. She is a Titan, though she betrayed them to aid the Greeks when they claimed the heavenly throne."

Lucien recalled the goddess, though the image inside his head was fuzzy. Tall, dark-headed and slender. An aristocratic face and fine-boned hands that fluttered as she spoke. Some days she'd been gentle, others unbearably harsh. "What do you remember of Themis?"

"Only that she was wife to Tartarus, the prison guard."

Lucien frowned. "Perhaps she cursed Anya to punish her for hurting Tartarus in order to escape?"

Reyes shook his head. "If the scroll's timeline was correct, the curse came *before* Anya's imprisonment." He clicked his tongue on the roof of his mouth. "Perhaps Anya is exactly like her mother. Perhaps she slept with Tartarus and infuriated the goddess. Isn't that why most women wish ill upon other females?"

The suspicion did not settle well with Lucien. He scrubbed a hand over his face, the scars so puckered they abraded his palm. Had they scratched Anya? he suddenly wondered. Beneath the damaged tissue, his cheeks heated in mortification. She was probably used to smooth perfection from her men, and would remember him as the ugly warrior who had irritated her pretty skin.

Reyes traced a fingertip over one of the empty glasses perched on the tabletop. "I do not like it that we are in her debt. I do not like it that she came to the club. As I said earlier, Anya leaves a trail of destruction and chaos everywhere she goes."

"*We* leave a trail of destruction and chaos everywhere we go."

"We *used* to, but we never enjoyed it. She was smiling as she seduced you." Reyes scowled. "I saw the way you looked at her. Like I looked at Danika."

Danika. One of the humans Aeron had been ordered to slay. Reyes wanted her more than he wanted to take his next breath, Lucien suspected, but had been forced to let her go in hopes of saving her from the gods' brutality. Lucien thought perhaps the warrior had regretted the decision ever since, wishing to protect her up close and personal.

What am I going to do? Lucien knew what he *wanted* to do. Forget Anya, and ignore Cronus as Aeron had. To ignore the king of gods, however, was to invite punishment—just as Aeron had. His friends could endure no more. Of that, he was certain. Already they were poised on the edge between good and evil. Any more and they would fall, just give in to their demons and stop fighting the constant urge to destroy.

He sighed. Damned gods. The heavenly command had come at the worst possible time. Pandora's box was out there, hidden somewhere, a threat to his very existence. If a Hunter found it before he did, the demon could be pulled out of him, killing him, for man and demon were inextricably bonded.

While Lucien did not mind the thought of his own demise, he refused to allow his brethren to be hurt. He felt responsible for them. If he had not opened the box to avenge his stinging pride at not being chosen to guard it, his men would not have been forced to house the demons inside their bodies. He would not have destroyed their lives—lives they had once enjoyed as elite warriors to the Greeks. Blithe, carefree. Happy, even.

He exhaled another sigh. To protect his friends from further pain, he would have to kill Anya as ordered, Lucien decided with a pang of regret. Which meant he would have to hunt the goddess down. Which meant he would have to be near her again.

The thought of being in Anya's presence once more, of smelling her strawberry scent, of caressing her soft skin, both tantalized and tormented him. Even forever ago, when he'd fallen deeply in love with a mortal named Mariah, and she with him, he had not desired like this. A hot ache that infused every inch of his body and refused to leave.

Mariah…sweet, innocent Mariah, the woman he'd given his heart to shortly after learning to control his demon. By then, he'd lived on earth a hundred—two hundred?—years, time seemingly nonexistent, one day the same as any other. Then he'd seen Mariah, and life had begun to matter. He'd craved something good, something pure to wipe away the darkness.

She'd been sunshine to his midnight, a bright candle in merciless gloom, and he'd hoped to spend an eternity worshipping her. But all too soon, disease struck her. Death had known immediately she would not survive. Lucien should have taken her soul that very moment, but he had been unable to force himself to do it.

For weeks, the sickness ravaged her body, destroying her piece by piece. The longer he'd waited, hoping she would heal, the more she'd suffered. Toward the end, she'd begged, sobbed and screamed for death. Heartsick, knowing they would never again be together, he'd finally broken down and done his duty.

That was the night he'd obtained his scars.

Lucien had carved himself to ribbons using a poisoned blade; every time the wounds had tried to heal, he'd prayed for scars and carved himself up again. And again. He'd even burned himself until the skin no longer rejuvenated. In his grief, he'd hoped to ensure that no female would ever again approach him, that he would never again have to suffer the loss of a loved one.

He'd never regretted the action. Until now. He'd ruined any chance of being a man Anya could truly desire. A woman as physically perfect as she deserved a man equally so. He frowned. Why was he thinking like that? She had to die. Desire on either side would only complicate matters. Well, complicate them more.

Once again, Anya's image etched itself into his mind, consuming his thoughts. Her face was a sensual feast and her body a sexual high. As a man, he howled with rage at the thought of destroying that. As an immortal warrior, well, he howled, too.

Perhaps he could convince Cronus to rescind his command. Perhaps... Lucien snorted. No. That would not work. Trying to bargain with Cronus was more foolish than ignoring him. The king of gods would only order him to do something worse.

Damn this! Why did Cronus want her dead? What had she done?

Had she spurned him for another?

Lucien ignored the haze of jealousy and possessiveness that fell over his eyes. Ignored the *mine* ringing in his ears.

"I am waiting," Reyes said, breaking into his thoughts.

He blinked, trying to clear his mind. "For?"

"For you to tell me what happened out there."

"Nothing happened," he lied smoothly, and hated himself for the need.

Reyes shook his head. "Your lips are still bruised and swollen from kissing her. Your hair is in spikes around your head from where she plowed her fingers through. You stepped in front of her when we meant to take her, and then she disappeared altogether. Nothing happened? Try again."

Reyes had enough to worry about without having to carry Lucien's burden, as well. "Tell the others I'll meet them in Greece. I won't be traveling with them as planned."

"What?" Reyes frowned. "Why?"

"I've been commanded to take a soul," was all he said.

"Take a soul? Not just escort it to heaven or hell? I don't understand."

He nodded. "You do not need to understand."

"You know I hate when you turn cryptic. Tell me who and why."

"Does it matter? A soul is a soul, and the outcome

is the same no matter the reason. Death." Lucien slapped Reyes's shoulder and pushed to his feet. Before the warrior could utter another word, Lucien strode out of the club, not stopping until he reached the very place he'd kissed—and lost—Anya.

In an unwieldy corner of his mind, he could almost hear her moaning. He could almost feel her nails digging into his back and her hips rocking into his erection. An erection that had not dissipated. Despite everything.

Need still clawed through him, but he shoved it aside and closed his right eye. Surveying the area with his blue eye—his spiritual eye—he saw a rainbow of glowing, ethereal colors. Through those colors he could interpret every deed that had occurred here, every emotion ever felt by visitors. Sometimes he could even determine exactly who had done what.

Having done this infinite times before, he easily sorted through the morass to find signs of the most recent activity. There, against the freshly erected and painted boards of the brand-new building, were sparkling stars of passion.

The kiss.

In this spiritual realm, Anya's passion appeared a blazing pink. Real. Not faked, as a part of him had assumed. That pink trail glittered with a dazzle unlike anything he'd ever seen. Had she truly desired him, then? Had a creature so physically perfect found *him* worthy? That did not seem possible, and yet the proof was shining at him like a pathway to salvation in the middle of a storm.

His stomach tightened, heat shooting through him. His mouth watered for another taste of her. His chest ached, a sharp and hungry throb. Oh, to hold those breasts in his hands again and feel the nipples stiffen against his palms. To sink his fingers into her wet sheath this time and pump in and out, slowly at first, then faster and faster. She would come, maybe even beg for more. He groaned.

She has to die by your hand. Do not forget.

As if he could, he thought, hands fisting. "Where did you go?" he muttered, following the sparks to where she'd stood when she'd pushed him. Blue winked at him. Sadness. She had been sad? Because he'd said she did not matter? The knowledge filled him with guilt.

He studied the colors more closely. Interspersed with the blue was a bright, pulsing red. Fury. He must have hurt her feelings, and that in turn must have angered her. The guilt intensified. In his defense, he had assumed she'd been playing with him, that she hadn't really wanted him. He hadn't thought she would care whether he wanted her or not.

That she had utterly amazed him.

As he continued to sort through the colors, he found the faintest trace of white. Fear. Something had scared her. What? Had she sensed Cronus? Seen him? Known he was about to deliver her death sentence?

Lucien didn't like that she'd been scared.

Every muscle tensed as he followed the muted trail of white. As he moved, he allowed his body to fuse with the demon of Death, becoming nothing more than a spirit, a midnight mist that could flash from one location to another in an instant.

Anya's essence led to his fortress, he was startled to find. His bedroom, more specifically. Clearly she hadn't stayed long, but seemed to have paced from one side of the chamber to another, then had flashed away to—

Maddox and Ashlyn's bedroom. Lucien's brow furrowed in confusion. Why here? The couple was asleep in bed, twined together, cheeks rosy and flushed from a recent sexual marathon, he was sure.

Lucien tried to tamp down a sudden rush of envy before picking up Anya's trail and flashing—

Into an apartment he did not recognize. Moonlight seeped inside through cracks in the black window coverings. Still dark. Was he still in Budapest, then? The furnishings here were sparse: a brown, thread-bare couch pushed against the wall, a wicker chair with slats that had come unraveled and would poke the sitter in the back. No TV, no computer or any of the other modern luxuries Lucien had grown accustomed to over the years.

From the next room echoed the clatter of one dagger slapping against another. It was a sound he knew well. He allowed himself to float toward it, knowing whoever was inside would not be able to see him.

He reached the doorway and gaped, waves of shock pummeling through him. Danika, the doomed woman Reyes lusted after, was thrusting two daggers repeatedly into a man-sized dummy hanging from the wall. A dummy that, surprisingly, looked like a cross between Reyes and Aeron.

"Kidnap me, will you?" she muttered. Sweat trickled down her temples and chest, soaking her gray tank to her body. The long length of her blond ponytail was plastered to her neck. To work up such a sweat in so cold an apartment, she must have been at the exercise for hours.

Why had Anya come here? Danika was—or had been—in hiding. Temporarily letting her go had been the only way to give the mortal some semblance of a life before Aeron hunted her down on the wings of Wrath as the gods had ordered. And he would. It was only a matter of time before Aeron escaped the dungeon. Not one of the warriors had been able to bring themselves to take any more of his freedom by binding him with the only thing that could truly hold him: unbreakable links forged by the gods. So yes, Aeron *would* eventually escape.

Lucien was tempted to reveal his presence and talk to Danika, but didn't. She had no good memories of him and would not be willing to help in his search for Anya. He worried two fingers over his jaw. Whatever the goddess of Anarchy's purpose, she had clearly taken an interest in all things Underworld.

He was more baffled than ever.

There were no answers here, only more questions, so he didn't waste another minute. He followed Anya's lighted trail, which was now a bright red—anger was taking root again—and found himself flashing to—

A convenience store. He believed that was what mortals called the small shop.

His eyebrows furrowed together. He was no longer in Budapest, he knew, for sunlight glowed brightly through the store's windows. A multitude of people milled about, paying for fuel and buying snacks.

Unseen, Lucien ventured outside. A horde of yellow cars sped along a nearby street, and mortals rushed along the crowded sidewalks. He found a shadowed alley and materialized without anyone the wiser. Curiosity propelling him, he strode back into the store. A bell tinkled.

A woman gasped when she saw him, then looked away as quickly as possible. A child pointed at him and was reprimanded by his mother. *Everyone* backed away from him, inching as far from him as they could without seeming blatantly rude. There was a line leading to the cash register, which he bypassed without apology.

No one protested.

The cashier was a teenager, a boy who looked a lot like Gideon. Blue hair, piercings, tattoos. However, he lacked Gideon's savage intensity as he smacked his gum and shuffled the money in his drawer. A quick glance at the tag on the boy's shirt provided his name.

"Dennis, did you notice a pale-haired female in a short black skirt—"

"And ice-blue barely-there top? Hell, yeah, I noticed," Dennis finished for him as he closed the register. Lucien recognized the accent. He was in the States. The boy's gaze lifted, and he stilled. Gulped. "Uh, yeah." His voice shook. "I did. May I ask why?"

Three emotions skidded through Lucien, none of them welcome: jealousy that another man had enjoyed the sight of Anya, eagerness that he was closer to finding her and *dread* that he was closer to finding her. "Did she speak to anyone?"

The boy took a step backward and shook his head. "No."

"Did she buy anything?"

There was a heavy pause, as if he was afraid his answer would send Lucien into a rage. "Kind of."

Kind of? When Dennis failed to elaborate, Lucien gritted his teeth and said, "What did she kind of buy?"

"Wh-why do you want to know? I mean, are you a cop or something? An ex-husband?"

Lucien pressed his tongue to the roof of his mouth. *Calm, stay calm.* He fixed his eyes on the paling human, capturing Dennis's gaze and refusing to release it. The scent of roses began to drift from him, thickening the air.

Dennis gulped again, but his eyes began to glaze over.

"I asked you a question," Lucien said softly, "and now you will answer. What did the woman buy?"

"Three strawberry-and-cream lollipops," was the trancelike reply. "But she didn't buy them. She just grabbed them and walked off. I didn't try to stop her or anything, I swear."

"Show me the lollipops."

With people moaning and muttering in protest at the delay—until Lucien glared at them and they quickly hushed—Dennis left the register and led him to the candy aisle. He pointed to a half-empty box of lollipops.

Lucien pocketed two, not allowing himself to smell them as he so badly wanted, and withdrew several bills. Wrong currency, but giving the boy *something* was better than nothing. "How much do I owe you?"

"They're on me." Dennis held up his hands in a pretend show of friendship.

He wanted to force the boy to take the money, but did not want to cause even more of a scene. In the end, he stuffed the bills back inside his pocket. "Return to your register," he said, then pivoted to slowly survey the rest of the store. On the spiritual plane, there were millions upon millions of colors. Sorting through them proved tedious, but no one dared bother him and he was finally able to locate Anya's unique essence.

His blood heated.

Everything about her, even the minute mist she left behind, called to him, drew him. And, if he wasn't careful, would ensnare him. She was just so…captivating. A beautiful enigma.

Lucien left the store and returned to the abandoned alleyway, where he once again dematerialized into the spirit realm. He flashed to Anya's next location—

And found her in a park. Finally.

Looking at her, the sharp ache returned to his chest and he suddenly had trouble drawing in a breath. Right now, she appeared serene, not at all like the temptress in the club. She sat on a swing, sunlight bathing her in a golden halo. Back and forth she rocked.

She seemed to be lost in thought, her temple resting against the chain that anchored the swing to the rail. That silky, silvery hair cascaded down her arms, wisping across her pixie face every few seconds as the wind rolled.

He was struck by a nearly inexorable urge to fold her in his arms and simply hold her.

Had a woman ever looked so vulnerable? Had a woman ever looked so alone? She licked one of the lollipops she'd stolen, the pink tip of her tongue flicking out, circling the rosy candy. His cock jumped in response. *No. None of that.* But the command failed to lessen his desire.

However long it takes, whatever you have to do,

you will bring her to me, Cronus had said. *Or all those you love will suffer.*

Lucien felt a spark of anger leap through himself, but he quickly tamped it down. No anger. He was Death. Right now he had no other purpose. Emotion would only hinder him; he knew that well.

However longs it takes. Cronus's voice once again echoed in his mind.

For a moment, only a moment, Lucien entertained the possibility of taking forever. An eternity. *You know what happens when you hesitate. The one destined to die suffers a far worse fate than originally intended. Do it! Or your friends, too, will suffer a far worse fate.*

Determined, Lucien materialized and stepped forward. Gravel crunched under his boots, and Anya's head snapped up. Instantly their gazes locked. Her crystalline eyes widened, filling with such intense heat and longing they singed him.

Her mouth fell open in shock as she popped to her feet. "Lucien."

The sweetness of her voice blended with the strawberries-and-cream scent she emitted. As his body tensed erotically, his resolve weakened. Again. *Stay strong, damn you.*

Not realizing the danger she was in, she remained in place, still peering over at him through the thick shield of her lashes. "How did you find me?"

"You are not the only being capable of tracking

an immortal," he replied, giving her only half of the answer.

Her gaze traced over him, so hot he thought she might be mentally stripping away his clothing. Women simply did not look at him like that. Not anymore. And that this one did… He was having more and more trouble controlling his reactions. His cock grew harder with every second that passed.

"So you've come to finish what we started, have you, Flowers?" She sounded eager.

"That is not why I've come." He spoke the words precisely. *There is no other way. You must do this deed.*

Her lush red lips edged into a frown. "Then why—" She gasped and anchored one hand on her suddenly cocked hip. "Did you come to insult me some more? Because you should know, I'm not going to tolerate it. I am *not* unimportant!"

Oh, yes, he had hurt her, and the knowledge once again filled him with guilt. Foolish to feel guilt when he'd come here to hurt her irrevocably, but the emotion proved too strong to fight. Still he repeated, "That is not why I've come," this time adding, "I'm sorry, Anya, but I've come to kill you."

HQN™

We *are* romance™

HAPPY READING!

As part of our special sizzling summer reads offer, you can now **SAVE $1.00** on the purchase of **THE DARKEST KISS** by *New York Times* bestselling author **Gena Showalter**, available in June wherever books are sold, including most bookstores, supermarkets, drugstores, department and discount stores.

If you've enjoyed this sizzling excerpt,
purchase

Available in June

THE
DARKEST
KISS

by *New York Times* bestselling author

Gena Showalter

at Borders and **SAVE $1.⁰⁰**
on your purchase!

NEW YORK TIMES
BESTSELLING AUTHOR

carly phillips

Hot PROPERTY

Dear Reader,

I love writing, but no series has given me more joy than THE HOT ZONE, maybe because of the many personal connections for me in these books. Uncle Yank is based on my Grandpa Jack, may he rest in peace, and macular degeneration runs in my family. Giving Uncle Yank a love of life despite his limitations has truly been a labor of love. From your many wonderful letters, I sense you have the same warm fuzzy feeling for the Jordan sisters and the Hot Zone characters as I do. Thank you so much for letting me know!

Hot Property is the last in THE HOT ZONE series of books. John Roper (Micki's best friend and high-maintenance client) and Amy Stone (Riley's cousin from Florida) are about to meet— and when they do, sparks fly!

So enjoy the heat and the fun, and the next time you write to me, I hope it's because you miss these characters as much as I will!

Best wishes always and happy reading!

Carly

www.carlyphillips.com
e-mail: carly@carlyphillips.com

PROLOGUE

AMY STONE WAS SURROUNDED by testosterone. Not everyday, average testosterone but the heavy-duty testosterone that could only belong to athletes. She couldn't stop staring at the quarterbacks, the baseball stars and other large, muscular guests attending her cousin Riley's wedding reception. The bride, Sophie Jordan, her sisters and their friends appeared unfazed by so many hot men in one place. As publicists for the Hot Zone, a PR firm specializing in athletes, they were probably used to the sight. As a single woman more accustomed to living and working as a social director at a Fort Lauderdale retirement community owned by her relatives, Amy was out of her element.

But that was about to change. Starting in January, Amy would be working at the Hot Zone, too, and she'd have to learn how to handle herself around these big-shot athletes without melting at their feet. She'd already made a few trips to the city and had begun settling into the apartment Micki Jordan Fuller had leased to her. After spending the holidays with her family, Amy would be leaving her easy life behind.

The sun beat down on her head and she envied the senator's guests who had parasols to shade themselves from the heated rays. The humidity was really getting to her. Her skin was sticky beneath her dress as she strode to the bar.

"Can I get you a drink?" a deep male voice asked.

Amy turned, shading her eyes against the glare of the sun, and stared into the most gorgeous face she'd ever seen on a man. His eyes were a deep shade of green, his features more chiseled than rugged, and when he smiled, dimples embraced his white teeth and oh-so-sexy smile.

"I was just about to order a cola," she said.

"I think I can manage that for you." His easy-going smile grew wider. "Do not go anywhere."

Amy wouldn't dream of it. It was one thing to be surrounded by testosterone, another to have one of these men turn his attention her way. Heat suffused her and her pulse rate kicked up so she found it hard to breathe. Amy wasn't a nun and she'd been with her share of men, but she'd never dated a guy as rugged and…well, hot as this man.

He eased his way between the people at the bar and quickly returned with her drink in one hand, one for himself in the other. "Here you go."

She accepted the glass. "Thank you."

"My pleasure." He nodded and tipped his glass, clinking it against hers. "So, pretty lady, are you a guest of the bride or the groom?"

She tried not to preen under the compliment, but he'd gotten under her skin already. "I'm a guest of the groom. Riley is my cousin," she explained, before taking a cool, welcome sip of her soda.

"Are you related to the senator?" he asked.

"No, actually, Spencer Atkins is my uncle." Riley had a complicated family situation, but Amy figured this man, probably an athlete, knew of renowned sports agent, Spencer Atkins, who was Riley's biological father. "What about you? Which side of the family do you know?"

"I'm a guest of both, actually."

"Which would make you a client of the Hot Zone PR and Athletes Only?" she said, referring to her uncle's sports agency.

"Not only beautiful but perceptive, as well."

She was certain she blushed. "What sport do you play?"

"You don't know who I am?" His eyes widened. "I'm wounded," he said in an affected tone with a little boy's hurt in his expression. But immediate laughter let her know he was just teasing.

Amy smiled, enjoying his sense of humor and easygoing personality. The attraction went without saying. The man was definitely irresistible.

"John Roper, New York Renegades center fielder at your service." He tipped his head toward her, then extended his hand.

"Amy Stone." She placed her palm inside his.

Searing heat branded her, sizzling up her arm and into her chest, knocking the wind out of her completely.

Wow.

She'd *never* had such an intense reaction to a man before. She caught a whiff of his sensual cologne, which caused an erotic spike in her body temperature. "It's nice to meet you, John."

A cute smile pulled at his lips. "It's nice to meet you, too, Amy Stone." His voice dropped a husky octave.

She ran her tongue over her dry lips. "So what table are you seated at?" she asked him.

He'd been holding her gaze with a look hot enough to melt the ice sculptures she'd seen earlier, but suddenly he twisted his body, looking around before turning back to her again. "Listen, the seating is…um…complicated."

"Tell me about it. It's a wedding. Seating is always complicated. I'm just hoping I'm not at the same table as my mom and her sister."

"It's not that kind of complicated." He mulled something over in his mind for a while before finally speaking. "I just didn't expect to meet someone like you here," he said, warmth and something inherently more in his tone.

"Tell me about it." She hadn't come here with a date or intending to meet a man, either, but she was definitely glad she had met one. Now she didn't have to survive those awkward moments during slow songs. If John didn't ask her to dance, maybe she'd just ask him instead. Though that sounded more like something her mother would do than Amy, this man was worth stepping out of her comfort zone for. A tingle of anticipation rippled through her at the thought of a slow dance, his arms wrapped around her waist....

He bent his head close to hers. She inhaled and his aftershave filled her with deep yearning. He leaned closer. For a whisper? Not a kiss, it was way too soon.

But her heart pounded in anticipation.

"Roper! Roper!" A shrill female voice called out his name.

The chance for her to discover his intentions disappeared as Amy and John jerked back and turned toward the sound. A beautiful woman walked, teetering on high heels, across the lawn, making a beeline his way. Her long dress kept catching beneath her shoes, and although she held up the hem with both hands, the trip was obviously a difficult one.

"There you are," she said. "Didn't I ask you to stay on the patio? I told you I didn't want to ruin my dress on the lawn." She whined through heavily glossed lips that turned downward in what was obviously meant to be a pretty pout.

It *was* pretty, though Amy hated to concede the point. The other woman was model-thin and attractive in a waiflike sort of way, elegant despite her awkward trek across the lawn. And judging from the possessive way she aligned herself against John, she was his date.

His date. Disappointment rushed through her. All the while he'd been initiating conversation and coming on to her—at least that's how she'd read his words and his body language—he'd had another woman waiting for him.

How naive could she be, thinking a hot baseball player would be interested in a country bumpkin? And that's what she felt like compared to the chic woman standing next to him. She resented the emotion, hating that she allowed herself to feel inferior.

"I leave you alone for five minutes and I find you racking up another conquest in my absence," the other woman said.

"I—" He paused. Obviously he couldn't find an acceptable excuse because there was none.

Amy's heart beat hard and fast while nausea overwhelmed her. She turned and started for the house, trying to get as far away as she could get from John Roper.

"Amy, wait!" He called after her. "I know this looks bad, but—"

She refused to turn around. It looked like what it was. He'd brought a date to the party, but he'd definitely come on to *her.*

He caught her arm, forcing her to face him.

His date followed, coming up beside them. "You're worried about her and not me? You *jerk!* I flew out to this godforsaken place to be with you and this is how you repay me? By trying to hook up with a local bimbo?"

Before anyone could blink, the woman grabbed his drink from his hand and deliberately poured it down his shirt.

"Come on, Carrie. This is a Hugo Boss shirt!" He pulled at the stained material and glared at his date. "Was that really necessary?"

She forced a smile. "I think it was."

Amy couldn't believe this. The crowd around them grew silent and began to edge closer for a better look. Amy cringed. She hated being the center of attention and she resented that this man had done it to her now.

"You two obviously need privacy." This time she ran from the circus act that was John and his date.

She slowed as she approached the patio, disappointment in John Roper and the way this day had turned out as strong as the sun overhead. She'd really been attracted to him, but she didn't need a man like that in her life. She would begin her new job as a publicist for the Hot Zone, operating behind the scenes. But she definitely had to grow a thicker skin if she was going to deal with this kind of high-maintenance client on a daily basis.

And when the New Year arrived and with it, her new life, Amy swore to make it her new life's mission not only to succeed, but to thrive.

CHAPTER ONE

One month later

SPORTS AGENT YANK MORGAN sat in the backseat of his Lincoln and rubbed a hand over his scruffy beard. Scruffier now since his wife, Lola, had thrown out his razor to prevent him from accidentally slitting his throat. Dang woman had also somehow discovered where he'd hidden his spares. Apparently an almost-blind man had no privacy in his own bathroom.

Normally he'd be angry, but considering his eyesight had gotten worse, he was forced to admit Lola had a point. Macular degeneration was messing with the balance of power in his marriage. Telling a woman she was right about anything, though, especially his woman, would be the equivalent of relinquishing his throne. And that wasn't happening at home or at work.

"We're here, Mr. Morgan," J.D., the ex-football player he'd hired as his driver, said. "Want me to walk you inside?"

Yank shook his head. "No, thanks. It's bad enough

you had to drive me here. I don't need you as my guide. I got Noodle for that." His Labradoodle sat beside him and Yank patted her furry head. He'd got the dog when she was a pup, but now she was the size of her standard poodle mother.

"Be careful. I don't want to end up at the emergency room again because you tripped over something you and the mutt didn't see."

"She's not a mutt, she's a mix of two pure breeds," Yank said proudly as he opened his car door.

"I still say you should have bought a real guide dog and not a pet." J.D. came around and met him.

Yank frowned. "Keep sounding like my wife and you'll have to find yourself a new job."

J.D. merely laughed. "You say that every day," he said as he helped Yank out of the car.

"Wait till you get older before passing judgment. I'll only be about fifteen minutes." Yank pulled his heavy jacket tighter around him and let the dog lead him toward the door of the gym.

Part Labrador retriever, part poodle, completely dense when it came to being in charge, Noodle wasn't the guide dog Yank should have gotten, but he enjoyed the pretense. It was fun making people think he was a little bit crazy. There were worse ways to spend his life, he thought, laughing.

He made his way to the weight room in the back of the gym. The trainers and employees were used to him visiting clients and bringing Noodle along. He headed for where he knew he'd find John Roper, letting years of experience lead the way. The main part of the gym was noisy and crowded, but as he approached the private rooms in the back, Yank could hear that there weren't as many people there.

Which Yank figured was the reason his not-so-star baseball player client John Roper chose to work out here and now. Unfortunately, the televisions were on and the sound coming from the speakers told Yank that morning sports talk-show host, Frank Buckley, was spouting off at the mouth as usual.

"Spring training is around the corner and this New York Renegade fan still hasn't gotten over John Roper's disastrous last season or his role in the Renegades Game 5 World Series loss. Call in and let me know if your lack of expectations match mine for the highly overpaid hero. The Buck Stops Here, folks."

The television station went to commercial at the same time Roper yelled aloud, "Somebody shut that damn thing off before I rip the speakers off the wall."

When nobody moved, Yank added his two cents. "Can't you hear the man? Shut off the noise or we'll sue you for intentional infliction of emotional distress."

The weights clanged hard as Roper dropped them to the floor. "Morgan, what are you doing here?" he asked.

"Visiting the dumbbells." Yank laughed at his own joke.

Roper didn't.

"You still upset over Buckley the Bastard's tirade? Grow up and get over it," Yank said. He'd already tried coddling Roper through his rough patch and it hadn't worked. He was moving on to tough love.

"Someone dropped off a Roper bobblehead doll with my doorman. Damn thing had a knife stuck in the shoulder."

"Are you sure Buckley doesn't have a personal grudge?" Yank asked.

Roper rose to his feet, looming large over Yank. "I screwed his ex-girlfriend. She just didn't see fit to mention she was no longer his ex on the night in question."

Yank chuckled. "He oughta let it go."

"She's his wife now," Roper said.

"Shit."

"Yeah," Roper agreed. "You do realize that if this was a lesser market, nobody would pay attention to anything Buckley said?"

Yank shook his head. "But it isn't a lesser market. It's New York." And that said it all.

Athletes were like movie stars here, back- and front-page news and fodder for gossip. "You used to love the attention," Yank reminded him.

Prior to his funk, Roper had been known for being a high-maintenance outfielder. ESports TV, Magazine and Radio named Roper among the top metrosexual athletes of the year. Yank didn't get why grown men like Roper spent good money on the best clubs, gyms and hairdressers. What normal man had his back waxed? Yank had no idea. But Roper's good-looking mug had made them both a boatload of money, so Yank wasn't about to complain.

"I did love the attention," Roper said. "Until my talent went south." Roper leaned forward on the bench, elbows on his knees, and stared ahead at nothing in particular. "So what are you really doing here?" Roper asked.

"I came to cheer you up. I don't want the media to see you down and I sure as hell don't need you taking a swing at one of them, no matter how much they provoke you."

"That sounds like a message from Micki."

Yank's niece, Michelle, was Roper's close friend, as well as his publicist. She was the resident expert at the Hot Zone for keeping her high-maintenance client out of trouble and out of the press.

Then again, maybe some good press was exactly what Roper needed. "I have a present for you. Here's a gift certificate." Yank pulled a piece of paper from his back pocket. "Go get yourself a massage and a manicure."

"Not in the mood."

Yank didn't know what else to do in order to help his dejected client. "Don't you want to look your best for the annual Hot Zone New Year's party?"

"I'm not going."

Yank smacked him upside the head. "You sure as

hell are. You're going to hold yourself up and make like life's grand. Attitude is everything and right now yours sucks."

Yank couldn't see well but he figured Roper was scowling at him about now. "I'm sure you're having a rough time after the series, but obviously something more has you bent out of shape. The happy-go-lucky guy I know wouldn't be sulking like a pansy."

Roper rose and Yank felt the other man's height close beside him.

"You want to know what's bothering me? Where should I start? I could live with last year's disaster if I thought I was definitely coming back, but we both know the shoulder's not healing the way it should. That means my career may be shorter than we'd anticipated. Not a financial problem given my huge contract, right?"

"Unless you pissed it away…" Yank said, not at all serious.

"You know me better than that. But my family's working hard at doing it for me."

Yank blinked. "Ever hear *just say no?*"

"You try telling them that."

Yank wasn't worried about Roper's future. The younger man had come to him for investment advice and Yank knew he'd diversified wisely. But if his career was shortened due to injury and his family was going through his money like water, Yank could understand the man's distress. "Slow 'em down, then," Yank suggested.

"Yeah, I'm trying," Roper muttered. "Do me a favor? Tell Micki I need time to myself. If she doesn't quit worrying and sending you around to check on me, I'm going to let the Hot Zone go. Who knows? If I can't play this season, I may not need a PR firm at all."

Yank frowned. "Micki's not worried about you as a client, you ass. She's worried about you as a friend."

"I know that," Roper said, sounding more subdued and apologetic. "I appreciate her concern, but there's nothing she can do unless she's got a magic cure for the shoulder."

Even Yank knew when to give a man space, and John Roper needed it more than Yank had realized. "I'll make you a deal," he said to the man he both liked and admired.

"What's that?"

"Come to the party and I promise nobody will be talking business. You could use some time to relax. No media invited. What do you say?"

Roper remained silent for too long.

Obviously the man was tense and strung tight if he couldn't bring himself to say he'd come to a party. "When was the last time you got laid?" Yank asked, voicing the first question that came to mind.

"None of your damn business."

Yank chuckled at the quick answer. "Then it's been too damn long."

Roper shrugged. "Okay, then. Why the hell not?"

Yank tugged on Noodle's leash, and as they

walked out the door, Yank whistled, pleased with his handiwork.

J.D. met him by the car. "Why are you in such a good mood?"

"Because I'm not a Boy Scout and I never have been," Yank said, laughing. John Roper was about to benefit from Yank being a lying, meddling son of a bitch.

AMY LOVED FLORIDA. SHE enjoyed the warm weather all year, the ease of never having to wear a winter jacket. It was one of the reasons she'd stayed down south instead of going away to college. She also was a person who appreciated comfortable surroundings, and her home and family in Florida represented the familiar.

But it was time for a change and uprooting herself from the familiar was the first step in forging a new life. One that included a new career—with the Hot Zone thanks to her uncle Spencer and the generosity of the Jordan sisters in giving her a chance.

Now, on New Year's Eve, she stepped off the elevator at the Park Avenue offices of the Hot Zone and glanced at the guests, the male ones in particular, and an immediate feeling of déjà vu swept over her. Just like at Sophie and Riley's wedding, she felt out of her element. Would she ever get used to being surrounded by buff, hot men? She hoped not, she thought, as she glanced around at her new normal.

The coat-check woman greeted her and took her

jacket. A server offered her a glass of champagne, which Amy declined. She wanted a clear head for all the new faces and names she'd encounter, as well as access to her memories of those she'd already met at the wedding. Those memories were vivid. Especially the ones of John Roper and how disappointed she'd been by his deception. Of course, maybe he'd have told her about his date given more time.

And maybe he hadn't leaned close enough to kiss her cheek, she thought, still disappointed by the outcome. No matter how much she wanted to believe he'd been as blindsided by their attraction as she'd been, that he couldn't help but act on it, date or no date, she knew she was deceiving herself. In all likelihood, the man was exactly what he seemed to be— a guy trying to juggle more than one woman at a time.

The man was a superstar athlete, a celebrity who was probably used to women falling at his feet. Amy had grown up listening to her uncle's stories of his famous clients. And Amy had inadvertently played the role of doting admirer. But that wasn't who she was. Amy wasn't into the glitz, glamour and fame celebrity brought.

She exhaled a stream of air, annoyed at herself for giving Roper any thought at all. She forced herself to focus on the holiday decorations that lingered from Christmas and the pretty silver balls hanging from the ceiling. A professionally decorated tree sat in the corner twinkling with lights that were sure to be taken down soon after the first of the year. The decor outdid anything she, her mother and aunt back in Florida had managed to set up in the clubhouse each year.

"Amy?"

She turned at the sound of her name above the noise of the happy crowd. Sophie Jordan approached quickly, a warm smile on her face. No matter how many times Amy saw Sophie, she was always shocked by her beauty and perfection. Tonight her honey-blond hair was pulled back in a neat knot, her face beautifully made up.

Amy hugged Sophie, the sister who was the organizer behind the Hot Zone. She had met Sophie for the first time in Florida last year. Though Sophie wasn't as touchy-feely as Amy, she hugged right back.

"You look happy. Marriage to my cousin must agree with you," Amy said, taking in Sophie's glowing face.

Sophie grinned. "Well, marriage to Riley *is* pretty darn good."

"I just bet it is. Where is my cousin, anyway?"

"He'll be here soon."

"And your sisters?" Amy glanced over Sophie's shoulder. "Are they around here somewhere?"

"Unfortunately Micki's still on the island—her husband, Damian, owns a slice of paradise. Her daughter had a respiratory infection and Damian insisted on taking the family to a warmer climate for a little while. From what they say, it seems to be helping. But Annabelle is here working the crowd. I'm sure you'll see her soon."

Amy nodded. "Well, please send Micki my love."

"I will. And you can do it yourself at the first staff meeting in a few days."

Amy already knew she was stepping into a high-profile, high-pressure place with loyalty and dedication in spades, and she wanted to play a successful part. Nepotism might have gotten her the job, but only proving herself would keep her here. She was definitely ready for the challenge.

"Well, look who's here!" a booming male voice said. Her uncle's partner, Yank, pulled her into a big hug at the same time Amy caught sight of his wife, Lola, standing behind him.

Amy waved to the other woman, who smiled right back.

"Just tell me your crazy mother and aunt are still at home in Florida," Yank said as he stepped back.

Lola groaned. "Ignore him. He's had a drink or two and doesn't know what he's saying." She smacked her husband on the shoulder.

"I'm stone-cold sober. You've been watering down my drinks all night." He leaned closer to Amy. "She thinks just because I can't see, my taste buds have gone, too."

And he thought Amy's relatives were crazy? She shook her head and laughed. "No problem, Lola. I've heard from Uncle Spencer that Yank says whatever's on his mind." She shot the older man a grateful look. "Thank you for giving me a chance here," she told him.

Yank grinned, obviously pleased. "You see? The only one who's got a problem with me is you," Yank said to his wife.

Sophie rolled her eyes. "Okay, you said your hellos, Uncle Yank. How about giving me a chance to introduce Amy to some other people at the party?"

"I'd like that." Amy rubbed her hands together.

"Why not start with someone she knows and ease her in. John Roper's over there in the corner," Yank said without much tact.

Amy's stomach flipped. "Oh, I think we can skip over him," Amy said, only partially meaning it. A traitorous part of her wanted to get a glimpse of him again.

"Nonsense. Amy wouldn't want him to think she was avoiding him, considering he's been eyeing *her* since she walked into the room," Yank said.

"He has?" Amy asked, then wished she could bite her tongue and take it back. Still, she had to admit it stroked her ego to know Roper's eyes had been on her since she'd arrived. She had to force herself not to glance at the corner and look over at *him*.

Lola scowled at her husband. "Leave Amy alone," she instructed.

"Lola's right," Sophie said. "But tell me something. Just how would you know where Roper is, considering you can't see well enough to identify anyone?" Sophie perched her hands on her hips and eyed her uncle warily.

"She's got your number, old man," Lola said, laughing.

"Who are you calling old?" he grumbled.

Lola ignored him, meeting Sophie's gaze instead. "Actually, Yank's been checking up on Roper ever since he arrived. I feel like the man's personal GPS system."

"Speaking of guides, where is Noodle?" Sophie asked.

"One of the staff took the dog out for a walk." Lola gestured toward the windows overlooking the city. "They'll be back soon."

Sophie nodded. "Gotcha. Well, I can understand your concern for Roper. We've all been worried about him lately. The papers have been brutal."

Despite her better judgment, Amy's curiosity got the better of her. "Why? What's going on?"

The other three stared at one another, wide-eyed and surprised.

"I guess New Yorkers forget that not everyone else's world revolves around sports," Sophie said, realization dawning. "You know that the Renegades made it to the World Series?"

Amy nodded. She just hadn't kept up with the details since the opposing team hadn't been from Florida.

"Roper went into the post season in a serious slump," Sophie said in a low whisper. "He didn't play well at all in the series, struck out in the clutch and injured his shoulder in an attempt to stop a home run. The team lost the series and Roper became the media scapegoat."

"Ouch." Poor man, she thought, then caught herself. The *poor man* didn't need her pity, that much she knew for sure.

Despite herself, Amy's gaze came to rest on the sexy guy who had made her pulse kick up a notch and her mouth go dry.

And he still had a female cozying up to him just like the last time.

"He doesn't look happy," Sophie murmured.

She was right. Despite the attention of a woman who appeared to be hanging on his every word, Roper appeared dazed and bored.

"How odd," Lola said. "Normally Roper loves every bit of attention he can get, female or otherwise."

Amy pursed her lips and kept silent. She'd once been all too happy to shower him with that attention. Thanks to the scene made by his date at the wedding, everyone here knew it.

"Must be today's paper that's getting to him," Yank said. "Lola read it to me earlier. The *News* ran a list of New Year's resolutions. Said if Roper didn't get a renewed dose of talent from Santa, he should resolve to take a one-way ticket to Siberia as his contribution to the team."

"That's awful," Amy said, shocked by the brutal

treatment despite her feelings about Roper at the moment.

"That's New York," Sophie replied. "Something you'll be getting used to, I promise."

Amy nodded. "Still, I can't imagine being the center of such negative press day in and day out."

Yank shrugged. "In this city, it comes with the territory. The bigger the contracts, the worse the scrutiny and the higher the expectations. Let's go save him," Yank said. He practically gave Amy a shove forward, calling Roper's name at the same time.

So much for steering clear of him, Amy thought. And one glance his way had her wondering why she wanted to.

"I'm sorry," Sophie whispered, catching up with her.

"Not a problem," Amy said with a forced smile as they walked forward.

Yank Morgan trailed right along with them until Lola deliberately pulled him away for a scolding.

Amy chuckled at the family dynamic, one to which she could relate. But she had something more important to focus on now than Yank and Lola.

Roper's gaze locked on Amy's and her insides twisted with the familiar sense of awareness he'd invoked in her once before.

"Ladies, please come rescue me from wedding talk," Roper said, reaching out and putting an arm around Sophie's shoulder.

But he never broke eye contact with Amy.

"Wedding?" Sophie asked, her voice rising. "I didn't know you were even seeing someone special."

Wedding? A voice inside Amy's head echoed and her stomach cramped.

"As in, you and a member of the opposite sex making a permanent commitment? Someone give me a fan. I think I'm going to faint." Sophie waved a hand in front of her face, mocking him and chuckling at the same time.

"Did you hear that, John? They think *you're* getting married." The woman by his side, a different woman from the last one Amy had seen him with, laughed in real amusement.

When she turned around, Amy realized the other woman was much younger than she'd originally thought. Certainly younger than Amy and definitely younger than John Roper.

"John's not my fiancé, he's my brother," the other woman explained.

Amy let out a breath she hadn't realized she'd been holding. She wanted to dismiss the wave of relief washing over her, but she couldn't. Roper wasn't getting married and she could breathe again. Obviously, despite her frustration with him over their first meeting, the attraction was still there, strong as ever.

"Ah, now that makes more sense." Sophie nodded in understanding. "I couldn't see you taking yourself off the market, and I definitely couldn't see the papers missing out on the courtship."

"Ha, ha," Roper muttered.

While they were sparring, Amy took a moment to look at the younger woman with fresh eyes. With the family connection made, Amy saw the resemblance now—the sandy-blond hair, the shape and color of their green eyes and the matching dimples.

"Sabrina, meet everyone here." Roper inclined his head towards his sibling. "Everyone, meet my sister, Sabrina." He finished the introductions with a quick wave of his hand.

"Nice to meet you all." Sabrina smiled, once again reinforcing the family resemblance. "I wish I could stay and hang out, but I've got to go find my fiancé."

"Nice to meet you," Amy murmured, but Roper's sister had taken off before she could hear the reply.

Sophie glanced at her watch. "I should follow her lead. Riley should have been here by now."

"Go on. I'll take good care of Amy while you're gone."

Sophie shot Amy a look of concern, but Amy didn't want the other woman worrying about her or thinking she couldn't handle herself with one of the Hot Zone's clients.

Amy put on her brightest smile. "Say hi to Riley and tell him I'll catch up with him in a few minutes," Amy said.

"Are you sure?" Sophie's gaze bounced between Amy and Roper.

Roper pushed off from where he was leaning against the wall and rose to his full, overwhelming height.

"Don't worry about me," Roper said, treating Amy to a wink and a grin that caused a tingling straight down to her toes.

"I wasn't. Amy?" Sophie asked.

"Go find my cousin and give him a kiss for me." She dismissed the other woman's worry with an encouraging smile.

Sophie turned to Roper. "You know that Riley will kick your ass if you misbehave, so be good to Amy. She's new in town."

He cocked an eyebrow, throwing a sexy look her way. "When am I ever not good?"

Which was exactly what had Amy on edge. But she was a big girl. She could handle herself, as well as John Roper.

Sophie frowned, but after a lingering glance at Amy, took off to find her husband, leaving them alone.

Roper stepped closer. And Amy knew she was in deep trouble.

CHAPTER TWO

WHEN YANK INSISTED ROPER show up at this gig, he'd agreed under duress. Now Roper realized fate wanted him here so it could present him with the one thing he needed—a distraction from his career problems, his sister's wedding and his brother's constant whining about a loan. Amy Stone provided that distraction. Apparently life had given him a second chance, and he decided to take this as the first positive sign in ages. Maybe things were looking up after all.

He vividly recalled the instant attraction he'd felt for Amy the first time he'd laid eyes on her. And the stirring in his body told him *that* much hadn't changed. He'd gone to the wedding out of obligation, still in a funk over the blown World Series. But one look at the pretty brunette and all thoughts of his problems had fled. She'd been a breath of fresh air in his down-and-out life. He'd actually forgotten all about his date, mostly because she was simply arm candy and hadn't meant anything to him at all. Not that that was an excuse. Although Roper liked women, all women—blond, brunette or redhead, natural or from a bottle—when he looked at Amy, the punch in the gut had been harder and more defined.

He hadn't lost sight of the fact that he'd made an ass of himself the last time they were together and he owed her an apology for what had transpired. Now, with everyone gone, he and Amy were alone in their own corner of the party and she met his gaze head-on, not blinking or backing down.

He admired the fact that he couldn't rattle her and refused to rush his perusal. She had tanned skin only someone from a southern state could manage, a fresh, unjaded look in her eyes, and curly hair that didn't appear overly set with sprays or products. He could definitely get into tangling his hands in the soft brown curls.

But most of all he wanted to be with a woman who in all likelihood didn't keep up with New York sports news and Roper's humiliations. One who wouldn't pity him, judge him or want something from him in any way. Of course, he was getting ahead of himself. Chances were good she hadn't forgiven him for the scene at the wedding, and he couldn't blame her.

"So how have you been?" he asked once they were alone, or as alone as they could be in a room full of people.

"Just fine, and you?" She folded her arms across her chest, causing her cleavage to swell above the glittery gold tank she wore beneath a white silk blouse.

He knew Amy's movement was unintentional, and

he had to admit her lack of pretense was one of the things he found most appealing about her. "I've been better," he admitted, opting for honesty.

But he didn't want to get into his recent problems. He cleared his throat and asked, "Been in town long?" Not his best line, but he wanted to change the subject.

She shook her head. "Not very."

She wasn't making this easy. For the first time, he was uptight around a woman and unsure of how to reach her. "So, um, when do you leave?" he asked.

She raised an eyebrow. "Anxious to get rid of me already?"

He shook his head, exhaling hard. "I'm blowing this big-time. Let's backtrack, okay? It's good to see you again."

"Same here." She immediately pursed her lips.

He'd bet she wished she could take that comment back, but he liked her refreshing honesty.

She turned, obviously scanning the crowd.

He followed her gaze but couldn't pinpoint anyone or anything that would have distracted her. "Looking for someone?"

"As a matter of fact, I am," she said as she pivoted back to face him. "I was trying to locate your date."

A grin tugged at his mouth. "What makes you think I brought one?" he asked.

"Experience."

"Touché."

She shrugged. "I can't imagine you spending New

Year's Eve alone." She reached her hand out, tapping a finger against his pink Ralph Lauren dress shirt.

She was bolder than he thought she'd be, but the slight trembling of her fingers told him the movement was forced. He'd bet she didn't want him to think he could get to her again.

Well, hell. *She* got to him. "You wound me," Roper said.

"You'll live."

He laughed hard, something he hadn't done in way too long. "I suppose I deserved that."

She grinned. "You supposed right." Her hand lingered. Her pink fingernails were short and blended with the color of his shirt.

His flesh burned hot underneath the material. He couldn't tear his gaze from her delicate fingertips lingering so close to the buttons that would let his skin touch hers.

She followed his stare, glanced down, realized she hadn't removed her hand and snatched it away, leaving him to wonder if she'd felt the same searing heat.

She cleared her throat. "Well, your shirt's clean so I assume you've been a good boy. You haven't ticked off your date, at least not yet. So where is she? Ladies' room? Buffet table?"

They were bantering easily and he was glad. But he'd like for her to get to know him better so he could erase the bad first impression he'd made. "If I admit that was tacky and I apologize, can we start over?" he asked.

"That depends." She narrowed her gaze, assessing him in silence, but assessing him nonetheless.

Roper decided the fact that she couldn't take her eyes off him was a good thing. At least it was mutual. He couldn't stop staring at her, either. The more he thought about it, the more he realized she'd be good for him. A welcome break from physical therapy for his sprained shoulder and from wondering whether or not he'd return in time for spring training.

"I didn't come with a date," he admitted, refocusing on Amy. "Lesson learned the hard way." Thank God.

She inclined her head. "That's a start," she murmured.

"What if I told you I was so taken by you at the wedding that I couldn't help myself, date or no date?"

She swiped her tongue over her lightly glossed lips. "I'd say you were pushing it and would be better off with just the apology."

"Even if I was telling the truth?"

"Especially then," she said, her voice huskier than before.

He stepped closer, so close he could examine each freckle on her nose and cheeks. "Come on, give me another chance. Let's start fresh." On impulse, he reached out and ran his finger down the tip of her nose. Skin touched skin and his hand sizzled on contact.

Her eyes widened with awareness, but she didn't back away.

Pleased, he tipped his head even closer. "So what do you say?"

She bit down on her lower lip, pausing in thought.

The seconds that he waited were the longest of his life.

"For the sake of peace, why not?" she finally said.

He had the second chance he'd sought, he thought with relief. "Can I get you some punch?"

She wrinkled her nose. "I think I'm going to stay away from alcohol. Besides, I should really get—"

A loud bell-like sound clanged, drowning out her voice.

"What's that?" Amy yelled over the noise.

"Sounds like a fire alarm."

And he must have been right because the guests, talking loudly among themselves, headed for the front of the offices leading to the hallway.

"Let's get moving," he said.

"Are you serious? We're twenty floors up!" Panicked, she grabbed for her heels.

"What are you doing?"

"I was going to take off my shoes so I could run downstairs easier!"

He swallowed a laugh, knowing her fear was real. "In my experience, more often than not it's a false alarm."

She narrowed her gaze. "Haven't you ever seen *The Towering Inferno?*"

He chuckled aloud this time. "It's a bad seventies

movie, not reality. But you have a point. Let's get going. If the shoes don't hurt, you can keep them on. We're not going to be running. Just moving quickly."

She nodded.

"Shoes on or off?" he asked, talking loudly to compensate for the clanging bell.

"On. The heels aren't that high. I'll be fine."

Before she could make a run for the stairs or push through the crowds, Roper slipped his hand into hers and took control. He led her to the fire exit along with the rest of the guests and they maneuvered the long walk down in silence, punctuated by the alarm but with no hint of smoke or fire. Finally they stepped into the front lobby and were greeted by firemen in uniform directing people to the sidewalk across the street.

From what Roper could gather, the fire chief thought it was a false alarm, but until they checked out the building, they couldn't be sure. Everyone needed to evacuate.

Outside, he caught up with one of his teammates.

Jorge Calderone lifted a hand in greeting. "Someone saw Yank Morgan trip on his Noodle and accidentally pull on the fire alarm," he said in his heavy accent.

Roper shook his head and laughed. "You're kidding. Was the old man hurt?"

"He's fine. But Sophia *mucho* angry that he ruined the party."

Roper thought of perfectionist Sophie and said, "I just bet she is."

"I'm not staying to freeze my ass off out here. See ya, *mi amigo*." Jorge strode away without looking back.

Roper turned to Amy. "I'd have introduced you to my friend but he took off too fast."

"Not a problem." Her voice shook as she spoke and she had wrapped her arms around her upper body as she shivered in the below-freezing temperatures.

He slipped his sport jacket off and wrapped it around her shoulders.

She smiled appreciatively. "Thanks. I left my jacket at the coat check when I arrived, and my body is used to much warmer temperatures."

"I should have figured as much. Can I take you somewhere for dinner? I know a nice place with good food." The party might be over, but he wasn't ready to part ways with Amy just yet.

"No thanks. I really should just go home, change and get warm. Oh, no." She swung around and glanced back at the building.

"What's wrong?"

She shut her eyes, frustration clear in her expression. "I left my key in my coat pocket."

He shoved his hands into his front trouser pockets for warmth. "I'm sure the hotel would issue you another one, unless your ID is in your pocket, too?"

"No. But I'm not talking about a hotel key card. I'm talking about the actual key to my apartment."

"Wait, you live here? In New York?" Suddenly he

was wary. Earlier when he'd pursued her, some-where in the back of his mind was the knowledge that Amy was in town for a short time. No hopes, no expectations to add to his burdens. Except, appar-ently, he was wrong.

"I just moved here. I'm subletting Micki's apart-ment since it's too small for her whole family and they stay at Damian's when they're in the city, anyway." Amy hopped from foot to foot in order to keep warm. "I take it Micki didn't mention it?"

Roper shook his head. He was going to strangle his best friend for the omission. If he'd known Amy was a permanent resident, he wouldn't have restarted his flirtation. He was looking for a quick fix and a good time. Not a relationship with a woman nearby who, though she kept her distance now, would un-doubtedly begin to expect something more eventu-ally. He'd had enough of that already.

"I could talk to Sophie or Yank and see if they have an extra key, but they look tied up with the firemen," she said, glancing over his shoulder. "I guess I'll just wait."

Her eyes were wide, her cheeks flushed red from the cold and her curls were tousled around her pretty face. Oh, hell, who was he kidding? Even if he had known she'd moved to town, he'd have had a hard time staying away. Besides, he wasn't going to over-think this, just make the most of it.

She shivered and he stepped toward the curb,

hailing the first yellow cab that appeared and opening the door so she could get in first.

"Where are we going?" she asked.

"My place." Where she could warm up before he took her back to her building to see if the doorman or super had a spare key.

It was New Year's Eve and he wanted to keep her with him for a while longer.

AMY HADN'T AGREED TO go to his apartment. She just wanted to get warm. She settled into the taxicab seat, then Roper sat down beside her. His body heat rippled through her, warming her when just seconds before she was chilled inside and out.

He rattled off an address to the driver.

"Wait."

"You need warm clothes and maybe some hot food before dealing with Micki's grouchy doorman," he said, before leaning forward and telling the driver to go.

She knew better than to sound like an ungrateful brat, considering she was freezing, hungry and she had nowhere else to go. "Good point. Thanks." Teeth chattering, she leaned back in her seat for the duration of the ride to his high-rise farther uptown.

When she finally walked into his apartment twenty minutes later, she was immediately reminded that she still wasn't used to city living. In her old world, one-floor ranch homes were the norm. Her house in Florida hadn't been huge, but because everything was spread out on one level, the square footage seemed larger. Her father had left her mother with enough insurance money to let them live comfortably, and once her uncle had bought the real estate he'd turned into a retirement community along with his fellow investors, he'd insisted his sisters move there, as well. Amy had lived in one of the smaller units, paying token rent. Here in New York, her new apartment was small and quaint.

Roper's place was enormous. She sensed how large it was just by looking across, past the sliding doors to the terrace off the living room. Then there was the decor. In a masculine cocoa-and-cream color scheme, the living room held a plush suede sofa and ottoman, two club chairs and a rectangular marble cocktail table in the center. A massive large-screen TV hung on the wall across from the sitting area, while behind the couch, framed artwork made the room come alive.

"Like it?" Roper asked as he tossed his keys into a bowl in a practiced movement.

"It's gorgeous."

He grinned. "Thanks. I decorated it myself." The pride in his voice was unmistakable.

"I'm impressed." What other hidden talents did he have? Amy wondered.

He shrugged. "Why pay a professional if I can just as easily do it myself? That's my motto. Anyway, let me get you something to change into. My sister leaves comfortable clothes here in case she's too lazy to go home, which used to happen pretty often before she met her fiancé. She won't mind if you borrow them."

Amy rubbed her hands up and down her arms, covered only by her thin blouse. "Thanks."

"After you warm up, we'll talk about what to eat. I'll be right back."

She turned to study her surroundings once more, her gaze coming to rest on the trophies in a dark wood cabinet with glass doors. MVP, Golden Glove and other notable mentions were inscribed on plaques with John Roper's name.

He walked back into the room with a stack of clothes in his hand. "Take your pick."

"Nice set of awards. Once again, you've impressed me," she said as she accepted a sweat outfit.

"I hope the awards aren't the only things you like about me, because you know what they say, all good things come to an end." He studied her through narrowed eyes.

"I don't know you well enough to know what I like about you." She knew better than to mention the career problems she'd just learned about tonight.

"Good answer." He smiled and his eyes softened, warming her a bit more.

She supposed it couldn't be easy to meet women and not know whether they were interested in him or in his status and money. Amy had no use for either. She'd grown up comfortable and didn't need excessive luxury, although what her mother couldn't afford, her uncle had always provided. But Amy never took having material things for granted. Love and family were much more important than money. But he didn't know enough about her to understand she was a genuine person and she knew better than to try to convince him with mere words.

She had already seen there was more to Roper than the player she'd assumed him to be. Like his ability to apologize for mistakes and his chivalry in bringing her back here to warm up with seemingly no ulterior motive.

"Let's get to know each other better over a good meal. While you change, I'll fix us up something to eat," he said.

"There's no need for you to go to any trouble. We can order in. It's easier. And I ought to know—I've been living on takeout."

Although she had essentially been the caretaker in the family, keeping everyone busy and out of trouble, she'd also been spoiled by living near her mother and aunt. They'd served her home-cooked meals and delivered them to her doorstep if she wanted to be alone. She hadn't had to worry about fixing things for herself, which was a good thing, because she was a hazard in the kitchen. Here in New York, she'd been too busy making Micki's apartment her own and learning her way around the city to attempt making meals, too.

"That settles it, then. I'm definitely cooking. It

relaxes me, and besides, it's healthier than eating the fried food and heavy sauces you'll find in takeout."

She couldn't help but laugh. "A man who cooks? Now, *there's* something to like about you. I knew that list wouldn't be all that hard. I'll change and then maybe you can give me some pointers in the kitchen."

"I'd be happy to." His eyes sparkled with pleasure. "Bathroom's down the hall on your right." He pointed toward the back of the apartment.

She headed to change in his spare bathroom, something her apartment didn't have, and a few minutes later she returned to the kitchen dressed in sweats that were a little snug but much warmer and more comfortable than the outfit she'd worn to the party.

She stood in the doorway and took in the gorgeous state-of-the-art kitchen. "Wow. My mother would be impressed."

"I'm impressed, too." His gaze traveled leisurely over her, his eyes darkening with distinct approval. "You dress down as well as you dress up. The rumpled, fresh-out-of-bed look suits you," he said with a sexy grin.

Her face warmed at the compliment and her body followed suit.

"I didn't realize you were that much taller than my sister," he said, taking in the sweats that she'd rolled around her calves.

She glanced down at her bare ankles. "Well, at least capris are in style."

"They are and they look great on you."

"Thanks." A flush rose to her cheeks. She could say the same about how good he looked, too.

He'd opened the first few buttons on his shirt and rolled up his sleeves, giving him an edgy, sexy look. "So let's get started. You said you wanted lessons. I take it cooking's not your thing?"

She sighed and lifted her hands uselessly in the air. "Nope. They say children learn by watching, but I'm afraid I never picked up Mom's talent. Not even the basics."

"Well, then, sit and I'll teach you."

She realized he'd already taken out presliced chicken strips and now he was slicing fresh vegetables on a cutting board. A wok sat ready and waiting for him to use.

"Starting with precut and sliced food helps," she said, laughing.

He raised an eyebrow. "So you're that much of a novice, hmm?"

"And you're that much of an expert?"

He nodded.

Everything about the man took her by surprise. A really pleasant surprise.

She settled herself onto a barstool near the island, where he was working.

"I buy presliced chicken because my schedule's so hectic I never know how much time I'll have. On a night like tonight, it comes in handy. You can buy precut vegetables, as well, but it takes me no time and I'd rather eat fresh. Now I'm nearly ready to toss the vegetables into the wok."

She blinked at how fast he'd prepared a meal that would have taken her an hour minimum. "Maybe I should be taking notes," she mused as she reached over and plucked a carrot from the cutting board.

"Hey, quit nibbling or you won't be hungry enough to enjoy my masterpiece." He playfully smacked at her hand, but she was faster.

She nabbed another carrot before he could stop her.

In two steps he stood by her side, his presence big and overwhelming, the heat in his eyes matching the desire pulsing through her veins. From the moment she'd laid eyes on this man, she'd been seduced by his looks. What sane woman wouldn't be?

But in the short time she was with him tonight, she'd seen glimpses of the everyday guy he really was. She really liked what she saw.

He reached for the carrot and she tucked it tighter into her hand.

"Give it up," he ordered, clearly amused by her game.

She bit the inside of her cheek. "Make me."

He tickled her but she held on fast, eagerly anticipating his next method of extraction.

Their eyes met and held. Her pulse pounded hard in her throat and the anticipation of his lips hot and hard on hers sent tremors quaking through her body.

She slid her tongue over her mouth, moistening her lips, waiting, hoping…

The jarring ring of the telephone broke the thick silence surrounding them. His head jerked toward the sound.

Needing space, Amy jumped up from her chair. "You should answer it," she said, her voice unusually shaky.

He shot her a glance filled with equal parts heat and regret before grabbing the portable phone behind him. "Yeah," he barked into the phone, then listened to whoever was on the other end.

"Sorry. Happy New Year to you, too, Mom. Why aren't you out at one of those Hollywood parties you love so much?"

Hollywood? That was an interesting tidbit of information, Amy thought. And far better to focus on that than how close they'd come to kissing.

"Oh, right. Time difference. I forgot. I'm distracted, that's all." His gaze settled on Amy, his stare deep and consuming, letting her know he hadn't forgotten what had almost happened between them. What could still happen if she let it.

He cleared his throat. "That's okay. What's going on?" he asked. His expression darkened the longer his mother spoke. "No, Mom, I'm not giving Ben money to invest in a gym."

He listened, then said, "Because giving money to my brother is like throwing it away, that's why."

Roper pinched the bridge of his nose. "Have you forgotten about all the failed businesses that I did subsidize for him? Never mind. I can't talk about this now. I have company."

He winked at Amy, but she didn't miss the fact that his previously playful side had disappeared.

"Yes, Mom, *female company.* Just how long am I supposed to compensate Ben because I made it in the majors and he didn't?"

Obviously his mother wasn't listening to what Roper said, and Amy winced. As an only child, she wasn't used to dealing with siblings. But she *was* used to coping with stubborn adults who acted like kids and who wouldn't take no for an answer. She was being given an inkling into Roper's family dynamics, and they seemed to be in as much turmoil as his career.

"I didn't say family wasn't important, Mom. Go to your party and we'll talk about this tomorrow," he said, his voice softening.

He obviously loved his mother. He also had a complex family situation, but really, who didn't? She'd had to leave home to get a life, but that didn't mean she wasn't worried about every move Rose and Darla made. She loved them, but there were times they grated on her nerves, pushing every emotional button she possessed.

Roper obviously felt the same way about his family. His life wasn't easy, she thought. She quietly slipped the carrot they'd fought over into her mouth and waited for him to finish his call.

"Yes," he said, raising a finger toward Amy to indicate he'd be off soon. "Yes, I know. Go enjoy and forget about it for now. Oh, and Mom? Happy New Year," Roper said.

He hung up the phone and turned her way. A flush highlighted his cheekbones and a muscle ticked on one side of his face. "Nothing like a call from Mom to kill the mood," he said too lightly.

Amy figured he needed a minute or two to calm down, so she let him turn away and place the food into the heated wok.

She tried to use the minutes wisely, reminding herself she wasn't going to be taken in by his charm, something he possessed and no doubt knew how to use in spades. After all, he was not just an athlete but a showman. Yet already she was coming to know him better and to like him despite all common sense. She tried to calm her still-racing heart, but Roper's effect on her was very strong. And the whole night lay ahead….

CHAPTER THREE

ROPER COULD NOT BELIEVE his mother was bugging him about helping Ben yet again. On New Year's Eve. Just as he was finally going to kiss Amy.

Still wound tight, he tossed the last handful of vegetables into the wok with too much force and oil splattered up at him. He stepped back to avoid being hit.

"Families can be a bitch," Amy said at last, breaking the tension.

He turned toward her. "Especially mine. Here's the thing." He set two full glasses of water on the table. "I love my family, but everyone needs something from me. They pull at me from every direction and like you said, I feel guilty not responding on the minute."

"Because you always have before."

"Exactly." He placed his hand on the top of his chair. "Now, how about some champagne? It *is* New Year's Eve."

She crinkled her nose in that cute way she had whenever she wasn't sure she wanted to do something. "Maybe just one glass."

He obliged, pulling a bottle from the fridge, popping

the cork, pouring and finally sitting down beside her at the table. "A toast," he said, raising his glass.

She raised hers, as well.

"To…new friends," he said. He hadn't known how much he needed someone like Amy in his life until tonight. She was special.

A warm smile tilted her lips. "To new friends," she said, a gleam in her eyes as she touched her glass against his and took a sip.

"Good?"

She nodded. "Excellent. Now, you were saying that everyone in your family needs something from you. Care to elaborate beyond Ben?"

He lifted his fork and tasted his meal. "Mmm. Care to compliment the cook first?"

Laughing, she took a bite and paused.

And paused. And paused so long he nearly fell off the edge of his chair waiting for her opinion.

"This is unbelievably good!" she said at last with a smile on her face that bordered on orgasmic.

All he could imagine was putting that same expression on her face in a more intimate setting. But somehow, he managed to clear his throat and continue their discussion. "Thank you," he said, ridiculously thrilled that he'd pleased her palate.

He loved to cook and often did so to relieve tension when he had home games or just to help himself relax during the off-season. And he'd needed one helluva lot of relaxing lately.

"Well? You were saying about your family?" Amy prodded without shame.

"Anyone ever tell you you're like a pit bull when you get your teeth into something?" he asked. She didn't reply, merely continued eating and waiting, knowing he'd have to answer eventually. "Oh, all right. I'll tell you, but I'll probably put you to sleep with my family saga."

She shook her head. "Try me."

He shrugged. "Mom's an actress, or at least she was until she aged beyond the point where cosmetic surgery enabled her to take youthful roles."

"Would I know of her?" Amy asked.

"Her stage name is Cassandra Lee."

Amy's eyes lit up. "From the movies *Maiden Lane* and *On Sandy Shores!* My mother is a huge fan and took me to her movies all the time when I was growing up!"

"That's her," Roper said. "These days she's too vain to accept the more mature roles, so she's settled into living her life with me supporting her. Not that I mind, since she worked hard to take care of us while I was a kid."

"It must be hard aging in Hollywood."

"There are plenty of better-known actresses who've handled it. Sharon Stone, Meryl Streep, Annette Bening. Mom has truly made *Poor Me* into an art form. But I'm used to it by now."

Amy finished her meal, leaving nothing on her

plate. She wasn't one of those women who pushed the food around instead of eating, and that pleased him.

She raised her glass and sipped her champagne. "What about your father? Is he still alive? Mine isn't. He passed away a few months after I started junior high," she said, her tone wistful.

"I'm sorry." He wanted to squeeze her hand, but she didn't seem to want or need sympathy.

She finished her champagne and smiled.

He poured them both another glass. "My father is still alive. He just wasn't ever much of an influence in my life, except for the fact that I inherited my baseball talent from him. Eduardo Montoya. He was a bigtime player in his day. And before you ask, Roper was my mother's name before she had it changed."

Amy inclined her head. "I've never heard of him, but that isn't saying much."

He nodded. "It's kind of nice that you don't know the professional me."

She nodded in understanding. He couldn't get over how much he'd revealed to her tonight. Other than with Micki, he never discussed his famous parents with anyone. He didn't need another reason for people to be impressed with something about him that had nothing to do with who he was inside. Amy was different. She was easy to talk to and genuinely interested in him, unlike the usual women he dated, ones who were more interested in his career, status and what he could buy them. Before now, all he'd wanted from his companions was a good time, in bed and out. Yet here was a woman he could talk to….

Unwilling to think about that, he rose and started to clean up. Amy helped and in the process, they managed to finish the bottle of champagne. Once the plates were in the dishwasher, and the kitchen was sparkling, he finally led Amy into the family room and turned on the big-screen TV to watch the ball drop in Times Square. He'd have offered to take her home, but he was enjoying her company too much and he didn't want to ring in the New Year alone.

She snuggled into the corner of the couch and didn't object when he eased in close beside her. From the way she'd tripped once on her way into the den and giggled a few times over a joke he hadn't made, Roper knew the champagne had gone to her head.

She was adorable to watch, and he liked having her in his home. Another first.

She narrowed her gaze at the TV screen depicting Times Square. "I can't believe all those people are standing outside in that freezing-cold weather. It was awful when we were there and it wasn't by choice!" She shivered at the memory, giving him just the excuse he needed.

"Spoken like a true Florida girl." Roper pulled her close at the same time the countdown to the New Year began.

"Know what I was doing last year at this time?" Amy asked him, her eyes wide, her face close to his.

"What?"

"Breaking up a fight between two men who wanted to kiss Aunt Darla first once the ball dropped," she murmured. "It's been ages since I spent New Year's with someone my own age."

"Oh, yeah? And when was the last time you were kissed?" he asked, staring at her moist lips.

"Way too long," she said as her eyes fluttered closed.

He knew she had to be slightly tipsy, because he couldn't imagine her letting her guard down this easily otherwise. Still, she'd seemed willing enough earlier in the evening before they were interrupted by the telephone.

He had every intention of taking that next step with her now.

AMY'S STOMACH FLUTTERED as she waited, delicious ripples of anticipation licking at her from deep inside. Roper's eyes darkened and he lowered his head, slowly dragging out the anticipation until finally his mouth came down on hers.

The initial touch set off more sparks. Spiraling whirlpools of desire started slowly and built larger, filling her from inside out. His kiss was silky smooth, the stuff of sensual dreams as he drew his mouth back and forth over hers and lulled her into a hazy stupor of wanting. She lifted her hands and wrapped her arms around his neck, pulling him closer, something he seemed to appreciate because he slid his tongue over the seam of her lips, teasing her back and forth until she opened her mouth and let him inside.

Her tongue tangled with his, matching every fantasy she'd ever had of him and providing even more. He ran his thumbs over her cheek, gently caressing her face while he ravished her mouth. She didn't need food, not when she had this. Wanting to taste more of him, she curled her hands into the hair at the nape of his neck, then tilted her head back, giving him better access. He swept his tongue one last time around her mouth, then began a warm, wet trail of kisses down the side of her face, her neck, her throat, until his head came to rest on her chest just above her cleavage.

Her heart pounded and her breasts felt full, her nipples tightening into hardened peaks at the thought of his wicked mouth suckling her hard. Moisture pooled between her legs, dampening her panties as desire pulsed through her body.

"You taste sweet," he said against her skin.

She moaned. The sound tore from deep inside her at the same time the crowds cheered at the dropping of the ball.

"Happy New Year," she said, drunk with happiness.

"Happy New Year." He pulled back, and she tilted her head, smiling at him, expecting him to kiss her again. After all, the first time had been spectacular and he obviously wanted her, too.

Instead, he pushed himself up and rose to his feet.

"Where are you going?" she asked.

"To get you a blanket so I can tuck you in. Much as it kills me, I'm going to be a gentleman."

She started to rise, then decided it was too much effort. She hadn't had alcohol in a long time and the champagne had gone straight to her head. Of course, it could also be his kisses that made her feel light-headed and dizzy.

"Sit tight," he said, a sexy smile lifting his lips. "I'll be right back."

Amy laid her head back against the couch and shut her eyes, waiting for him to return. Maybe she'd be able to pull him down so they could finish what they'd started. Her mind might be hazy, but she was clear on what she wanted.

Amy wanted John Roper.

HQN™

We *are* romance™

HAPPY READING!

As part of our special sizzling summer reads offer, you can now **SAVE $1.00** on the purchase of **HOT PROPERTY** by *New York Times* bestselling author **Carly Phillips**,

available in July wherever books are sold, including most bookstores, supermarkets, drugstores, department and discount stores.

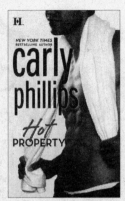

If you've enjoyed this sizzling excerpt,
purchase the complete book

Hot
PROPERTY

Available in July

by *New York Times* bestselling author
carly phillips

at Borders and **SAVE $1.⁰⁰**
on your purchase!

159032490000000000

BORDERS®

NEW YORK TIMES Bestselling Author

SUSAN MALLERY

Sweet Talk

"Smart, sexy romance doesn't get any better than this."
—DEBBIE MACOMBER, #1 *NEW YORK TIMES* BESTSELLING AUTHOR

Dear Reader,

Welcome to the first book in my new trilogy,
THE BAKERY SISTERS. These stories are about
sisters who—you guessed it—own a bakery. But
as in many families, the people who should love
each other the most often don't get along at all.

In *Sweet Talk*, Claire Keyes returns home to find
what she's always missed most. Only, her sisters
aren't that happy to see her. They're also not
talking to each other, and neither wants to tell
Claire why. Claire has her own problems. She's
a concert pianist who can't perform. Every time
she steps on stage, she has a panic attack. She's
totally freaked, terrified about her future, and this
is possibly the worst time in the world to meet the
man of her dreams. But when has love ever had
good timing?

So grab a cupcake or a cookie and enjoy this
yummy taste of *Sweet Talk!*

Susan

CHAPTER ONE

CLAIRE KEYES jumped to answer the phone when it rang, deciding an angry call from her manager was more appealing than sorting the pile of dirty clothes in the middle of her living room.

"Hello?"

"Hi. Um, Claire? It's Jesse."

Not her manager, Claire thought, relieved. "Jesse who?"

"Your sister."

Claire kicked aside a blouse and sank onto the sofa. "Jesse?" she breathed. "It's really you?"

"Uh-huh. Surprise."

Surprise didn't begin to describe it. Claire hadn't seen her baby sister in years. Not since their father's funeral when she'd tried to connect with all the family she had left only to be told that she wasn't welcome, would never be welcome and that if she was hit by a bus, neither Jesse nor Nicole, Claire's fraternal twin, would bother to call for help.

Claire still remembered being so stunned by the verbal attack that she'd actually stopped breathing.

She'd felt as if she'd been beaten up and left on the side of the road. Jesse and Nicole were her *family*. How could they reject her like that?

Not knowing what else to do, she'd left town and never returned. That had been seven years ago.

"So," Jesse said with a cheer that seemed forced. "How are you?"

Claire shook her head, trying to clear it, then glanced at the messy apartment. There were dirty clothes piled thigh-high in her living room, open suitcases by the piano, a stack of mail she couldn't seem to face and a manager ready to skin her alive if that would get her to do what she wanted.

"I'm great," she lied. "And you?"

"Too fabulous for words. But here's the thing. Nicole isn't."

Claire tightened her grip on the phone. "What's wrong with her?"

"Nothing…yet. She's going to have surgery. Her gallbladder. There's something weird about the placement or whatever. I can't remember. Anyway, she can't have that easy surgery with the tiny incisions. The lapi-something."

"Laparoscopic," Claire murmured absently, eyeing the clock. She was due at her lesson in thirty minutes.

"That one. Instead, they're going to be slicing her open like a watermelon, which means a longer recovery time. With the bakery and all, that's a problem. Normally I'd step in to help, but I can't right now. Things are…complicated. So we were talking and Nicole wondered if you would like to come back home and take care of things. She would really appreciate it."

Home, Claire thought longingly. She could go home. Back to the house she barely remembered but that had always placed so large in her dreams.

"I thought you and Nicole hated me," she whispered, wanting to hope but almost afraid to.

"We were upset before. It was an emotional time. Seriously, we've been talking about getting in touch with you for a while now. Nicole would have, um, called herself, but she's not feeling well and she was afraid you'd say no. She's not in a place to handle that right now."

Claire stood. "I would never say no. Of course I'll come home. I really want to. You're my family. Both of you."

"Great. When can you get here?"

Claire looked around at the disaster that was her life and thought about the angry calls from Lisa, her manager. There was also the master class she was supposed to attend and the few she had to teach at the end of the week.

"Tomorrow," she said firmly. "I can be there tomorrow."

"JUST SHOOT ME NOW," Nicole Keyes said as she wiped down the kitchen counters. "I mean it, Wyatt.

You must have a gun. Do it. I'll write a note saying it's not your fault."

"Sorry. No guns at my house."

None in hers, either, she thought glumly, then tossed the dishcloth back into the sink.

"The timing couldn't be worse for my stupid surgery," she muttered. "They're telling me I can't go back to work for six weeks. *Six*. The bakery isn't going to run itself. And don't you dare say anything about me asking Jesse. I mean it, Wyatt."

Her soon-to-be-ex-brother-in-law held up both hands. "Not a word from me. I swear."

She believed him. Not because she thought she frightened him but because she knew he understood that while some of the pain in her gut came from an inflamed gallbladder, most of it was about her sister Jesse's betrayal.

"I hate this. I hate my body turning on me this way. What have I ever done to it?"

Wyatt pushed out a chair at the table. "Sit. Getting upset isn't going to help."

"You don't actually know that."

"I can guess."

She plopped into the chair because it was easier than fighting. Sometimes, like now, she wondered if she had any fight left in her.

"What am I forgetting?" she asked. "I think I've gotten everything done. You remembered that I can't take care of Amy for a while, right?"

Amy was his eight-year-old daughter. Nicole looked after her a few afternoons a week.

Wyatt leaned forward and put his hand on her forearm. "Relax," he told her. "You didn't forget anything. I'll look in on the bakery every couple of days. You've got good people working for you. They love you and are loyal. Everything will be fine. You'll be home in a few days and you can start healing."

She knew he meant from more than just the surgery. There was also the issue of her soon-to-be ex-husband.

Instead of thinking about that bastard Drew, she stared at Wyatt's hand on her arm. He had big hands—scarred and callused. He was a man who knew how to work for a living. Honest, good-looking, funny.

She raised her gaze to his dark eyes. "Why couldn't I have fallen in love with you?" she asked.

He smiled. "Back at you, kid."

They would have been so perfect together…if only there had been a hint of chemistry.

"We should have tried harder," she muttered. "We should have slept together."

"Just think about it for a minute," he told her. "Tell me if it turns you on."

"I can't." Honestly, thinking about having sex with Wyatt kind of set her teeth on edge, and not in a good way. He was too much like a brother. If only his stepbrother, Drew, had caused the same reaction. Unfortunately with him, there had been fireworks. The kind that burned.

She pulled back and studied Wyatt. "Enough about me. You should get married again."

He reached for his mug of coffee. "No, thanks."

"Amy needs a mother."

"Not that badly."

"There are great women out there."

"Name one that isn't you."

Nicole thought for a minute, then sighed. "Can I get back to you on that?"

CLAIRE ARRIVED at the SeaTac Airport early in the afternoon, feeling very smug about making her own travel arrangements. She'd even booked a car for herself. Normally she would have used a car service, but she would have to drive back and forth to the hospital, then to the bakery. Nicole might need her to run errands. Wheels of her own made sense.

After wrestling her two very large suitcases off the baggage claim belt, she grabbed one in each hand and dragged them toward the escalator. The catwalk to the parking garage was long and the bags heavy. She was breathing hard by the time she reached a bank of elevators she had to take down to the rental car place. By the time she got to the Hertz office, she was regretting the long wool coat she'd shrugged on. Sweat trickled down her back, making her cashmere sweater stick to her.

She waited in line, excited about being here, nervous and filled with resolve to do whatever it took to reconnect with her sisters. They were being given a second chance. *She* wasn't going to blow it.

The woman at the counter waved her forward. Claire dragged the two suitcases along as she approached.

"Hi. I have a reservation."

"Name?"

"Claire Keyes." Claire handed over her driver's license and her platinum credit card.

The woman studied the driver's license. "Do you have insurance or do you want coverage on the car?"

"I'll take your coverage." It was easier than explaining that she didn't own a car and had, in fact, never owned a car. The only reason she had a driver's license at all was because she'd insisted on lessons when she'd turned eighteen and had studied and practiced until she'd passed the test.

"Any tickets or accidents?" the woman asked.

Claire smiled. "Not one." Getting a ticket or an accident would require actual driving. Something Claire hadn't done more than once or twice in the past ten years.

There were a couple of forms to sign, then the woman handed back the license and credit card.

"Number sixty-eight. It's a Malibu. You said midsize. I can get you something bigger, if you want."

Claire blinked at her. "Number sixty-eight what?"

"Your car. It's in slot sixty-eight. The keys are inside."

"Oh, great. I'll pass on something bigger."

"Okay. You need a map?"

"Yes, please."

Claire tucked the map into her purse, then dragged her suitcases out of the glass structure. She saw rows of cars and numbers at the end of each parking space. Counting as she went, she found number sixty-eight and stared at the silver Malibu.

It had four doors and looked huge. She swallowed. Was she really going to drive? A question for later, she told herself. First she had to get out of the parking lot.

Challenge number one turned out to be getting her luggage into the trunk. There didn't seem to be any way to open it. No buttons, no knobs. She pushed and pulled, but it wouldn't budge. Finally she gave up and maneuvered her two big bags into the backseat. Then she slid behind the wheel.

It took her a couple of minutes to get the seat moved up so she could actually reach the pedals. She managed to get the key in the ignition and turned it. The engine caught immediately. Claire carefully adjusted her mirrors, then drew in a breath. She was practically on her way.

Next she turned to the GPS system. It greeted her in French.

Claire stared at it. What on earth?

She pushed a few buttons. Yup, it was speaking French. Okay, sure, she also spoke the language, but not well enough to deal with it while driving. The potential to freak while on the road seemed big enough without adding a foreign language to the mix.

She punched buttons until she'd scrolled through Dutch and Japanese. Finally she heard the pleasant female voice in English.

The need to run screaming into the night faded slightly.

She continued reading the instruction card, then carefully punched in the address of the bakery. She'd forgotten to ask Jesse for the name of the hospital where Nicole would have her surgery, so the bakery seemed like the best place to start. Finally, she braced herself to drive out of the space.

Her chest was tight. She ignored that, along with the prickling that started on her back and moved over her whole body.

Not now, she thought frantically. Not now. She could panic later, when she wasn't about to drive.

She closed her eyes and breathed, pictured her sister lying in a hospital bed, in desperate need of help. That's where she needed to be, she reminded herself. With Nicole.

The sense of panic faded a little. She opened her eyes and began her journey.

The parking structure seemed dark and closed. Fortunately there weren't any cars in the row in front of her, so she would have extra room to turn as she drove out.

Slowly, carefully, she put the car in Drive. It started

to move right away. She jammed her foot on the brake. The whole car jerked. She eased up on the brake and it moved again. Moving six or eight inches at a time, she managed to make it out of her space. Fifteen minutes later she'd made her way out of the parking structure and onto the road that led out of the airport.

"In five hundred feet, stay to the right. I-5 is on the right."

The voice from the GPS system was very commanding, as if it knew Claire was totally clueless about driving in general and where she was going in particular.

"I-5 what?" Claire asked before she saw a sign for the I-5 freeway. She shrieked. "I can't go on the freeway," she told the GPS. "We need to go on regular streets."

There was a ding. "Stay to the right."

"But I don't want to."

She looked around frantically, but there didn't seem to be any other way to go. The road she was on just sort of eased into the freeway. She couldn't move to her left—there were too many cars in her way. Cars that suddenly started going really, really fast.

Claire clutched the steering wheel with both hands, her body stiff, her mind filled with images of fiery crashes.

"I can do this," she whispered to herself. "I can do this."

She pressed a little harder on the accelerator, until

she was going nearly forty-five. That had to be fast enough, didn't it? Who needed to go faster than that?

A big truck came up behind her and honked its horn. She jumped. More cars came up behind her, some getting really, really close. She was so busy trying not to be scared by the cars zipping around her that she forgot about merging until the GPS system reminded her, "I-5 north is to the right."

"What? What right? Do I want to go north?"

And then the road was turning and she was turning with it. She desperately wanted to close her eyes, but knew that would be bad. Fear made her sweat. She really wanted to rip off her coat, but couldn't. Not and keep from crashing. She was clutching the steering wheel so hard, her fingers ached.

She was doing this for Nicole, she reminded herself. For her sister. For family.

Her lane merged onto I-5. Still going forty-five, Claire eased into the right lane and vowed to stay there until it was time to exit.

By the time she got off, just north of the University district, she was shaking all over. She hated driving. Hated it. Cars were awful and drivers were rude, mean people who screamed at her. But she'd made it and that was what mattered.

She followed the directions from the GPS and managed to make her way into the parking lot next to the bakery. She turned off the car, leaned her forehead against the steering wheel and did her best to breathe.

When her heartbeat had slowed from humming-bird rate to that for a medium-size mammal, she straightened, then stared at the building in front of her.

The Keyes bakery had been in the same location for all of its eighty years of operation. Originally, her great-grandparents had rented only half the store-front. Over time, the business had grown. They'd bought out their neighbor's lease, then had bought the whole place about sixty years ago.

Pastries, cakes and breads filled the lower half of the two display windows. Delicate lettering listing other options covered the top half. A big sign above the door proclaimed Keyes Bakery—Home of the World's Best Chocolate Cake.

The multilayer chocolate confection had been praised by royalty and presidents, served by brides and written into several celebrity contracts as a "must have" on location shoots or backstage at concerts. It was about a billion calories of flour, sugar, butter, chocolate and a secret ingredient passed on through the family. Not that Claire knew what it was. But she would. She was confident Nicole would want to tell her immediately.

She got out of the car and smoothed the front of her sweater. It was cool enough that she kept on her coat, hoping it wasn't too wrinkled from the drive. After collecting her purse, she carefully locked the driver's door. Taking a deep breath, she walked into the bakery.

It was midafternoon and relatively quiet. There were two young moms sitting at a corner table with pastries and coffee. Two strollers with babies were between their chairs. Claire offered a smile as she made her way to the long counter. The teenage girl there looked at her.

"Can I help you?"

"Yes. I hope so. I'm Claire. Claire Keyes."

The teenager, a plump brunette with big, brown eyes sighed. "Okay. What can I get you? The rosemary garlic bread is hot out of the oven."

Claire smiled hopefully. "I'm Claire Keyes," she repeated.

"Heard that the first time."

Claire pointed to the sign on the wall. "Keyes, as in Nicole's sister."

The teenager's eyes got even bigger. "Oh, my God. No way. Are you really? The piano player?"

Claire winced. "Technically I'm a concert pianist." A soloist, but why quibble? "I'm here because of Nicole's surgery. Jesse called and asked me to—"

"Jesse?" The girl's voice came out as a shriek. "She didn't. Are you kidding? Oh, my God! I can't believe it." The teenager backed up as she spoke. "Nicole is so going to kill her. If she hasn't already. I just…" She held up her hand. "Wait here, okay? I'll be right back."

Before Claire could say anything, the girl took off toward the back.

Claire adjusted her bag on her shoulder and

looked at the inventory in the glass case. There were several pies, a couple of cakes, along with loaves of bread. Her stomach growled, reminding her she hadn't eaten all day. She'd been too nervous to have anything on the plane.

Maybe she could get some of that rosemary garlic bread and then stop at a deli for—

"What the hell are you doing here?"

Claire looked at the man walking toward her. He was big and rough looking, with tanned skin and the kind of body that said he either did physical work for a living or spent too much time at a gym. She did her best not to wrinkle her nose at the sight of his plaid shirt and worn jeans.

"I'm Claire Keyes," she began.

"I know who you are. I asked why you were here."

"Actually you asked me why the 'hell' I was here. There's a difference."

He narrowed his gaze. "Which is?"

"One question implies a genuine interest in the answer, the other lets me know that somehow I've annoyed you. You don't really care why I'm here, you just want me to know I'm not welcome. Which is strange, considering you and I have never met."

"I'm friends with Nicole. I don't have to have met you to know all I need to about you."

Ouch. Claire didn't understand. If Nicole was still mad at her, why had Jesse called and implied otherwise? "Who *are* you?"

"Wyatt Knight. Nicole is married to my step-brother."

Nicole got married? When? To whom?

A deep, deep sadness followed the questions. Her own sister hadn't bothered to tell her or invite her to the wedding. How pathetic was that?

Emotions chased across Claire Keyes's face. Wyatt didn't bother to try to read them. Women and what they felt were a mystery best left unsolved by mortal man. Trying to make sense of the female mind would drive a man to drink, then kill him.

Instead he studied the tall, slender blonde in front of him, looking for similarities to Nicole and Jesse.

Their eyes, he thought, taking in the big, blue irises. Maybe the shape of the mouth. The hair color…sort of. Nicole's was just blond. Claire's was a dozen different shades and shiny.

But nothing else was the same. Nicole was his friend, someone he'd known for years. A pretty enough woman, but regular looking. Claire dressed in off-white—from her too-long coat to the sweater and slacks she wore underneath. Her purse was beige, as were her boots. She looked like an ice princess…an evil one.

"I'd like to see my sister," Claire said firmly. "I know she's in the hospital. But I'm not sure which one."

"No way I'm going to tell you. I don't know why you're here, lady, but I can tell you Nicole doesn't want to see you."

"That's not what I heard."

"From who?"

"Jesse. She said Nicole was going to need help after her surgery. She called me yesterday and I flew in this morning." She raised her chin slightly. "I'm not going away, Mr. Knight, and you can't make me. I *will* see my sister. If you choose not to give me the information, I'll simply call every hospital in Seattle until I find her. Nicole is my family."

"Since when?" he muttered, recognizing the stubborn angle of her chin and the determination in her voice. The twins had that much in common.

Why had Jesse done this? To make more trouble? Or had she been trying to fix a desperate situation? The truth was Nicole *would* need help and she was just difficult enough not to ask. He would do what he could, but he had a business to run and Amy to look after. Nicole wouldn't want Drew around, assuming his good-for-nothing brother hadn't run off somewhere to hide. Jesse was a worse choice. Which left exactly no one else.

Why did he have to be making this decision? He swore under his breath. "Where are you staying?"

"At the house. Where else?"

"Fine. Stay there. Nicole will be home in a couple of days. You can take this up with her then."

"I'm not waiting two more days to see her."

Selfish, spoiled, egotistic, narcissistic. Wyatt remembered Nicole's familiar list of complaints about her sister. Right now, every one of them made sense to him.

"Listen," he said. "You can wait at the house or fly back to Paris or wherever it is you live."

"New York," she said quietly. "I live in New York."

"Whatever. My point is you're not going to see Nicole until she's had a couple of days to recover, even if that means I have to stand guard on her hospital room myself. You got that? She's in enough hurt right now from the surgery without having to deal with a pain in the ass like you."

CHAPTER TWO

CLAIRE DEFLATED like a punctured balloon, leaving Wyatt feeling like the biggest asshole this side of the Rockies. He told himself it was just an act, that she was born to play people and had only gotten better at it as she'd gotten older. For someone who claimed to care so much for her sister, she'd never once shown up here in all the years he'd known Nicole. Not for birthdays or even her sister's damn wedding. She'd missed Jesse's high school graduation. She was good at playing the victim, that was all, and he wasn't going to get sucked in to her game.

Just when he thought she was going to turn around and go away, she straightened. Her shoulders went back, her chin came up and she looked him square in the eye. "My sister called me."

"So you said."

"You don't believe me."

"I don't care enough to think about it one way or the other."

She tilted her head so that her long, shimmering

blond hair fell over one shoulder. "Nicole has a good friend in you. I hope she appreciates that."

So she'd moved on to sucking up. Probably an effective plan on anyone who wasn't clued in to her style.

"Jesse called me," she continued. "She told me about the surgery. You have to know that much is true, otherwise how would I know? Jesse also told me that Nicole wants me to help out afterward and is happy I'm here. Under the circumstances, I'm more inclined to believe her than you."

"I can tell you that as of twenty minutes before the surgery, Nicole had no idea you were going to show up. Trust me. She would have mentioned it."

Claire frowned slightly. "Nothing about this makes sense. Why would Jesse lie? Why would you?"

"I wouldn't."

She looked genuinely confused and Wyatt almost believed her. This messed-up situation had Jesse written all over it. The question was, why had the kid done it? To make a bad situation worse or did she really want to help Nicole? With Jesse it wasn't easy to tell.

"I'm staying," Claire told him. "Just so you're clear. I'm staying. I'm going to the hospital and—"

"No."

"But I—"

"No."

She looked at him. "You're very determined."

"I protect what's mine."

Something flickered in her eyes. Something sad and small that he didn't want to identify.

"Fine. I'll wait at the house until Nicole is ready to come home," Claire said at last. "Then she and I can figure out what's going on."

"It would be easier if you just went back to New York."

"I don't do easy. Never have. Career hazard, I suppose."

He had no idea what she was talking about. Did she think anyone believed that playing the piano for a bunch of rich people in fancy European cities was hard?

He shrugged. He couldn't force Nicole's sister to disappear. As long as she didn't try to bug Nicole in the hospital, he would stay out of it.

"So Nicole will come home in a couple of days?" Claire asked.

"Something like that."

She smiled at him. "You're very determined not to give up any information, Mr. Knight, but as I'm going to be living in the same house it will be difficult to conceal Nicole's arrival from me."

"Wyatt. I'm not your boss and you're not my banker."

"Your employees call you by your last name?"

"No. I was making a point."

"My banker calls me Claire."

"My banker doesn't."

Her smile faded. "You don't like me very much."

He didn't bother to answer that.

"You don't even know me," she continued. "That hardly seems fair."

"I know enough."

She stiffened, as if he'd hit her. Egotistical and sensitive, he thought grimly. Hell of a combination.

Claire turned and walked out of the bakery. Wyatt followed to make sure she really did get into her car and drive away.

He glanced around the parking lot, half expecting to see a stretch limo or a Mercedes. But Claire's rental was a midsize four-door with luggage piled in the backseat.

"How much crap did you bring?" he asked before he could stop himself. "It wouldn't even fit in the trunk?"

She came to a stop and looked at him. "No. That's all I brought."

"What have you got against the trunk? Afraid you'll break a nail?"

"I, as you put it so elegantly, play piano. I don't have long nails." She straightened again and seemed to brace herself. "As I said before, I live in New York, where I don't keep a car. I don't drive much anywhere. I couldn't figure out how to open the trunk."

Now he knew why she'd braced herself. She was waiting for him to rip her a new one. It was a pretty sweet setup and he could think of a hundred cheap shots. Who didn't know how to open the trunk? His eight-year-old could do it.

What stopped him from saying that and more was the fact that she was expecting to be trashed and that, even knowing he didn't like her, she'd still exposed a vulnerable spot. Wyatt didn't mind being a mean bastard, but he wouldn't be a bully.

He moved next to her, took the keys from her hand and pointed to the attached fob. "Ever see one of these before? The little pictures tell you what the buttons do." He pushed the one that opened the trunk. It popped open.

Claire grinned at him. "Seriously? That's it?" She walked over and stared down into the space. "It's huge. I could have brought more luggage. Are there more buttons?"

She was thrilled on a level the key fob didn't deserve. "You don't get out much, do you?"

The smile widened. "Even less than you think."

"Door lock, door unlock, panic button."

"That is so cool."

She was like a kid with a new toy. She had to be jerking him around.

"Thank you," she told him. "Seriously, I felt like such an idiot at the car rental place, standing there not knowing what to do." She wrinkled her nose. "If only driving were this easy. Do people have to go so fast on the freeway?"

He had no idea what to think of her. Based on Nicole's infrequent comments about her sister, he knew not to trust her. But while she was as useless as Nicole had claimed, she wasn't nearly as cold and distant.

Not his problem, he reminded himself.

He handed the keys back to Claire. She reached out and took them. For a second, maybe two, they touched. His fingers on her palm, a brush of skin. Inconsequential. Except for the sudden burst of fire.

Goddamn sonofabitch, he thought grimly, jerking back his hand and stuffing it in his jacket pocket. No way. Not her. Dear God, anyone but her.

Claire was babbling on, probably thanking him. He wasn't listening. Instead he was wondering why, of all the women in all the world, he'd had to feel that hot, bright, sexual heat with her.

THE CALM-VOICED WOMAN in the GPS system led Claire to the house where she'd spent the first six years of her life. She found a parking space on the narrow street in front. It was by a driveway, so all she had to do was pull forward to claim it. There was no way she would ever be able to parallel park.

She turned off the engine, got out of the car and locked it, using the fob. Feeling foolishly proud of herself, she walked around to the back of the house and found the spare key where Jesse had said it would be. She unlocked the rear door and stepped into the house.

She hadn't been inside it for years. Nearly twelve, she thought, remembering the single night spent under this roof after her mother had died. One night with Jesse staring at her as though she was a stranger and Nicole glaring with obvious loathing. Not that Nicole had settled on communicating silently. At sixteen she'd been very comfortable speaking her mind.

"You killed her," she screamed. "You took her away and then you killed her. I'll never forgive you. I hate you. I hate you."

Lisa, Claire's manager, had taken her away then. They'd checked into a suite at the Four Seasons where they'd stayed until after the funeral. From there they'd gone to Paris. Springtime in Paris, Lisa had said. The beauty of the city would heal her.

It hadn't. Only time had closed the wounds, but the scars were still there. Springtime in Paris. The words always made her think of the song and whenever she heard the song, she thought about her mother's death and Nicole screaming that she hated her.

Claire shook off the memories and moved into the kitchen. It looked different, more modern and bigger somehow. Apparently Nicole had renovated the place, or at least parts of it. She continued through the downstairs and found several small rooms had been opened up into a larger space. There was a big living room with comfortable furniture, warm colors and a cabinet against one wall that concealed a flat-screen TV and other electronics. The dining room looked the same. The small bedroom on this floor had been converted into a study or den.

The place was dark and cool. She found the thermostat and turned up the heat. A few lamps helped add light, but didn't make the house any more welcoming. Maybe because the problem wasn't the house. It was her and the memories that wouldn't go away.

The last time she'd come to Seattle had been for their father's funeral. She'd received a terse phone call from a man, probably Wyatt, Claire thought as she sat on the edge of the sofa, saying her father had died. He'd given the date, time and place of the funeral, then had hung up.

Claire had been in shock. She hadn't even known he was sick. No one had told her.

She knew what they thought—that she couldn't be bothered with her own family. That she didn't care. What she'd tried to explain so many times was that she was the one who had been sent away. They'd been allowed to stay here, where it was safe, where they were loved. But Nicole had never seen it that way. She'd always been so angry.

Claire rubbed her hands against the soft fabric on the couch. None of this was familiar. Wyatt had been right—she didn't belong here. Not that she was leaving. Nicole and Jesse were the only family she had left. They might have ignored her phone calls and letters over the years, but she was here now and she wasn't leaving until she somehow got through to them. Until they made peace.

Claire stood and went up the stairs. There were

three bedrooms on the top floor. She paused by the master suite. Based on the color scheme and items scattered across the dresser, she would guess that Nicole slept there now. At the other end of the hall were the two remaining bedrooms and the bathroom they shared.

One looked like a typical guest room with a too-tidy bed and neutral colors, while the last was done in purple, with posters on the walls and a computer on a desk filling one corner.

Claire walked into that room and looked around. The space smelled of vanilla.

"What have you done?" she asked aloud. "Jesse, did you set me up? Is Nicole really ready to forgive me?"

She desperately wanted to believe her sister, but found herself doubting. Wyatt had been very convincing in his dislike of her.

The unfairness of it, a stranger judging her, made her chest hurt, but she ignored the sensation. Somehow she would get this all fixed.

She returned downstairs and walked toward the front door. On the way, she saw a narrow staircase leading to the basement. She knew what was down there.

Every cell in her body screamed at her not to do it—not to go look—yet she found herself walking toward the opening, then slowly, so slowly, moving down.

The stairs opened into a basement. But what should have been an open space was closed off with a wall and a single door. Nicole hadn't destroyed it, Claire thought, not sure what to make of that. Did it mean there was hope, or had the project simply been too much trouble?

Claire hesitated, her hand on the doorknob. Did she really want to go in?

When she and Nicole had been three, their parents had taken them to a friend's house. It was a place neither girl had been before. At first the visit had been unremarkable. A rainy Seattle day with two toddlers trapped inside a house full of adults.

One of the guests had tried to entertain the girls by playing the piano. Nicole had grown bored and wandered away, but Claire had sat on the hard bench, entranced by the keys and the sound they made. After lunch, she'd gone back on her own. She'd been too short to see the white and black keys, but she'd known they were there and she'd carefully reached above her head and started to play one of the songs.

Despite how young she'd been, Claire remembered everything about that afternoon. How her mother had come looking for her and stared at her for the longest time. How she'd been put on her mother's lap in front of the piano, where she could make the pretty music more easily.

She had never been able to explain how she knew which key produced which sound, how the music had seemed to begin inside of her, bubbling up until it spilled out. It was just one of those things, a quirk of an, until then, unremarkable gene pool.

Nicole had also sat on her mother's lap, but she'd shown no interest in the piano and when she put her tiny hands down, there was only noise.

That moment had changed everything. Within two days, Claire started lessons. Then the work on the basement began and a soundproof studio was built. For the first time in their lives, the twins weren't doing exactly the same thing at exactly the same time. Music, and Claire's gift, had come between them.

She pushed the door open. She could see the piano that had seemed so beautiful and perfect when she'd been a child. She would guess the cost of it had decimated her parents' savings account and then some. Claire had played on many of the most famous pianos in the world, but this was the one she remembered most.

She stared at it now, at the dust on the cover. It probably hadn't been touched in years. It would need tuning.

She had no desire to play. Just the thought of sitting down on the bench made her chest tighten. She forced herself to keep breathing. She didn't have to play if she didn't want to. Everything was fine. She didn't even have to make up excuses to avoid her masters classes. She was a whole continent away from that world.

Panic haunted the edges of her conscious mind.

She pushed it away. When it stayed stubbornly in place, she retreated upstairs, to safer ground. Once on the main floor, she could breathe more easily.

She would ignore the piano, she told herself. Pretend it wasn't here at all. Except for getting it tuned. A lifetime of training wouldn't allow her to let it sit untended.

With the monster in the basement, if not vanquished at least momentarily glared at, she went out to the car and wrestled in her two suitcases. After dragging them up the stairs and putting them in the guest room, she returned to the kitchen to make herself something to eat.

There wasn't a lot of food in the house. She found a can of soup and started heating it on the stove. In the meantime, she located a phone book and started calling hospitals until she found one that said her sister had been admitted and offered to connect her to the nurses' station. Claire declined and hung up.

The good news was the surgery had gone well, since Nicole's room had been on a regular floor, not in ICU. The bad news was that according to Wyatt, Nicole knew nothing about Claire's visit and had no interest in seeing her. Had she come all this way for nothing?

She checked her cell phone out of habit and saw she had two messages from Lisa. As her manager couldn't possibly say anything she wanted to hear, Claire deleted them without bothering to listen.

Standing at the sink, she ate soup out of the pot and stared into the small, fenced backyard.

She knew when things had gone wrong with Nicole. She knew what the problem was. So why couldn't she fix it?

Did it matter? She was here now. Here and determined to make Nicole and Jesse a part of her life. No matter what they said or did, they weren't getting rid of her. She was going to make them love her and she was going to love them back. They were her family and that mattered more than anything.

NICOLE DID HER BEST not to move. She hurt. The pain was dulled by the miracles of modern drug therapy, but it was still there, lurking, threatening. She ignored the heat of it and blessed whoever had invented beds that raised and lowered with the push of a button. She would just lie here for the next six or eight years and eventually she would be fine.

Someone walked into her room. She heard the footsteps and braced herself for the inevitable poking and prodding that followed. Instead, there was only silence. She opened her eyes and saw Wyatt standing next to the bed.

She felt like crap and figured she didn't look a whole lot better. At times like this she was grateful they had only ever been friends.

"It's going to be a hell of a scar," he told her.

"Guys are into scars," she whispered, her mouth dry. "I'll have to beat them off with a stick. Not that I can ever imagine having the strength to lift a stick. Can I beat them off with a straw? I could handle a straw."

"I'll be there to help."

"Lucky me."

He touched her cheek, then pulled up a chair and sat down. "How are you feeling?"

She managed a smile. "That falls under the category of really stupid questions. Did you get the whole concept of surgery? I've been sliced and diced and I'm thinking of getting hooked on painkillers."

"You won't like rehab. You're too cynical."

"And crabby. Don't forget crabby." She pointed to the plastic cup on the tray beside her bed. "Could you hand me that?"

Wyatt picked it up and passed it to her. She took it and risked a sip. The last one had nearly made her throw up but a very mean-looking nurse had informed her she had to start drinking and peeing. Nicole didn't see the point, but the nurse had been insistent.

She took a tiny sip and winced as a wave of nausea washed through her. At least it was less intense than the previous one. She sipped again and didn't feel much of anything. Progress.

She handed him the water and drew in a breath. "You talk. I'll listen. But please, don't be funny. I don't want to laugh. It will hurt too much."

Wyatt leaned forward and took her fingers in his. "I went by the bakery. Everything is fine."

"Good. They'll be okay without me. They know

how to handle the business. I don't have to worry about anything."

She would worry because it was her nature, but it was nice to know it wasn't required.

"So, um, I met someone there."

Despite the pain and the drugs, Nicole opened her eyes. There was something about the way Wyatt wouldn't look at her. Something almost…guilty.

"A woman?"

He nodded.

She didn't understand. What was the big deal? He'd met someone. That was a good thing. "So ask her out."

"What?" He straightened and stared at her. "You're not—" He leaned toward her again. "I didn't mean I'd met someone I liked. I met someone I didn't expect to be there."

"Maybe it's the surgery and everything, but you're not making sense."

"I met Claire."

Claire who? But even as the question formed, she already had the answer. Claire, her sister. Claire, the perfect one, the princess. The concert pianist and soloist. World traveler. Rich bitch. Her selfish, narcissistic, shallow, cruel, awful sister.

"Not possible," she murmured as her eyes closed. Sleep would be good, she told herself. She would sleep now and this would all go away.

"Apparently Jesse called and told her about your surgery and she flew in."

Nicole's eyes opened. "What?"

"She's here to help during your recovery."

If Nicole hadn't been so uncomfortable and drugged, she would have laughed. "Help? She wants to help? Where the hell has she been for the past twenty-two years? Where was she while I was stuck here, raising Jesse and working in the bakery? Where was she when our mother went off to be with her and then died? Where was she when Dad died? Does she bother to show up even once? I can't believe it. She needs to leave right now. She needs to get her designer-wearing ass out of my city and back to her cocktail party circuit or wherever it is she spent her—"

Nicole made the mistake of trying to sit up on her own. Pain ripped through her, stealing her breath and making her moan. She sank back into the bed and closed her eyes. Claire here? Because Nicole's life wasn't sucky enough already?

"I hate her."

"I know." Wyatt squeezed her fingers. "She thinks she's helping."

It was too much, Nicole thought. "I can't deal with her right now. Just keep her away from me. I mean it, Wyatt. Don't let her come to the hospital."

"I won't," he promised, then kissed her forehead.

He was a good guy, she thought as sleep beckoned. One of the best. Why hadn't she been smart enough to fall in love with him? Instead she'd fallen for Drew. Talk about a disaster. All of it. And now Claire? What was next? Locusts?

CLAIRE ARRIVED at the hospital in plenty of time to take Nicole home. The previous day she'd made the drive twice so she was familiar with the route. Driving was a little less scary, as well. As long as she stayed off the freeway, she felt almost competent. She'd also talked to Nicole's nurse, explaining that they were family and that she, Claire, wanted to pick her up. They had given her the approximate time of release. Now Claire was here and ready to help.

She tried not to think too much about Wyatt's claim that Nicole knew nothing about her visit and wasn't going to be happy to see her. Despite repeated calls to Jesse's cell phone, she'd been unable to catch her, nor had Jesse answered any of her messages. Obviously something was going on, but Claire was confident it was little more than a misunderstanding that could be easily cleared up. At least that's what she told herself every time her stomach flipped over or her chest started to constrict.

She tightened her grip on her handbag as she exited the elevator and started down the long hallway. The signs pointed to the nurses' station, but before she got there, she saw Nicole in a wheelchair being pushed by a nurse, with Wyatt bringing up the rear.

Emotions flooded Claire, bringing her to a stop as she just stared at the sister she hadn't seen in years.

Nicole looked good, pale, but that made sense. The woman had just had surgery. She wore a zip-up hoodie over a T-shirt, with her hair pulled back in a ponytail. Claire instantly felt overdressed.

"Nicole," she whispered, fierce joy filling her. They were together again. Finally.

"Oh, crap," Nicole muttered. "Can I get more drugs?"

"Your sister?" the nurse asked. "You look alike. Almost like twins."

"Fraternal and don't make a bad situation worse by talking about it," Nicole said.

Wyatt put his hand on her shoulder. "I'll take care of this." He walked to Claire. "What are you doing here? I told you not to come."

She ignored him and Nicole's snarky comments, instead rushing forward, then crouching in front of her sister. She wanted to hug her, but was afraid of hurting her. She settled on touching her arm and smiling into her eyes.

"You look great. How do you feel?"

Nicole stared at her. "Like I had an organ ripped out. What are you doing here?"

"I'm taking you home."

"No, you're not," Wyatt said. "That's why I'm here."

"What are you doing in Seattle?" Nicole asked. "Please tell me it's a short visit that ends in an hour."

"I heard about your surgery, so I flew here to take care of you."

"That's so sweet," the nurse said.

"I don't need your help," Nicole said. "Go away."

Claire was doing her best not to react to all the hostility. She told herself that her sister was in pain, that Wyatt didn't know her and that a lot of time and bad feelings had come between the Keyes sisters. It was going to take more than a day to heal old wounds.

What she wanted to do was stand up, stomp her foot and point out that she was the wronged party here. That Nicole had turned her back on Claire years ago and refused to reconsider her position. That she'd been blamed for things that had hurt her just as much as them. But there was no point in starting there. She was here for a purpose.

She stood. "I'm not going anywhere. You need me."

Nicole groaned. "I need a lot of things, but you're not one of them. Wyatt, did I tell you to shoot me before? Did you listen?"

Wyatt put his hand on her shoulder. "I told you I couldn't do that."

"All men are useless," Nicole muttered, then looked back at Claire. "You want to get up so I can get out of here? I hurt, I'm tired and I just want to go home."

"My car is right out front," Claire told her. "I know the way. I practiced the drive."

"We're all so proud."

The nurse gave Claire a sympathetic smile, then pushed her patient toward the elevators. Claire trailed after them, not sure what to say or do. She couldn't force Nicole into her car. Maybe it would be better to let Wyatt deal with getting Nicole to the house and Claire could take over from there.

Still, it hurt to be rejected and ignored. She'd hoped things would be different.

"I'll change them," she told herself as they walked out into the cool, spring morning.

There was a large truck parked in front of the entrance. Wyatt opened the passenger door, then lifted Nicole inside and put her on the seat.

Claire watched, aching at the sight of the tenderness and care Wyatt displayed. She wanted a little of that for herself. Not from Wyatt, but from someone. She wanted a man to care about her, worry about her. She wanted friends and family. She wanted a life.

Which was mostly what she'd come home to find.

CHAPTER THREE

"I THOUGHT YOU WERE LYING," Nicole said as they pulled out of the hospital parking lot. "I thought I was having drug-induced hallucinations. I can't believe she's here. She's possibly the most useless human being on the planet. Why me? Why now?"

Wyatt didn't have any answers, so he kept quiet. He'd heard enough about Claire over the years to form an unflattering opinion of her. But today, at the hospital, she'd looked so hopeful and wounded at the same time. He'd almost felt bad for her.

Which only proved what a fool he was when it came to women. He always picked wrong. He had the divorce to prove it. Nicole knew her sister a whole lot better than he did, and he trusted Nicole. What she said went.

"What are you going to do about her?" he asked.

"I supposed asking you to shoot her would be a waste of time." She sighed. "I don't know. Ignore her and hope she goes away."

"You're going to need some help, at least for a couple of days. You won't be able to take care of yourself."

He kept his eyes on the road, but felt Nicole's angry stare. "You have got to be kidding me. You're not suggesting I let her stay and attempt to take care of me. Do you know how incredibly useless she is? She's not a person, Wyatt. She's a trained monkey. I'm amazed she can even drive a car. Oh, wait. I haven't seen the car. I'll bet you money it's a limo, with a driver. Claire wouldn't want to risk her delicate and valuable hands by actually doing work. Holding the steering wheel might impact her performance and we wouldn't want that."

He'd known the sisters didn't get along and the bare bones of the estrangement, but he'd never understood the depth of Nicole's anger and bitterness before.

Nicole had been hurt when Claire had gone away, but until now, he'd never known the wounds went so deep. Sarcasm and black humor concealed a lot of pain. It was just like her to play the bitter bitch to protect herself.

"I can come over in the evenings," he said. "After work."

She slumped down in the seat, then pressed her arm into her midsection and groaned. "I don't want that. You have to take care of Amy. I'll be fine."

"No, you won't."

"I don't want to think about it. Not right now."

None of this was supposed to be a problem, he reminded himself. When the surgery had been scheduled, Drew, Nicole's husband, had still been in the picture.

Wyatt thought of his stepbrother and instantly wanted to pound him into the ground. What a total idiot. Talk about screwing up big-time. Drew had crossed the line and Nicole was never going to forgive him. Wyatt wasn't sure he would be able to forgive his brother either.

He glanced in his rearview mirror and saw Claire in the car behind them. Even from a couple of car lengths away, he could see her death grip on the steering wheel and the determination in her face.

"You should move in with me and Amy," he said. "That's the easiest solution."

"No."

"You're being stubborn."

"It's part of my charm."

Under normal circumstances, Jesse could have pitched in, but that wasn't going to happen anytime soon.

"If you don't want me, you'll have to have someone," he said. "At least for the first couple of days. Claire can keep food in the house, bring it to you."

"Ha. You think the piano princess can cook?"

"She can order takeout."

"I can do that."

"And check on you."

"Did I mention a trained monkey? It would be a lot more helpful. Or one of those service dogs."

"She's your sister."

Nicole glared at him again. "She was the start of my bad luck streak."

"You're overreacting. Use her. There should be some pleasure in that."

"Less than you would think."

They arrived at the house. After parking, Wyatt came around to the passenger side and opened the door.

Nicole looked at him. "Don't even think about carrying me. I can walk."

"When was the last time you let a man sweep you off your feet?"

"I would never do that."

"You need to work on your trust issues."

With that, he gathered her in his arms. Claire had already opened the back door. She followed them inside.

He went up the stairs and into Nicole's bedroom. Someone, probably Claire, had pulled back the covers. When he set Nicole in the bed, she sucked in a breath, then forced a smile.

"Thank you."

She'd gone pale. He knew she had to be hurting. "When can you take something for the pain?"

"Not for a while. I got a shot in the hospital. I'll be fine."

She didn't look fine.

He pulled off her athletic shoes, then unzipped her sweatshirt. She eased out of it and he tossed it on a chair.

She wasn't wearing a bra. He could see her breasts moving under her thin T-shirt and wished the curves tempted him. Falling for Nicole would solve a lot of problems. Unfortunately, he felt nothing.

He pulled the covers over her, then sat on the edge of the bed.

"It's just for a few days," he told her. "I'm happy to hang out here in the evenings and you know Amy loves you but you'll need help during the day."

She closed her eyes.

"It won't be so bad," he said.

"I hate you."

"Is that a yes?"

She sighed. "Yes."

He stood. Claire hovered in the doorway. He went past her then waited until she'd trailed after him into the hallway and downstairs. Once they were in the kitchen, he faced her.

"You said you came here to look after your sister," he said.

"Yes. Obviously. Why else?"

"Fine. Then that's what you're going to do. Help. This isn't about you. Nicole is in a lot of pain. She's going to be healing and your only job is to make her life easier. You don't get to run off to visit clubs or hang out with your friends. You're to be here and be responsible. This is a serious commitment. I'll be checking in every night and I promise you, if you screw this up, you'll be sorry."

Claire looked at him as if he were an alien life form. "I have no idea what you're talking about."

"What was unclear?"

"Is that really what you think of me?" She shook her head. "Never mind." She crossed to the counter and leaned against it. "Part of me wants to ask what she's told you, but I don't really want to know. I mean, why would I set myself up that way? I'm bad and she's good and that's how it's always been."

She paused and swallowed. Wyatt had the sudden sense that she was fighting tears. While he was a typical guy and would do almost anything to make a woman stop crying, he told himself that this was nothing more than an expert performance. He refused to be engaged by the play.

But Claire didn't cry. She took a couple of breaths, then faced him.

"You don't know me. Regardless of what Nicole has told you, you know nothing about me. I could say the same her, which is sad. We're twins. Fraternal, but still. I hate how much we've messed over each other's lives. I hate how things are now. I don't…" She stopped and pressed her lips together. "Sorry. You don't actually care about any of this, do you."

He watched her without saying anything.

She squared her shoulders and raised her chin. "I'm here to help. I have no interest in nightclubs, I never have. I don't have any friends here in Seattle, so you don't have to worry about distractions. I want to take care of Nicole and reconnect with her. Nothing more. Those are the only words I have. You'll either believe them or you won't. The bottom line is, I'm not going anywhere. Not until Nicole is better."

She spoke with a quiet dignity that appealed to him. His instinct was to believe her, but Nicole had always talked about how Claire played people with the same easy skill that she played the piano.

Still, he didn't have a choice. He couldn't take off from work and he had a daughter to deal with.

"I'll be around," he told her. "Watching."

"Judging. There's a difference."

He shrugged, not caring if he offended her.

He pulled a business card out of his shirt pocket. "My cell is on this. You can always reach me on it. If there's a problem, call."

"There won't be."

He handed her the card, instead of just putting it on the counter, then realized his mistake the second their fingers touched.

The heat was so bright and raw, he expected the kitchen to explode. He swore under his breath as he glared at Claire, blaming her for the unwelcome chemistry flaring between them. She stared at the card, then looked at him.

"That was weird," she said.

There was genuine confusion in her voice and questions in her eyes, as if she'd felt it, too, but didn't know what it meant.

Yeah, right, he thought to himself. She *was* playing him.

Play away. He didn't care. It didn't matter how he reacted when he touched her—he would never act on those feelings. He wasn't controlled by his hormones. He was a rational man who thought with his head, not his dick.

Still, when she smiled at him and said, "Thank you for taking care of her," putting her hand on his arm, he wanted to pull her hard against him and kiss her until she begged for mercy. The image was so powerful, his mouth went dry and he got hard in a heartbeat. Talk about humiliating.

He stalked out of the kitchen without saying goodbye and vowed he would keep his distance from Claire. The last thing he needed in his life was another useless woman making him crazy and ruining everything she touched.

CLAIRE STARED at the clothes she'd laid across the bed and sighed. Apparently packing was not an intuitive skill. She'd been so careful with everything. Yet here were all her clothes, horribly wrinkled.

Normally Lisa's assistant du jour would whisk the clothes away and bring them back perfectly pressed. If she wasn't around, Claire could call the valet service at the hotel herself. But this wasn't a hotel.

She studied a silk blouse and wondered if it was safe to iron. With another sigh, she reminded herself she didn't know how to use an iron and if she wanted to practice, perhaps a designer silk blouse was not the place to start.

"Am I really totally useless, or is this an isolated incident?" she asked herself, speaking the words softly aloud. Better to know the truth than pretend. Her goal was to change—to fit into the real world. She needed to know where she was to find out how much work was required to get where she needed to go.

A sound from down the hall caught her attention. Still holding the blouse, she hurried toward Nicole's room and found her sister coming out of the bathroom. She was bent over at the waist, one arm pressed across her midsection. Her face was drawn, her mouth pulled in pain.

"You should have yelled for me," Claire said as she hurried to her side. "I'm here to help."

"If you figure out a way to pee for me, I'm all ears. Otherwise, stay out of my way."

Claire ignored the snarky comment and rushed to the bed where she quickly smoothed the sheets and pulled back the covers. Nicole ignored her and what she'd done as she slowly, carefully, crawled back in bed. Claire reached for the covers.

"If you tuck me in, I swear I'll kill you. Not today, but soon and when you least expect it."

Claire stepped away from the bed.

When Nicole was settled she closed her eyes.

After a second, she opened them again. "Are you just going to stand there?"

"Do you need anything? More water? Ice chips? They'll help you stay hydrated without making you nauseous."

"How do you know that?"

"I was reading some articles on the Internet."

"Aren't you mama's little helper?"

Claire clutched her blouse in one hand. "They didn't say anything about surgery making one ill-tempered, so I guess the sarcasm is all you."

"I wear it proudly, like a badge of honor." Nicole shifted and winced. "What are you doing here, Claire?"

"Jesse called me a few days ago and told me about the surgery. She said you were going to need my help." Claire didn't want to say the rest when it was obviously untrue, but she couldn't think of a way to avoid it. She'd already told Wyatt and she suspected he had passed it on to Nicole. "She said you were sorry we were still estranged and that you wanted us to be a family."

She spoke without shaking, without her voice giving away her potential hurt. But it was still there, hidden. Because connecting was the one thing she wanted.

"You believed her?" Nicole shook her head. "Seriously? After all this time, you think I'm suddenly going to change my opinion of you?"

"Your opinion of who and what you *think* I am," Claire told her. "You don't actually know me."

"One of the few blessings in my life."

Claire ignored that. "I'm here now and you obviously need help. I don't see anyone else lining up for the job. Looks like you're stuck."

Nicole's expression tightened. "I have friends I could call."

"But you won't. You hate owing anyone anything."

"Like you said, you don't actually know me."

"I can guess." Claire hated being obligated, too.

"Don't pretend we have anything in common," Nicole snapped. "You're no one to me. Fine, if you think you can help, help. I don't care. The good news is I don't think you're capable of anything beyond being served, so my expectations are fairly low."

This was so not what she'd imagined, Claire thought sadly. She'd hoped they would be able to find their way back to each other. She and Nicole were twins...fraternal, but connected from conception. Had all the time apart, the anger and misunderstandings really broken that bond?

She was here to find out.

"You probably want to rest," Claire said. "I'll get out of your way."

"If only."

She ignored that and started to leave, then paused. "Do you have a cleaning service you use?"

"For the house? No. I managed to scrub it all by myself."

"Oh. Okay. I didn't mean... Never mind."

Nicole stared at her. "What didn't you mean?"

Her gaze dropped to the blouse in Claire's hand. "You mean a service to clean my clothes?"

Claire took a step back. "It's not important."

"Yeah, right. Let me guess. A piano princess like you couldn't possibly be expected to take care of your own clothes. I'd tell you how to use the washer, but that's probably not going to help, is it? Too much silk and cashmere, I'll bet. Poor, poor Claire. Never owned a pair of jeans. You must cry yourself to sleep every night."

Claire did her best to deflect the hurtful darts that jabbed at her. "I won't apologize for my life. It's different from yours, but that doesn't make it any less valuable. You've changed, Nicole. I've always remembered you being angry before, but I don't remember you being mean. When did that happen?"

"Get the hell out of here."

Claire nodded. "I'll be down the hall if you need me."

"That is not going to happen. I'd rather starve than deal with you."

"No, you wouldn't."

Ignoring the burning in her eyes and sense of loss weighing her down, Claire returned to her room, determined to fix whatever had gone wrong.

THE ALARM WENT OFF at three-forty-five in the morning. Claire turned it off and then stared at the unblinking red light. What had she been thinking? Who got up this early?

People who worked in a bakery, she reminded herself. She was one of the Keyes sisters. She had an obligation to the family business. As Nicole was in no position to check on things and Jesse had disappeared for reasons still not clear, it was left to Claire.

She got up and pulled on clothes. Wrinkled clothes made only marginally better by their time in a steamy bathroom. She washed her face, applied some light makeup, pulled her long hair back in a ponytail and quietly crept downstairs. Less than fifteen minutes later, she had arrived at the bakery and parked in the back by the other employee cars.

There were lights on in the building. Claire hurried to the rear door and walked inside.

The space was warm and bright, smelling of sugar and cinnamon. Equipment filled counters and lined walls. Huge ovens radiated an impressive amount of heat. There were deep fryers and massive mixers, stacks of flour and sugar and what smelled like the richest chocolate in the world.

Claire paused and breathed in the delicious scents. She'd only been able to fix soup again the previous night, not that Nicole had been all that interested in eating. But three days of a nearly liquid diet had left Claire starving.

A middle-aged man dressed entirely in white saw

her and frowned. "Hey, you. Get out of here. The bakery opens at six."

She gave him her best smile. "Hi. I'm Claire Keyes. Nicole's sister. I flew in because of her surgery. I'm helping out."

"Sister? She doesn't—" The man was small—a couple of inches shorter than her, but built like a bull. He drew his bushy eyebrows together. "You're the one who plays the piano? The snooty one?"

"I do play the piano," Claire said, wondering what Nicole had been telling people about her. "I'm not really snooty. Nicole, um, asked me to come by to help, what with her being laid up and all."

The man frowned. "I don't think so. She doesn't like you."

Something she'd apparently shared with the entire world. Claire had felt guilty about lying, but she didn't anymore. She was going to find a way to fit in and the bakery was the obvious place to start.

"We've come to an understanding," she said, still forcing a smile. "There must be something I can do to help. I'm her sister. Baking is in my blood."

Or it should be. Claire had never tested the theory by actually baking anything.

"Look, I don't know what's going on, but I don't like it. You need to leave."

The man walked away. She trailed after him. "I can help. I'm a hard worker and I'm really good with my hands. There has to be something. I'm not asking to work on the famous Keyes chocolate cake or anything."

The man spun back to face her. "You stay away from the chocolate cake, you hear me? Only Nicole and I do that. I've been here fifteen years and I know what I'm doing. Now get out of here."

"Hey, Sid? Come here for a sec."

The voice calling came from behind a wall of ovens. Sid gave her a scowl, then hurried off in the direction of the voice. Claire used the alone time to explore the inner workings of a real bakery a little more. She smiled at a woman injecting yummy-looking filling into pastry shells. The woman ignored her. Claire kept moving.

She found another woman working a machine that applied frosting to doughnuts. The smell was heavenly and Claire's stomach began to grumble in anticipation. She took a step toward the machine and bumped into a man carrying something.

As they struggled to get their balance, the bag he'd been carrying flew up in the air. Claire instinctively reached for it. But instead of catching it, she only bumped the side, sending it tumbling, sprinkling its contents on them, the floor and onto the already frosted doughnuts moving on the narrow conveyor belt. It spun and spun before landing, open end up, in a massive vat of dough.

"What the hell did you do?" the man demanded, as he began to swear in a language she didn't recognize.

Sid came running. "You! You're still here?"

The woman managing the doughnuts flipped off the belt and hurried over to inspect them. "Salt," she muttered. "It's everywhere. They're ruined."

Claire wished she could slink away. "I'm sorry," she began. "We ran into each other and—"

"You're not supposed to be here," Sid yelled. "Did I tell you to leave? Did you listen? Jesus, no wonder Nicole talks about you the way she does." He leaned over the vat of dough and swore. "Salt," he yelled. "There's a five-pound bag of salt in the French bread dough. You think anyone's going to want that? It's our batch for the day. The *day*."

Oh, no. "Can't you make some more?" she asked in a tiny voice, feeling so awful.

"Do you understand anything about making bread from scratch? What am I asking? Of course you don't. Get out. Just get out. We can't afford any more disasters this morning."

Claire wanted to say something to make it better, but what was the point? All four of them stared at her as if she was the lowest form of life they'd ever seen. They wouldn't care that she'd only been trying to help. That she hadn't meant to run into the other guy. That it had only been an accident.

Not knowing what else to do, she turned and left.

It was after five when she arrived back at the house. Claire checked on Nicole, who was still sleeping, then went down to the kitchen and made coffee. The first pot smelled funny and tasted worse. She threw it out and started over.

The second batch was drinkable. She poured herself a cup and sank into a chair at the table.

How could her day have started so horribly? How could she have messed up so badly without even trying? It wasn't fair. She wasn't a bad person. Okay, yes, she lived a strange, twisted life that most people couldn't relate to, but that didn't change who she was on the inside.

But it seemed existing outside of her gilded cage was going to be harder than she'd first realized.

"I'm not giving up," she said aloud. "I'm going to figure this out."

She didn't have much choice. If she couldn't play the piano anymore, she was going to need to have a life without music.

No music. The thought of it made her sad. Music was everything to her. It was her reason for breathing.

"I'll find another reason," she told herself. "I have unexplored depths." At least she hoped she did.

A little after six, she went looking for the toaster. There was plenty of bread in the freezer. She managed to burn the first three slices she put in before getting the adjustment right. She was digging around for a tray when the back door opened.

She straightened and saw Wyatt walking into the kitchen. Wyatt, who hated her nearly as much as

Nicole. Wyatt, who'd made her hand tingle so strangely the previous day.

But before she could wonder what that all meant, she saw the pretty little girl who trailed behind him.

Wyatt set several grocery bags on the counter. "Something smells bad."

"I burned some toast." Claire couldn't look away from the girl. "Your daughter?" she asked. Wyatt had a daughter? Which meant he had a wife.

The realization caused her to take a step back, although she couldn't say why. Still, she wanted to meet the girl. Claire had always liked children and dreamed of a family of her own.

"This is Amy," he said, moving his hands as he spoke. "Amy, this is Claire." He used his fingers in an odd way. "Amy's deaf."

"Oh." She looked at the child and noticed hearing aids in both ears.

She'd never known a deaf person before. No sound. What would that be like? Never to hear a Mozart concerto or a symphony? No melody or rhythm. Her whole body clenched at the thought.

"How horrible."

Wyatt glared at her. "We don't think so, but thanks for sharing your enlightened and sensitive opinion. When you see a one-legged guy walking down the street, do you kick it out from under him?"

She blushed and glanced at his daughter. "No. I'm sorry. I didn't mean it that way. I was thinking about music and how…" There was no recovery from this, she thought as guilt swamped her. "I didn't mean anything bad."

"People like you never do."

He wouldn't understand, mostly because he didn't want to. He assumed the worst about her and she seemed to do nothing but prove his point.

He began taking groceries out of the bags. She thought about offering to help, but knew he would refuse. Instead, she retreated to the living room and wondered if she should simply hire a nurse for Nicole and escape back to New York. At least there she fit in.

She sank onto one of the sofas and did her best not to cry. Why was everything going so wrong? How could she make things better? Because as easy as escaping would be, she didn't want to be a quitter. She'd never quit. Not once—no matter how hard things got.

But this situation was impossible.

Amy walked into the room. Claire started to apologize for what she'd said, only to realize the child probably hadn't heard her. Which meant she would have to explain why she was apologizing, assuming she could even get her point across. She sat there, feeling both stupid and awkward, not sure which was worse.

Amy didn't seem to pick up on any of that. Instead she walked over to a bookshelf in the corner and picked up a large picture book. She carried it back to the sofa and handed it to Claire.

"You want me to read to you?" Claire asked, looking at the book. "Aren't you too old for this book?"

Amy waved her hands to get Claire's attention, then touched her chin. She motioned to her lips, then her eyes.

"See you speak."

The words were spoken slowly, with exaggerated pronunciation.

Claire's eyes widened. "You can talk?"

Amy raised her right hand and waggled it sideways, then held her thumb and index finger an inch or so apart.

"A little," Claire said, feeling triumphant. "You can speak a little."

Amy nodded. "My school teaches me."

"Your school is teaching you to talk?"

Amy nodded. She pointed to her mouth again. "Lips."

"And read lips?"

More nodding. The girl smiled. She pointed at the book. Claire opened it. There was a girl holding a book. Amy pointed at the girl, then made a fist and rubbed her thumb across her cheek.

"Girl." Amy repeated the motion. "Girl."

Understanding dawned. "I get it," Claire told her. "This is the sign for girl?"

Amy grinned and pointed to the book. She held

both her hands together, as if she was praying, then opened them.

Claire repeated the gesture. "The sign for book?"

Amy nodded.

Claire flipped the page. "This is so cool. What else can you teach me?"

WYATT WALKED into Nicole's room with coffee and the bagels he'd brought.

"Hey, sleepy."

She opened her eyes and groaned. "Hey, yourself."

"How do you feel?"

"How do I look?"

"Beautiful."

She winced as she pushed into a sitting position, then leaned back against the pillows. "You are such a liar, but thank you for that. I feel awful. I have to tell you, the drugs in the hospital are much better than the stuff you get at the pharmacy. Is that coffee?"

"Yes, but I wasn't sure if you were allowed any."

"So you brought it to taunt me?" She reached for the mug. "I'm supposed to take it easy and eat what sounds good. Coffee sounds like a miracle, right now."

He set the tray on the nightstand, then pulled up a chair. After she'd taken her first sip and sighed with pleasure, he asked, "You doing okay with Claire?"

Nicole rolled her eyes. "Do I have a choice? She's staying away, which is my preference. Sid called my cell about a half hour ago." She motioned to the small phone by the tray. "She went to the bakery this morning, apparently to help. He sent her away. Instead she managed to run into Phil and dump a five-pound bag of salt into a batch of bread dough. It's totally ruined."

"How did that happen?"

"I have no idea."

"She didn't do it on purpose, did she?"

Nicole glared at him. "Probably not, but don't you dare take her side."

"Not my plan."

"Good, because I'm not sure I could handle that. She's even more useless than I'd first thought. She actually asked me about a cleaning service for her clothes. Apparently a few things are wrinkled and she doesn't know how to deal with that. We should all have such problems. I hate her."

"You don't hate her."

"I know, but I wish she'd go away."

So did Wyatt. As it was, he was keeping his distance. The last thing he needed was another raging fire keeping him up at night…in both senses of the word.

Why her? Why couldn't he have chemistry with someone else? Someone normal? Someone like Nicole? His body sure had a sense of humor.

Nicole glanced at the clock. "Where's Amy?"

"Downstairs with your sister."

"Check her before you leave. Who knows what Claire might do to her."

"I'll make sure she's in one piece." He stood and crossed to the bed, then kissed Nicole on the top of the head. "Call me if you need anything."

"I will."

"I'll be back soon."

"Come right away if you see smoke rising in the sky."

"Promise."

He went downstairs. As he entered the living room, he heard laughter. Amy sat next to Claire, watching intently as Nicole's sister carefully signed the story in the picture book on her lap. Her movements were studied, but she got all the words right. When his daughter signed the word *good,* Claire laughed again.

"You're a good teacher," she said slowly.

Amy signed, "Good student."

Claire reached out and hugged her.

Amy went easily into her arms.

Wyatt was unimpressed. Claire might be able to fool a child, but he knew better. She wasn't going to be able to suck him in so easily.

HQN™

We *are* romance™

HAPPY READING!

As part of our special sizzling summer reads offer, you can now **SAVE $1.00** on the purchase of **SWEET TALK** by *New York Times* bestselling author **Susan Mallery**,

available in July wherever books are sold, including most bookstores, supermarkets, drugstores, department and discount stores.

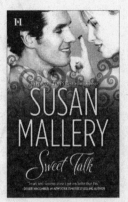

If you've enjoyed this sizzling excerpt,
purchase the complete book

Sweet Talk

Available in July

by *New York Times* bestselling author
SUSAN MALLERY

at Borders and **SAVE $1.⁰⁰**
on your purchase!

New York Times
Bestselling Author

Susan
Andersen

Cutting
Loose

He's getting under her skin…
in more ways than one

Dear Reader,

It wasn't easy growing up the only child of self-absorbed second-rate actors in a household full of stormy exits and theatrical reunions, but these days Jane Kaplinski has her life on track. The only thing on her mind is fulfilling the final request of a dear old lady who bequeathed her estate to Jane and her two best friends. She's certainly not looking for love—Jane is way too familiar with the damage done in its name. Still, if she ever *does* fall in love, she intends it to be with someone stable. A nice cerebral professor, maybe.

Then Devlin Kavanagh, a footloose international yacht sailor with *steamy* stamped all over him, comes home to help his family business during a crisis. And all Jane's careful plans go up in flames. Who knew arguing with an irresponsible heartbreaker could be so exciting? Or that they'd generate such heat? He's got issues of his own, of course, so this can't possibly last.

Or can it?

It was fun making sparks fly between Dev and Jane, and as always, I hope you enjoy my efforts. Happy reading!

Susan Andersen

PROLOGUE

Dear Diary,
Families suck. Why can't I have a regular
mom and dad?

May 12, 1990

"JANE, JANE, WE'RE HERE!"

Twelve-year-old Jane Kaplinski leaned out her bedroom window. Below, her friend's chauffeur-driven car was parked at the curb in front of her middle-class house, her friends Ava and Poppy spilling out the vehicle's back door.

"I'll be right down," she called, watching Poppy's cloud of blond curls swaying in the breeze, her filmy skirts plastered against her slender legs. She'd probably bought her outfit at Kmart, but as usual she looked stylish and pulled together, while Ava, who had developed a full year and a half ahead of everyone else in their grade level, looked sort of packed into her pale green dress, its expensive workmanship tugged akilter at bust and hips. But her sleek red hair, brighter than a four-alarm fire, blazed beneath the spring sunshine's sudden peekaboo appearance through the clouds and her dimples flashed as she grinned up at Jane.

Smoothing a hand down her own navy skirt, Jane flicked off her radio, aborting Madonna's "Vogue" midsong. The front door banged open downstairs as she picked up her backpack and carefully closed her bedroom door behind her. She smiled as she headed for the staircase, imagining Ava's usual insistence that they knock while Poppy countered they didn't need an engraved invitation.

But it was her mother's voice calling her name that froze Jane in place on the bottom step a moment later.

The suitcase in the foyer should have been her tip-off, but she'd been so focused on her outing with her best friends that she hadn't even noticed it. Now here came her mother, ice clinking a familiar Parent rhythm in the highball glass clutched in her hand as she bore down with frenetic joy on her only child.

Crapdanghell.

"You're back," she said flatly as her mother gathered her to her bosom, and choked when her nose sank into Obsession-scented cleavage. She stood rigid until Dorrie loosened her grip, then edged toward the door.

"Of course I am, darling. You know I could never stay away from you. Besides—" she gave her hair a pat "—your father simply begged me to return."

Dorrie slung an arm around Jane's shoulders and looked down at her, the aroma of Johnnie Walker Black wafting from her breath to clash with her perfume. "Look at you, all pressed and shiny! Are you going somewhere?"

Jane twisted away and took a giant step backward. "I've been invited to tea at Miss Wolcott's."

"Agnes *Bell* Wolcott?"

She nodded.

"My little girl is so highfalutin." Dorrie gave her a swift once-over. "You couldn't find something a little more colorful to wear?"

Casting a glance at her mom's neon-hued top, she merely said, "I like this."

"I have some nice red beads we could use to jazz it up." She lifted a shiny brown hank of Jane's stick-straight hair and rubbed it between her fingers. "Maybe fix up your 'do a little? You know how important staging is—if you want to look the role, you need to pay attention to the costume!"

Jane managed not to shudder. "No, thanks. I'm going for tea, not starring in one of your and Dad's productions. Besides, didn't you hear Ava's car pulling up out front?"

"Did I?" Dorrie dropped the tendril and took another sip of her Johnnie Walker. "Well, yes, I suppose I did, now that you mention it. I wasn't paying attention."

Big surprise. Mom was usually all about Mom.

Well, that or focused on the drama du jour of the Dorrie and Mike Show.

The doorbell rang and with a sigh of relief, Jane eased around her mother. "Gotta go. Me and Ava are spending the night at Poppy's, so I'll see you tomorrow."

And, boy, was she grateful to be spared tonight's theatrics when her dad discovered Mom was back. It was guaranteed to be filled with passion and fire-works, and having lived through both too many times to count she was just as happy to miss the show.

Ava and Poppy let themselves in before she could reach the door. They immediately surrounded her and, calling, "Hello, Mrs. Kaplinski, goodbye, Mrs. Kaplinski," hustled her to the car.

Daniel, the Spencers' chauffeur, opened the Lin-coln's back door. As Poppy dove into the backseat he tipped his neatly capped head at Jane. "Miss Kaplinski."

She always wanted to giggle at his formality, but she gave him a grave nod in return. "Mr. Daniel." She climbed in sedately after Poppy.

Ava plopped down next to her and Daniel closed the door.

The three friends looked at each other as the chauf-feur walked around to the driver's door, and, clutch-ing her hair, Poppy mimed a scream. "Can you believe this?" she stage-whispered. "Tea at the Wolcott mansion!" She looked past Jane at Ava and asked in her normal register, "Why did Miss Wolcott invite us again?"

"I told you, I'm not sure." Ava tugged on the hem of her dress to cover her pudgy thighs. "Maybe because we all talked to her at that dumb musicale thing my parents had. They were, like, so psyched that she accepted their invitation. I guess she turns down more than she accepts these days and everyone wants to have the party she comes to. But at the same time my mom says Miss Wolcott's a genuine eccentric and she was a little nervous that she might say or do something Not Done By Our Kind." She shrugged. "Dunno—she seemed pretty regular to me. Except maybe for her voice. My dad says it's like a foghorn."

"I thought she was interesting," Jane said.

"Well, *yeah*," Poppy said. "She's been everywhere and done everything. Can you believe that she's been to places like Paris and Africa and even flew her own plane until a couple of years ago? Plus, she's got that great mansion." She bounced in her seat. "It makes your place look like a shack, Ava, and I didn't think there was *any* place prettier than your house. I'm dying to see Miss Wolcott's on the inside."

"Me, too," Jane agreed. "It sounds like she collects all kinds of rad stuff."

Ava pulled a candy bar from her backpack, ripped the wrapper from one end and offered Poppy and Jane a share. When they declined, she shrugged and chomped off a large bite. "I'm just glad to get out of

Cotillion class. Any excuse to avoid Buttface Cade Gallari is a good one in my book."

Upon arriving at the three-storied mansion on the crowded western slope of Queen Anne Hill, they were ushered into a large parlor by an elderly woman wearing a severely styled black dress. She murmured assurances that Miss Wolcott would join them shortly and backed out of the room, rolling closed a long, ornate pocket door.

The high-ceilinged parlor was dim and cool, the windows all mantled in velvet curtains. Eclectic groups of artifacts cluttered every surface, making a space that could easily contain the entire first floor of Jane's house seem almost cozy.

"Wow." She turned in a slow circle, trying to take in everything at once. "Lookit all this stuff." She edged over to a glass-fronted case and peered at the crowded display of antique beaded bags. "These are awesome!"

"How can you tell?" Ava asked. "There's no light in here."

"Yeah," Poppy agreed. "Look at the size of those windows—I'd keep the curtains open all day long if I lived here. Maybe paint the walls a nice yellow to brighten things up."

"Ladies," a deep, distinctive voice said from behind them, and they all turned. "Thank you for coming." In tailored camel slacks and fluid jacket, with a high-necked blouse as snowy as her carefully arranged hair, Agnes Bell Wolcott stood framed in the now partially open pocket door. A beautiful antique-looking cameo nestled in the cascading ruffle at her throat. She glanced at Poppy. "You may open the curtains if you wish."

Without so much as a blush at being overheard, Poppy ran to do so and the high-cloud pearlescent glow of an overcast Seattle afternoon immediately brightened the southerly facing room.

"Well, now. Would you girls care to explore some of my collections or would you rather enjoy a light repast first?"

Before Jane could vote for option number one, Ava said, "Eat, please."

Their hostess led them to another room that held an exquisitely set table in front of a marble fireplace. A three-tiered pastry stand, set squarely in its middle, held an array of beautifully presented desserts and crustless sandwiches. They sat themselves according to the little name cards at each place setting and Miss Wolcott rang for tea.

She then focused her undivided attention on them. "I imagine you're wondering why I invited you here today."

"We were just talking about that on the way over," Poppy said frankly as Jane gave a polite nod and Ava murmured, "Yes, ma'am."

"This is my way of saying thank you for your company at the Spencer musicale the other night. It's not often young ladies will take the time to keep an old woman company, and I very much enjoyed talking to you." She regarded them with bright-eyed interest. "You girls are very different from each other," she observed. "I wonder if I might ask how you met?"

"We all go to Country Day," Poppy said. Intercepting Miss Wolcott's discreet inspection of her inexpensive clothing, she grinned. "My folks are all love, peace and joy types, but my Grandma Ingles is an alumna. She pays my tuition."

"And I get financial aid," Jane volunteered. Not that her parents had bothered to arrange it. If her second-grade teacher hadn't submitted the original scholarship application Jane would still be attending public school. Nowadays she filled in the annual paperwork herself, so all her folks had to do was sign it.

"I'm just a regular student," Ava admitted. "I don't do anything special for tuition and Jane and Poppy are better at school than I am." She smiled, punching dimples deep in each cheek. "Especially Jane."

Warmth flushed Jane's cheeks, ran sweetly through her veins. "Ava's special in other ways, though."

"I find it lovely to see such a close friendship between girls," Miss Wolcott said. "You're quite a sisterhood."

Jane savored the word as the black-clad woman entered the room, rolling a cart that bore an elegant tea service. Miss Wolcott indicated the rectangular packages lying across the girls' plates as her servant settled the silver teapot in front of her. "I got you a small token of my appreciation. Please open them while I pour."

Jane carefully untied silver ribbon and peeled gold-and-silver paper from her package while Poppy ripped hers off with abandon and Ava unwrapped hers with a just-right show of attention that she'd no doubt learned in one of the Miss Manners classes she was always attending.

Jane smiled to herself. Maybe it truly *wasn't* easy being a rich girl. Heaven knew Ava told them so often enough.

Nestled in the paper was a deep-green leather-bound book with her name engraved in gold on the front cover. Poppy's, she saw, was red, while Ava's was a rich blue. Wondering how the older woman had known green was her favorite color, she opened hers, but the gilt-edged pages within were blank. She glanced at Miss Wolcott.

"I've kept a diary since I was your age," the white-haired woman said in her deep basso voice. "And finding you all such interesting young women, I thought you might enjoy keeping one, as well. I find it a great place to share my secrets."

"Awesome," said Poppy.

Ava's face lit up. "What a great idea."

Looking from Miss Wolcott to the friends she'd known since the fourth grade, Jane thought of all the impressions and feelings that were constantly crowding her mind. Things weren't always great at home, but she didn't really like to talk about it—not even to her two best friends. Sometimes especially not to them. Poppy had great parents, so while she could and did sympathize with the way Jane's folks were constantly slamming in and out of her house, she didn't truly understand how shaky that could make the ground feel under a girl's feet. And although Ava's own home life was far from ideal, at least her parents weren't a couple of actors who lived for the drama of constant exits and entrances.

But the idea of writing down how she felt really appealed to her. She smiled.

"Maybe we could call them the Sisterhood Diaries."

CHAPTER ONE

I am so never wearing a thong again. Poppy swears they're comfortable—which probably should've been my first clue.

"OMIGAWD, JANE," Ava screeched. "Oh, my, gawd. It's official!"

Jane pulled the phone away from her ear. Her friend's voice had gone so high she was surprised the leashed dachshund sniffing the light standard down on First Avenue didn't start barking. But she clapped the receiver back to her ear as excitement danced a fast jitterbug in her stomach. "Probate finally closed, then?"

"Yes, two minutes ago!" Ava laughed like an escapee from a lunatic asylum. "The Wolcott mansion is officially ours. Can you believe it? I sure miss Miss Agnes, but this is just too thrilling. Omigawd, I can barely breathe, I'm so excited. I have to call Poppy and tell her the news, too." She laughed again. "We've gotta celebrate! Do you mind coming to West Seattle?"

"Lemme see." Stretching the telephone cord as far

as it would reach, she stepped out of her cramped sixth-floor office at the Seattle Metropolitan Museum to peer through the director's open door two doors down. The coveted corner office show-cased a panoramic view from Magnolia Bluff to Mount Rainier, with the Olympic Mountains rising dramatically across Elliott Bay and Puget Sound. Not that she could see more than a fraction of it from her angle, but she wasn't trying to scope out the scenery, anyway. Traffic flow was her objective. "No, that oughtta work. The freeway looks pretty clear your way."

"Good. Let's meet at the Matador in an hour. Overpriced drinks are on me."

She found herself grinning as she changed into her walking shoes and threw her heels into her tote in preparation to leaving. Swinging her butt to the happy dance song playing in her head, she freshened her lipstick, tossed the tube back in her purse and stuffed it into the tote as well.

"You look jazzed."

Jane let out a scream. "Good God!" She slapped a hand to her racing heart and whirled to face the man in her doorway.

"Sorry." Gordon Ives, her fellow junior curator, stepped into the room. "Didn't mean to startle you. What was the little dance for?"

Ordinarily she wouldn't consider telling him. She had a strict policy of keeping her private business out of the office that had worked well for her over the course of her career and saw no reason to change it now.

And yet...

Part of the inheritance was going to impact the museum, so it wasn't as if he wouldn't soon find out anyhow. And the plain truth was, she was excited. "I'm getting the Wolcott collections."

He stared at her, his pale blue eyes incredulous. "As in Agnes Bell Wolcott's collections? *The* Agnes Wolcott, who traveled the world wearing trousers when her generation's women stayed at home to raise the kids and didn't dream of stepping outside the house attired in less than dresses, gloves and hats?"

"Yeah. She didn't wear only trousers, though. She wore her share of dresses and gowns, as well."

"I've heard about her collections forever. But I thought she died."

"She did, last March." And grief stabbed deep for the second time today at the reminder. There was an unoccupied space in her soul that Miss Agnes used to fill and she had to draw a steadying breath. Then, perhaps because she was still off balance, she heard herself admitting, "She left them to me and two of my friends." Along with the mansion, but Gordon didn't need to know that as well.

"You're kidding me! Why would she do that?"

"Because we were friends. More than that, actually—Poppy and Ava and I were probably the closest thing Miss Wolcott had to family."

She rubbed a hand over her mouth to disguise its sudden tremble—then sternly pulled herself together again. This wasn't the place or person in front of whom she wanted to indulge her emotions. "Anyhow," she said briskly, "I'll only be around in the mornings for the next two months. A couple of the collections are being donated to the museum and Marjorie's letting me work afternoons at the Wolcott mansion to catalog them. Oops, gotta go. I've got a bus to catch." She grabbed up her tote and ushered him out of her office, closing the door behind her.

Emerging onto the street a few minutes later, she pulled on her little black cashmere sweater against the brisk wind and her sunglasses against the bright October sun.

She'd only mentioned the bus to get Gordon out of her office, but after a quick mental debate she decided against going home for her car and hiked up to Marion Street to catch the 55 instead.

As the bus approached the Alaska Junction a short while later she changed back into her heels, smiling down at the leopard-skin, open-toed construction. She loved these shoes and knew this would probably be one of the last times she'd get to wear them this season. According to the KIRO weatherman on the news this morning, their sunny days were numbered.

She beat Ava and Poppy to the restaurant, but even though it was a weeknight and early yet, the Matador's tequila bar was starting to fill up. She bought herself a club soda at the stained-glass-backed bar and staked out one of the few free tables.

She'd never been here before and spent a few minutes admiring the open-concept flow of bar into restaurant and the intricate metalwork on display. She killed another minute perusing the menu, but people-watching soon proved more compelling and she gave herself over to checking everyone out.

It was mostly a twenty-something crowd, but in the restaurant end of the room was a quartet of men who kept drawing her gaze. They ranged from late twenties to maybe forty and were holding what appeared to be an intense conversation across the room. Every now and then, however, they'd all shout with laughter, instigated for the most part, it appeared, by the redhead with the seam-threatening shoulders.

She'd never been particularly attracted to red-headed men, but this guy was something else. His hair was the dark, rich color of an Irish setter, his eyebrows blacker than crow feathers and his skin surprisingly golden instead of the creamy pale she associated with that coloring. Influenced, no doubt, by years of hanging around Ava.

Despite repeatedly redirecting her attention, it kept wandering back to him. He seemed very intent on the conversation with his friends, leaning into the table to speak, those dark brows pulled together in a frown one moment, then relaxing as he grinned and gestured animatedly the next. He talked with his hands a lot.

Big, tough, hard-looking hands with long, blunt-tipped fingers that could probably—

Jane jerked as if someone had clapped hands right in front of her face. Good God. What on earth was she doing thinking—what she was thinking—about some stranger's hands? This was *so* not like her.

And wouldn't you know he'd choose that exact minute to look across the room and catch her staring? She froze as he talked to the other guys at his table while his gaze skimmed her from the top of her head to the tips of her shoes, which he studied for a couple of heartbeats before beginning the return journey. When he reached her face once again, he tossed back a shot without taking his eyes off her, then pushed back from the table and climbed to his feet.

Was he coming over here? *Ooh.*

No! What was she, eighteen? She wasn't here to troll for a date—and wouldn't choose a bar if she had been.

"Hey, Jane, sorry I'm late. Poppy's not here yet, I take it."

She looked up to see Ava approaching the table and noticed that damn near every male head in the bar turned to follow her friend's progress. The redhead across the room was no exception. He checked Ava out for a moment before glancing at Jane again. For just a sec he stood there rubbing the back of his neck. Then he hitched a wide shoulder and headed in the direction of the men's room.

His butt was as nice as the rest of him. But giving it a final lingering glance before turning her attention to Ava, who was pulling out a chair, she noticed the telltale hesitancy in his step of a man who's had too much to drink.

"Well, shit." Her disappointment was fierce, which was pretty dumb considering she'd never even talked to the guy.

"What?" Ava tossed her Kate Spade clutch on the table and slid gracefully into the chair.

"Nothing." She waved it aside. "It's not important."

Ava just looked at her.

"Okay, okay. I was doing the eye-flirt thing with this buff redhead over in the restaurant part of the room and—don't turn around! For God's sake, Ava. He went to the can, anyhow."

"Eye flirting is good—especially for you, since you don't do nearly enough of it. So why are you cursing?"

"He's drunk. I didn't realize it until I saw him walking away."

"Aw, Janie. Not everyone who gets a little lit is a problem drinker. Sometimes it's just a once-in-a-while kind of thing."

"I know," she said, partly because she did but mostly because she really didn't want to argue tonight.

Ava knew her too well, however, and instead of letting it go, she leaned over the table, her bright hair swinging forward. Scooping it back, she tucked it behind her ear. "You've seen Poppy and me indulge a bit too much on occasion and you don't hold it against us."

"Yeah, because I know your history, and I know it's a rare thing for either of you to drink to excess." She gave an impatient shrug. "Look, I know I'm not completely rational on the subject and I don't need to put some shrink's kids through college to understand that Mom and Dad's drinking is the reason why. By the same token, Av, you know you're not going to change my mind. So let's just drop it, whataya say? We're here to celebrate."

Deep dimples indented her friend's cheeks. "Omigawd! Are we ever! Are you as excited as I am?"

"And *then* some. I'm so psyched at the thought of getting my hands on those collections I can hardly think straight. I didn't get a chance to talk to Marjorie this afternoon, but unless something special comes up at the Met—and it's been pretty quiet on the curator front for the past week or so—I'm hoping to dive right in and start sorting them on Monday."

"Sorry I'm late." Poppy arrived breathless at their table.

Ava made a rude noise. "Like we'd know how to act if you were ever on time. Where did you guys park, anyhow?" she asked as Poppy dumped her oversize handbag onto the floor and collapsed into the chair next to her. "Did you find a place on the street or park in the lot above the alley?"

"I'm in the lot," Poppy said.

"I took the bus."

Both her friends stared at her openmouthed, and she blinked. "What?"

"You're crazy, you know that?" Poppy shook her head.

"Why, because I'm a public transportation kinda gal?"

"No, because bus service drops way down in the evening and it can't be safe to hang around bus stops in the dark."

"Oh, as opposed to walking through a dark alley to get your car, you mean? Besides, I can always call a cab. I don't see what the big deal is. Ava said meet in an hour and I didn't think I could make it here in time if I went home first."

"And like Poppy's never on time, you're never late," Ava said.

She shrugged. "We all have our little idiosyncrasies. Shall we talk about yours?"

"We certainly could…if I had any. But I like to leave those to my lesser sisters." Serenely she waved over the waitress and ordered one of the tequila specials.

Poppy ordered tequila, as well, then turned to Jane. "How about you, Janie? Do you want your club soda freshened?"

"No, I think I'll have a glass of wine—whatever the house white is," she added to the waitress.

Her friends whooped and drummed the table and generally made a huge fuss over her unusual selection and Jane leveled a look at them when the waitress left with their order. "Contrary to popular opinion, you two, I do know how to make an exception on occasion." Then she grinned. "And this is definitely the occasion."

"Amen to that, sister," Poppy agreed.

When their order arrived, Ava raised her glass. "To being new home owners."

Jane and Poppy clinked glasses with her. "To new home owners!"

Jane took a sip of her wine, then raised her glass again. "To Miss Agnes."

They clinked again. "To Miss Agnes!"

"Man, I miss her," Poppy said.

"Yeah, me, too. She was like no adult I've ever known."

Then Poppy raised her glass. "To you, Jane. May you speedily catalog Miss Agnes's collections."

"To me," she said while Ava and Poppy exclaimed, "To Jane!" Then in a rare exhibition of uncertainty, she added, "What if I mess up the job?"

They stared at each other as the possibility of failure hovered in the air above them. Then Ava laughed, Poppy made a rude noise and Jane shook her head, her momentary nerves dissipating.

"Nah." If there was one thing she was completely confident about it was her abilities in her chosen field.

"That reminds me." Poppy twisted in her chair to

glance around the bar. "I asked the head of Kavanagh Construction to drop by if he had the chance so you guys could meet him. And there he is!"

To Jane's astonishment, Poppy hailed one of the men at the table she'd been watching earlier, then popped out of her chair and sashayed across the bar.

With her usual aplomb, she stooped down next to the bald guy Jane had thought was maybe forty and started talking with the confidence of a woman assured of her reception. After a brief conversation she rose to shake hands with the other three men at the table, then gestured in Jane and Ava's direction and said something.

To Jane's horror, not only did the bald guy get up and follow her back across the room, so did the hot redhead. The latter stumbled over an unoccupied chair a couple tables away and lurched the remaining steps to theirs, where he had to slap his fists down in order to catch his balance. He swore a blue streak beneath his breath.

"Dev!" the bald man snapped. "Cool it!"

"'Scuse my language, ladies." The redhead gave them all a loose, sheepish smile. "I'm seriously jet-lagged."

"More like seriously drunk," Jane said sotto voce.

"Jane, Ava, this is Bren Kavanagh and his brother Devlin," Poppy raised her voice to say over her. "As I told you earlier, the Kavanaghs are going to be in charge of our construction. Bren was just telling me that Devlin here will be the project manager on our remodel. He'll oversee—"

"No." Pushing back from the table, Jane surged to her feet, her heart slamming in outrage. It was one thing to put up with an inebriated man in a bar for a single evening. She'd be damned if she'd put up with one while she was trying to catalog the most important collection of her life.

Devlin, who'd been staring owlishly down at his knuckles where they bore into the rich wood tabletop, raised his hazel-green-eyed gaze and blinked at her. Then, apparently not liking what he saw in her expression, he narrowed his eyes, his devil-black brows snapping together over the thrust of his nose. "Say what?"

"No. It's a pretty simple word, Mr. Kavanagh— what part don't you understand?"

"Hey, listen—"

"No, you listen! I will not have some damn drun— Hey!" She yelped as Poppy grabbed her by the wrist and nearly jerked her off her feet.

"Excuse us," Poppy said as she turned and strode toward the back of the bar.

Leaving Jane no choice but to follow in her wake or be dragged behind her friend like a toddler's pull toy.

DEV WATCHED the uptight brunette being hauled from the table. "Okay, then, I'm outta here," he said, and knuckled himself erect. *Whoa.* He flattened his hand back against the wooden surface. Damn room was starting to sway.

Bren's eyes narrowed as he studied him. "Man, you *are* wasted. You'd better go sit down before you fall down."

Good plan. He started to pull out the chair next to the redhead with the great ti—

"At our table, bro."

"Oh. Yeah. Sure." He gave the redhead with the killer bod an acknowledging nod for her sympathetic smile, then made his unsteady way back to Finn and David.

What the hell was he doing here, anyway? He should have fallen straight into bed to sleep for ten solid hours. He'd sure as hell known better than to let Bren guilt him into going out to discuss how he could take over for his brother while Bren went through treatment. Or, alternatively, having caved, he at least should have been bright enough to forgo the two shots of tequila he'd slammed back after downing a generous dram or two of Da's treasured Redbreast. He was from good Irish stock; he could usually put away his fair share without showing the effects.

Tonight, however—well, he'd been up for more than thirty-five hours, nineteen of which had been spent traveling from Athens, Greece. He'd already been flattened with exhaustion when his brother Finn met him at the airport.

But there was no rest for the wicked as far as the Kavanaghs were concerned. When a chick came home to roost, a celebration was not merely expected, it was a given. And a get-together wasn't a get-together unless it included all six of his brothers and sisters, their respective spouses and kids, his folks, both grandmas and his grandpa, his two uncles, four aunts and their families. Fair enough—he knew the drill.

But he should have paid less attention to Da's whiskey and a little more to Mom's food.

"Way to go there, Dev," his youngest brother said with a sly grin when Devlin made it to their table. "Back in town a few hours and already you've managed to get sent back to the kiddie table so Bren can talk to the grown-ups."

"You're a riot, David, you know that?" Hooking the crook of his elbow around his brother's neck, he staggered slightly, steadied himself against his brother's side, then scrubbed his knuckles in David's brown hair. "You oughtta take it down to open mic night at the Comedy Underground." He turned him loose and dropped into the chair Bren had sat in earlier. "I gotta admit, though, that's kind of what it feels like. Apparently my drunkenness offended one of the potential clients."

"Can't imagine why," Finn said dryly.

He smiled crookedly. "Yeah, me, either. Shit." He rubbed his fingers over lips that felt rubbery. "I didn't realize how trashed I was until I stood up to go with

Bren to their table. Had to concentrate like a son of a bitch just to walk a straight line."

Finn looked at him, deadpan. "How'd that work for you?"

"Not so great." He glanced over his shoulder at his oldest brother, still talking to the redhead across the room, then turned back to the others, abruptly feeling a whole lot soberer. "So how's he doing, really?"

"He's got his good days and his bad. I think he'd rather tell you about it himself."

"Yeah, him being such a talkative son of a bitch so far." He gave his brothers a look. "I'm still hacked that I didn't even hear about it until three days ago."

Finn gave him a bland look in return. "You've been a little removed from the family for the past decade, little brother. Maybe we thought you wouldn't be interested."

He came up out of his seat, ready to brawl.

Finn merely looked at him with calm, dark eyes, however, and Dev sat back down. Shifted his shoulders. And leveled a hard look on his brother. "I might be removed geographically, but the last time I checked I was still a Kavanagh. I'm still family." Which, okay, conflicted the hell out of him every bit as much today as it had at nineteen. He loved the clan Kavanagh but couldn't be around them long before he started going insane. Yet while he'd moved to get away from everyone always knowing his business, this was not the usual oh-did-you-hear-Dev's-dating-the-O'Brien-girl, I-wonder-how-May-would-work-for-the-wedding kind of crap—this was Bren, sick with cancer. It pinched like hell that nobody had bothered to pick up a phone to let him know about it. "I'm still family," he repeated stonily.

"Yeah, yeah, Finn knows that," David said peaceably. "But that's something else you have to take up with Bren. It was his decision not to burden you with it when there wasn't anything you could do to help. But now you can. If you didn't blow it with the client, that is. So…what? She took a dislike to you because you didn't hold your liquor tonight? Didn't you explain you were jet-lagged?"

"'Course I did."

"So what was that all about then?"

He thought about the brunette. She'd caught his eye from across the room. She wasn't built like her redheaded friend or model-pretty like the blonde, and in their company he imagined she got overlooked a lot. God knew she wasn't his usual type, but she'd been alone and looking at him and he'd found himself abruptly interested.

It had been the contradictions, he thought. She wore a prim white blouse that showed such a meager hint of lace undergarments it might as well not have bothered and a straight midcalf-length black skirt whose center slit barely made it over her knees, let alone into interesting territory. But her shoes were leopard-print high heels designed to make a man realize that the pale, smooth legs they accentuated were pretty damn sleek. And while her shiny brown hair had been piled up on her head in an old-lady bun, it had listed to one side and looked as if it were about ten seconds from coming undone and sliding down that long neck.

But it was her eyes that had been the real contradiction. He hadn't been able to tell from across the room, but they were blue. And unlike her clothing, there wasn't a damn thing prim about them. They'd looked at him, in fact, as if she wouldn't mind giving him the hottest—

Shit. He shook aside the image that sprang to mind, because who the hell cared? She was obviously humorless and judgmental and he looked at David and shrugged. "Beats me, brother. I have no idea what her problem is."

"YOU WANNA KNOW what my problem is?" Jane wrenched her wrist free from Poppy's grasp and reached behind her to grasp the ladies' room counter at her back to keep from bopping her friend on her elegant chin. She might have thrown caution to the wind and taken her best shot when she was ten, but she had learned control since then.

Hell, she lived and *breathed* control these days.

"My problem," she said coolly, "is one, I don't like being manhandled by you, and two—and this is the biggie, Calloway—you're looking to saddle me with a drunk while I'm trying to get together the most important collection I've ever been asked to head. You know damn well that I'm on a time crunch to get it done for the January exhibit and the last thing I need is to waste time babysitting some lush. *That's* my problem."

"You think you're the only one with something on the line here?" Poppy thrust her nose right in Jane's face. "This is not all about you and you damn well know it. *None* of us want to fall short when Miss Agnes put so much faith in us. At least you have the experience to handle your challenge. Ava has to sell the place without benefit of any sort of real estate experience and I'm responsible for the remodel. And that's not small spuds, Kaplinski, given that I make most of my living designing menu boards!"

"Oh, please." Jane thrust her nose right back at her. "Like you don't know Miss A. requested you decorate because you've been trying to get her to redo the mansion since the first time we saw the place! How many suggestions have you given her over the years for improving the place? One million? Two? And I'm guessing she put Ava in charge of selling because she's the one who has contacts up the wazoo with the kind of people who will be able to afford it."

"All right, maybe you've got a point. But I've busted my butt researching and interviewing contractors, and the Kavanaghs are highly respected in their field. Not to mention that they agreed to work at twenty percent below their usual rate in exchange for the publicity that being associated with the Wolcott mansion will bring them. So get over it! Your hard-on against drinkers is not going to screw this up for Ava and me. Or you, either, when it comes to that."

She could see that Poppy was genuinely angry, and that was a rare enough occurrence to make her swallow her ire and give a jerky nod. "Give me some damn breathing room," she muttered and Poppy stepped back.

Jane smoothed her clothes, brushed back the strands of hair that had slid free of her bun. Then she met her friend's eyes.

"Fine," she said grudgingly, "he stays. But if he drinks on the job just once, I'm not accountable for my actions."

"Fair enough."

"I'm glad you think so. Because I'll be expecting you to help me bury the body."

"You wound me." Poppy pressed a hand to her breast. "After all, what are friends for?"

CHAPTER TWO

I will *do a good job of this. Miss Agnes obviously thought I could—believed all three of us could—and nothing and* <u>*NO ONE*</u> *is going to stop me from doing my best.*

"Looks like you've got your work cut out for you."

Jane tensed, recognizing the voice. The fact that she did after only one meeting made her want to string several nasty words together. Instead she composed her expression and slowly turned.

Devlin Kavanagh, all hard-bodied male in a navy T-shirt, worn jeans and scuffed boots, lounged in the doorway to the Wolcott mansion parlor, his auburn hair gleaming beneath all the lights she'd turned on. Her heart started thundering in her chest and, propping her fists upon her hips, she slammed her mind closed against his appeal. "What do you want, Kavanagh?"

"Oh, that's friendly." Shoving away from the door frame, he tipped his head back, closed his eyes and with wide, sweeping movements touched first his right forefinger, then his left, then his right again to the tip of his nose. Snapping erect, he gave her a level look. "Look, Ma, I pass the sobriety test."

"For now. It remains to be seen how long it will last, though, doesn't it?"

Eyes narrowing to glints of golden green between dense dark lashes, he demanded, "What is your problem? I wasn't kidding the other night when I said I was jet-lagged. Maybe I shouldn't have knocked back those tequilas at the bar, but give me a break. I'd been up for a day and a half and they hit me harder than usual."

Mortification suffused her. Because he was right: she was being a judgmental bitch and it wasn't an attitude that sat well with her. She didn't know this guy—it was hardly her place to criticize his actions. "My apologies," she said stiffly.

He made a skeptical sound. "Yeah, that sounds real sincere."

What the hell did he want from her? Her spine ached from holding herself so rigidly against the temptation to get close to him. She didn't understand this crazy attraction at all, but she knew one thing: she was stronger than a few stray hormones. Tipping her chin up, she looked him in the eye. "Then I apologize for that, as well. Your drinking issues are none of my business."

"Jesus, you don't give an inch, do you?"

"I said I was sorry!"

"In the most backhanded way I've ever heard. But

you're right about one thing, sister. *If* I had drinking issues they'd be none of your business."

It was one thing for her to criticize herself and something else for him to do so. "Was there something you wanted, Mr. Kavanagh?"

"Dev."

She gave him an *"and?"* look.

"Call me Dev. Or Devlin if you insist on being formal. Mr. Kavanagh's my dad."

"Okay. Is there something I can do for you, Devlin?" She stooped to fiddle with the collection of Columbia River basketry at her feet.

"I'm trying to locate updated blueprints for the mansion. A few of the rooms look off but the place is over a hundred years old and unfortunately I don't have the originals, either. For all I know the joint is riddled with secret passages or other hidey-holes. I'd like to know what we're dealing with before we start tearing things apart, though, because hidden spaces might actually be a selling point, which Bren tells me is your ultimate objective."

The idea of a secret passage intrigued her, but she refused to be sidetracked. The sooner she got rid of Mr. I'm-too-sexy-for-my-boots the better. Yet instead of simply giving him a straight answer, she heard herself demand, "And you're asking me because…?"

"You appear to be the go-to girl for all the odds and ends around here. So would you happen to know where the blueprints are?"

"No, I'm sorry." And she truly was because the more information Kavanagh Construction had, the better the restoration was likely to turn out. And she'd love to see this old mansion fixed up the way it deserved to be. "I'm sure there's more than one set, but I honestly don't know where Miss Agnes kept them. All I know is that she told us Wolcott had been renovated several times. The last was when she had the interior done in 1985."

He nodded. "The year the Wolcott diamonds were stolen by her construction foreman."

Jane quit pretending to pay attention to the work she should be doing and rose to her feet to face Devlin squarely. "You *know* about that?"

"Babe." He gave her a smile she'd bet her inheritance had gotten him into more than one woman's silkies. "I'm a Seattle boy. Those diamonds are an urban legend in this town. *Everyone* knows about them."

Well, she was a Seattle girl and— "I didn't. Not until recently. Miss Agnes never talked about their theft or the murder of her man Henry." She gave a shrug. "At least not before Poppy heard about it from someone and hounded her for the story." Her lips crooked at the memory. "Poppy can be a bit of a pit bull when she gets her teeth sunk into a subject."

He started to take a step into the room but must have noticed her stiffening, because he stopped where he was. Bracing a muscular shoulder against the doorjamb, he hooked his thumbs in his belt loops and studied her. "Henry, huh? Was that the business manager guy who was killed when the thief came back to recover the diamonds he'd hidden?"

"You're the expert, Seattle Boy."

"Hey, I was a kid when it all went down. I was interested in murder and mayhem but mostly fascinated by the idea of a multimillion-dollar set of jewelry still floating around somewhere."

"Yes, well, Henry was her man for all matters. He was her butler and secretary and advisor and I think probably her lov—" Jane cut herself off, appalled.

What was she doing? She'd already established she didn't know Devlin. And while assigning him dependency problems might have been jumping the gun a bit, there was no reason to offer him blanket trust, either. So why had she almost blurted out that she and her friends believed Henry had probably been more to Miss Agnes than a simple employee? It wasn't as if their mentor had admitted as much to them. But the way Agnes had looked when she'd talked about him and the fact he wasn't even supposed to have been there the night it was popularly believed that Maperton had broken in to retrieve the diamonds that had gone missing the year before, they had all sort of assumed Henry had probably been her lover as well as the man who kept her home and affairs running smoothly.

But she certainly didn't plan on cozying up to Devlin Kavanagh with the speculation.

"Well, listen." She gave him her best businesslike smile. "I have work to do. As I said, I really don't know where the blueprints may be. I'm not even sure any exist. But I will keep an eye out for them."

He looked at her for a moment, then stepped back, his hands shoved into his jeans pockets. "Thanks. I've got a partial set from the kitchen addition that was put on in 1909. I'll head downtown to see if King County records has the originals or any of the updates since then." He gave her a brief head-to-toe once-over, licked his bottom lip and nodded. "See ya around, Legs."

Legs? She stared from the now-empty doorway to the limbs in question, encased in plain old dark Levi's that she'd paired with a black blazer and a white shirt. She had fairly long legs, but they were certainly nothing to write home about. She'd always thought they were on the skinny side herself, which hardly qualified them as showgirl material.

Then she gave herself a mental shake and a stern directive to forget about it. But good grief. The man was a walking, talking Hazardous to Women zone. She imagined that with his confidence and those eyes and that body, females had been dropping at his feet since the day he hit puberty. Maybe even before.

Well, not her. As far she was concerned, he was Mr. Invisible from this point on. She was keeping her distance. Putting him out of her mind.

Getting her butt back to work.

Putting Miss Agnes's collections in order so she could start researching and cataloging them was a huge undertaking, and she was happy as a pig in a puddle at the prospect of getting her hands on them. At the same time she was a little daunted by the scope of the museum bequest, and she needed to get moving on it. She had never headed an undertaking of such scale before, and she was laboring under a deadline.

"So here the clock is ticking and I've been spinning like that Looney Tunes Tasmanian Devil all day long wasting time just trying to figure out *where* to start," she confessed to Ava when her friend dropped by to see how she was doing later that afternoon. "Then, too," she added wryly, "I keep getting caught up in the nostalgia of so many of the pieces—upshot of which is that I haven't actually started anywhere."

"Jane, Jane, Jane." Ava picked up a first-edition book, ran her fingers over the ancient leather binding, then carefully set the volume back on the shelf where she'd found it and looked up to pin Jane in place with her gaze. "It's a no-brainer. When in doubt, start with the jewels."

A startled laugh burst out of Jane and she gave her friend an impulsive hug. "You, Ms. Spencer, are a genius! I've been doing a bit of this and bit of that with all the collections, when I should be concentrating on the Met's stuff. The jewelry is an *excellent* place to start, since that's part of their haul." Grabbing up her slim Apple notebook, she started for the stairs. "Come on. I've got the codes for the safe in here. Let's go see what's in the vault."

IT WAS ALMOST 5:00 p.m. by the time Dev let himself back into the mansion. He probably should have called it a day and headed for the apartment his sister Maureen had rented for him in Belltown. But the skies had opened up, the place didn't feel like home yet and he'd just as soon build a fire in the little study up on the second floor, drink his Starbucks drip and listen to the rain bouncing off the windows while he went over the information he'd gathered from the County Assessor's Office and the Department of Development and Environmental Services.

Not that it was much. Before 1936 the records that the Assessor's Office kept for buildings had been compiled in longhand on four-by-six-inch cards with lots of revisions and cross-outs and not a single photograph. Pretty much useless, in other words.

But luckily he'd been able to get a Flexcar from the share-a-ride program he belonged to, and more helpful were the photos taken of the mansion from the late thirties on, which he'd run to ground at the Washington State Archives at Bellevue Community College. They weren't as helpful as blueprints, but they'd at least help him get a handle on the timeline for the various so-called improvements that had been made to the Wolcott mansion.

He frowned as he took the stairs two at a time. Because whoever was responsible for the additions on this grand ole dame ought to be stuffed and mounted. He'd seen some bad do-it-yourself jobs in his day, but he'd never seen a place butchered quite as badly as this one. Few of the structural changes added over the years had been made with the original architecture in mind. And rooms that once must have been spacious and full of grace had been divided to the point they had conceded all personality.

So deep was he in thought about how to undo the damage that he'd nearly reached the study before he realized that feminine voices drifted out of it. He faltered to a stop.

Well…shit. So much for a little time to nurse his coffee in front of a fire.

He was turning away to head back to his apartment after all when the murmur of voices gave way to a woman's deep, raucous belly laugh. The sound cut through him like a hot sword and he found himself following it back to the doorway as if he were one of those old-time cartoon characters wafting in the wake of a beckoning scent.

Since it never occurred to him that little Miss Bug Up Her Butt Kaplinski could be the woman laughing like she'd just heard a deliciously dirty joke, his gaze zeroed in on the voluptuous redhead seated in profile to him across the room. Unless Ava was a ventriloquist, however, the sound wasn't coming from her.

A slight smile curved her lips as she sat looking at her friend across the delicate oval coffee table. Dev turned his attention in that direction, as well.

Then he simply stood there feeling as if he'd just taken a roundhouse kick to the head.

Jane sat on a velvet love seat perpendicular to the crackling fire, her high-heeled ankle boots tumbled in a heap on the floor and her argyle-stocking-clad feet crossed at the ankles and propped amidst a tumble of velvet boxes and bags on the little coffee table. More neatly arranged containers surrounded her and her left hand curled over the top of an open notebook computer, preventing it from tumbling off her lap while she laughed with her head thrown back as if she'd just heard the raunchiest, most amusing story ever.

It was the first time he'd seen her with her spine fully unbent since stumbling into her table at the bar the other night. Not that he had seen her more than three times total, but on the other two occasions her posture had been rebar rigid, as if she were some secret princess wondering how the hell she'd gotten cast into this world of commoners.

As he watched her start gaining control of herself, a corner of his mouth ticked up. Because the royalty analogy wasn't half-bad, considering she was wearing a queen's ransom in jewels.

She'd removed her blazer and rolled up her shirt-sleeves, and ropes of emeralds and pearls adorned her wrists, looped in strand after lustrous, glittering strand from her neck. A diamond tiara perched at the fore of her listing bun, a cascade of some jewel he didn't recognize swung from her ears and each finger sported a gem-encrusted ring.

Ava was similarly decked out, but he barely spared her a second glance. Adorned with only a couple of select pieces, she had the look of someone who'd been born wearing this stuff. Jane looked like a little girl playing dress-up. And given her sober-puss personality he'd bet a position on the next America's Cup yacht—which, okay, he didn't actually have to wager—that she hadn't played a lot of little-girl games even when she'd been one.

"Your turn," she said, and Ava bent forward to pick one of the velvet containers from the table between them. The redhead's hand suddenly halted midreach, however, and she turned her head in his direction. He had a nanosecond, as their gazes connected, to wish he'd stepped out of sight while he'd still had the chance.

Then she inclined her head and said easily, "Hey, Dev."

Jane's head whipped around and she yanked her feet off the table so fast that several boxes and bags tumbled to the floor. Swearing beneath her breath, she bent to pick them up and her tiara tipped over one eye. She snatched the little crown from her head as hot color flowed up her throat. A minuscule comb that still anchored the tiara on one side ripped a hank of slippery hair free and it unfurled down to the corner of her mouth.

Blowing it off her face, she snapped upright to perch with that ramrod posture on the edge of the velvet seat. Raising her chin, she met his gaze. "Devlin."

He clicked his boot heels together and gave her a clipped bow. "Your highness." Okay, it was a cheap shot. But when the universe handed you an opportunity on a silver platter it was practically kicking karma in the teeth to ignore it. He swallowed a grin.

"What can we do for you, Devlin?" Ava asked.

"Huh?" He pulled his gaze away from Jane's flushed face and looked at her friend. "Oh. Nothing. I was going to build a fire and go over some photos of the mansion that I picked up at the state archives today, but I didn't realize the room was already occupied."

Straightening, the redhead extended an imperious hand. "Let's see them."

He crossed the room and handed her the manila envelope. Taking it, she patted the love seat next to her with her free hand. "Sit."

"Stay," Jane said in the same commanding-the-dog tone, and Dev looked at her in surprise. What the hell—did the woman have a sense of humor after all?

She returned his searching look with a bland one of her own and, rolling his shoulders, he sat down next to Ava. Nah. Probably not.

Ava started to pour the envelope's contents into

her lap, but he clamped his fingers over the opening to stay her. "Don't dump 'em—reach in and pull them out," he directed when she bent a queenly look of her own on him. "I'd just as soon not go to the trouble of putting them in order twice."

She did as he bid and a soft sound of pleasure escaped her when she looked at the topmost photograph. "Oh, this is wonderful. Janie, come see what the place looked like before that awful sunroom was added."

Somewhat to his surprise, Jane complied, setting aside her computer and rising to her feet. He felt Ava shift and once again she patted the cushion next to her. "Scoot over here," she commanded him. "We'll put you in the middle so we can all see."

He felt rather than saw Jane hesitate. But perhaps that was his imagination, because a second later she lowered herself next to him.

On a really small love seat. Now, normally he'd say being sandwiched between a couple of babes on a piece of furniture built for two was a good thing. For some damn reason, however, this was making him edgy as hell. "Uh, I don't think this love seat was designed with three people in mind." Aware of Jane's warmth all along his left side, he added, "Especially when one of us has such impressively curvy hips."

Okay, that didn't come out real suave, even though Ava did indeed have killer hips that cut down on the seating space. Still, he wasn't prepared for both women to freeze on either side of him. And he sure as hell wasn't prepared for the redhead to turn an expressionless face his way and demand with chill civility, "Am I taking up too much room, Devlin?"

"What? No! That's not what I meant at all. I just—" *What, genius?* The truth was, he hadn't been using his head at all, he'd simply rattled off the first excuse that popped to mind in order to get out from between the two. And now his brain, normally facile and quick around the opposite sex, was drawing a big, fat blank.

Jane's breast flattened against his biceps as she craned around to see her friend. "He said 'impressively curvy,' Av. *Curvy.* Not fat."

He jerked in shock and stared down at her for the first time since she'd squeezed in next to him. "Of course I didn't say fat! Jesus. No man in his right mind is going to look at her and think that. Hell, she's built like a walking wet dream." The blue eyes he was staring into widened and he felt like smacking himself in the head. *What the fuck is the matter with you, Dev? You had more savoir faire when you were nine.*

Except it appeared he'd actually said something right, because he felt Ava relax next to him even as Jane smiled slightly and said, "Damn straight she is. And it's your shoulders, Slick, not Ava's hips, that are taking up all the space."

"No, it's probably my hips." Ava handed him the

photos with a rueful smile. "I apologize, Dev. I didn't mean to freak on you. I was a fat kid, and I still have a few issues with my weight."

You *think?* With three sisters, one might reasonably imagine he had an inkling into the female mind, but he didn't have a clue. So he merely said, "Well, you shouldn't. There's not a man I know who wouldn't kill to get his hands on a body like yours."

Yet it wasn't Ava who commanded his awareness as the three of them pored over the photographs. It didn't make a lick of sense, but it was Jane who kept capturing his attention.

She might have a chilly personality, but as he'd already noted, the girl pumped out some serious body heat. He felt it radiating along his entire left side and had to peel himself free for a moment to set his coffee on the table. It was hard juggling the cup and the photos in these cramped quarters anyhow, and at this point he didn't need any additional heat from the inside, as well. He was plenty hot.

Plenty. Hot.

Shit.

He focused on Jane's unvarnished fingernails. They were bitten to the quick. It wasn't very big of him, but it gave him a little surge of pleasure all the same. Hah. Maybe she wasn't as aggressively confident as she appeared.

But she had skin like a baby. Not that he could see a hell of a lot of it—she was buttoned up from stem to stern. Still, he couldn't help but notice its soft texture when their fingers brushed as they exchanged photographs. Or how her bared forearms shone more luminous than the pearls twined around them.

He shifted uncomfortably. What the fuck was going on here? This was so not like him. He'd had more women over the years than you could shake a stick at, and he was a sailor and a carpenter, for cri'sake—he didn't think in words like *luminous*.

"Well, hey." He pried himself from between the two females and rose to his feet. "My eyes are starting to cross—I think I'm going to take off. I still haven't caught up with the jet lag. I need to hit the sack."

More like hit a bar and pick up a woman, he thought as he gathered his pictures, said his goodbyes and dashed through the rain to his car a few moments later after letting himself out of the mansion. Someone with cleavage, smiles and red lips. And nails long enough to drag down his back. Someone who'd look at him like he was the hottest stud to swagger down the pike, instead of a lush who was one drink away from oblivion.

Only…

Instead of heading out to one of Belltown's night spots when he reached his apartment house, he took a shower and went to bed.

Tomorrow, though. Tomorrow night he'd go out and find himself a woman. Because clearly if he was getting all hot under the collar over uptight, disapproving little Jane Kaplinski, it had been *way* too long since he'd gotten laid.

CHAPTER THREE

Sex is overrated. I for one can live just fine without it.
Really.

JANE SAT in the Wolcott parlor the next evening typing annotations into her notebook computer for a meeting with the museum director the following morning. Instead of focusing all her attention on the report, however, she found her thoughts constantly drifting to a certain buff redheaded man.

What was it about Devlin Kavanagh, anyway? This inability to concentrate whenever he popped to mind—which was far too often for comfort—was ridiculous, not to mention unprecedented.

Well, there was some precedent, she supposed. It wasn't as if she'd never been attracted to other men before, because naturally she had.

But not like this. Never had she been drawn to a guy in such an I-gotta-have-him, out-of-control sort of way.

And *that* was the problem in a nutshell. Because she didn't do out of control. Having grown up in a household that was always verging on or in the midst of some sort of drama, she'd made a firm decision about that before she was even ten years old.

What had she ever done to deserve parents who were actors? All she'd ever wanted was a nice, normal family, but had she gotten one? Oh, no. God was no doubt up in heaven slapping his knee at the thought of the Dorrie and Mike Show he'd sent her instead. It was unfair, that's what it was. Her parents didn't have simple differences of opinion; they had wars, crises of epic proportions. Which she almost could have lived with—had they just *once* not tried to drag her smack-dab into the middle of them.

So, no. She didn't do out of control.

Which ought to make matters simpler now, right? Except somehow this didn't feel simple. And she didn't understand why she was having so much trouble with this particular guy.

"Crap." She stared at her computer screen in frustration. "I have *got* to get a grip."

"Well, this doesn't bode well if the job already has you talking to yourself."

She gave an involuntary start, then scowled at Poppy as her friend strolled into the room. "Jeez, give me a heart attack, why don't you." Even if it was her own damn fault for allowing a man to distract her to the point where someone could sneak up on her.

"Sorry," Poppy said without noticeable contrition.

"So *is* it the job that's making you carry on conversations with yourself?"

"I wish," she muttered. "That would be so much easier." Then she gave herself a mental head slap. *Shut up, Kaplinski. Shut up, shut up, shut up.* She wasn't ready to spill her guts, and until she was she knew better than to give Poppy even an inkling that she might have a secret.

But of course it was too late. Because as she'd told Devlin just yesterday, Poppy was a pit bull once she sank her teeth into something. Already her friend, who looked deceptively soft and pliable with her curly blond hair, big brown eyes and today's floaty hippie-dippy-girl clothing, had Jane firmly in the crosshairs of the dreaded Calloway Evil Eye. "Spill," she commanded.

And like a leaky old oil tanker in a pristine harbor, she did just that. "I think I've gone and fallen face-first in lust."

"Ooh." Poppy plopped down on a nearby chair and wiggled her fingers in a gimme gesture. "Tell sister everything. And don't skimp on the details."

"Me. In lust. That is everything. There are no details, Pop, because there's nothing to tell."

Poppy pursed her lips to blow a skeptical *pfffft.* "Please. We're talking sexual attraction. Pounding hearts. Jingly-jangly nerve endings. Am I right?"

Oh, man. Was she ever. Jane nodded.

"Then of course there's something to tell. When

it comes to all things sexy there is *always* something to tell."

"Not this time."

Poppy gave her an indignant look. "Why the hell not?"

"Hey, just because I have certain urges doesn't mean I have to act on them. So I haven't—and I don't intend to." She saved the file she'd been working on and shut down her computer, gazing at her friend over its closing lid. "It's a random case of lust. I plan to get over it."

"Why would you want to?" Poppy blinked, clearly puzzled. "Lust is a good thing, right? I mean, it leads to sex, and sex makes you feel good. Not that I'd know from personal experience," she added virtuously.

"Of course not. You've only been disclaiming personal experience since you first misinformed Ava and me about sex back when we were nine." She gave her friend a lopsided smile. "The only difference being that you really were a total innocent then."

"What do you mean, misinformed? I was always first with the true scoop, and you know it."

"Please. Babies are made when you swap spit with a boy?"

"Oh. Yeah. That. Damn Karen Copelli's sister. I thought for sure she was a reliable source. After all, she was an older woman."

"I know. She must have been all of twelve, which made her a helluva lot nearer to being an honest-to-god teenager than the three of us. I gotta tell you, though, after hearing that spit thing I figured I'd probably never, ever have babies. Because, *ew*."

Poppy grinned. "Yeah, it didn't sound real appealing, did it? Luckily, actual kissing turned out to be so much cooler."

"Not that you'd know from personal experience."

"Of course not," she agreed with a serene smile, then brushed the topic aside with a long-fingered wave of her hand. "But we're not talking about me, Jane. So don't go changing the subject."

"Yes, let's. Let's change it to something else entirely."

"Okay then, how about this? Maybe what you're feeling isn't actually lust at all."

She considered the possibility for, oh, two full seconds before giving a definitive nod. "Trust me. It's lust." A big, fat, flaming-hot case of it. "Or, okay, I suppose it could be heartburn."

Her friend practiced the selective deafness that made her such a formidable meddler-with-a-mission and said with a perfectly straight face, "Maybe it was really a case of love at first sight."

"Uh-huh. Because everyone knows *that's* not a great big fairy tale, or anything."

"Hey, it worked for my parents. And Ava's mom and dad might be sort of benignly neglectful in the parental department, but look how long they've been married."

"I always sort of assumed that was because there

was too much money involved to go through the hassle of getting a divorce. But maybe not. They do seem to do a lot of stuff together."

"See? The world is simply lousy with True Love stories. So tell me your guy's name and maybe I can help you figure out how to handle the situation."

"I've figured it out for myself, thank you very much. It's pretty simple, really." She gave Poppy a level look. "I'm handling it by not doing anything at all."

"That's a *horrible* game plan."

"Yet all mine."

"Tell me, Jane-Jane."

"You don't really want to go there with that name—Pop-Pop."

"*Tell* me."

"No."

Poppy treated her to another Calloway Evil Eye. This time, however, Jane wasn't about to budge and she shot the Kaplinski version right back at her.

Her blond friend studied her for a moment. Then she gave a clipped nod. "Oh, all right. But you know I'll get it out of you sooner or later. I don't know why you don't just save us all some trouble and tell me now."

"I've never minded a little trouble."

"In what universe, pray tell?"

She merely gave the other woman her best inscrutable smile.

"Fine." Poppy heaved a disgruntled sigh. "Be that way. I didn't come here to see you, anyway. Ava told me Dev has some great photos from the Washington State archives. Have you seen him today?"

Jane's heart kicked hard, then commenced to gallop in her chest. Luckily, Poppy was busy glancing around as if she expected her question to make him magically appear and didn't notice her expression. Good thing, because Jane was pretty sure it would render the question about who she was lusting over obsolete.

She managed to compose her features in the moment it took Poppy to turn her attention back to her. "No, I haven't. Considering all the clomping around I've heard from up in the sunroom this afternoon, though, I'm gonna take a wild stab and guess he's upstairs."

Poppy studied her a moment. "Tell me you're not still holding on to that ridiculous grudge because he knocked back a few too many tequilas last week."

"Hey, I'll have you know I'm being incredibly open-minded. Of course, it doesn't hurt that he was sober when I saw him yesterday. Or that those footsteps I mentioned sounded fairly steady." Or the fact she'd already decided she'd been a bit precipitous passing judgment.

"Dammit, Jane! You have got to stop this judgmental shit, because I swear if you louse this up for us—"

"Oh, get a grip, I haven't done anything to upset your precious arrangement with Kavanagh Construction. As a matter of fact, I was the epitome of professionalism with him yesterday—and if you don't believe me, just ask Ava." Who luckily hadn't been around during her afternoon conversation with Devlin. "Not that I can swear she was actually paying attention, mind you. She was pretty jazzed about those photos."

The mention of which diverted Poppy's attention. "Av said you saw them, too?"

"I did, and they're every bit as great as she's undoubtedly told you."

"Hot damn. I'm gonna go find Devlin and see for myself." She started toward the doorway.

"I'll catch you later, then," Jane said to her friend's retreating back. "I'm going to call it a day and head home." Where she intended to put Devlin out of her mind once and for all and buckle down to finish her report.

Poppy paused to look back over her shoulder. "Hang around for another fifteen minutes. We can go grab some dinner."

She hesitated for a second, not sure she wanted to go another round defending her right to keep a few thoughts to herself. But visualizing her almost empty refrigerator and even sparser cupboards, she nodded. "Sounds like a plan to me."

"Okay, then, I'll be back in a few." She raised her brows. "Unless you wanna come up with me?"

Jane managed not to screech, *"Are you out of your freakin' mind?"* Her face even felt halfway composed when she said coolly, "No, you go ahead. We'll probably get to eat a lot sooner if only one of us is drooling over the pics. And this will give me a chance to get a little more done on my report."

"Okay, then. I won't be long."

"Hey, take your time." She didn't mind waiting. As long as she didn't have to endure any face-to-face time with The Incredible Radiating Pheromone Man, she was perfectly happy to have Poppy take just as long as her little heart desired.

HQN™

We *are* romance™

HAPPY READING!

As part of our special sizzling summer reads offer, you can now **SAVE $1.00** on the purchase of **CUTTING LOOSE** by *New York Times* bestselling author **Susan Andersen,**

available in August wherever books are sold, including most bookstores, supermarkets, drugstores, department and discount stores.

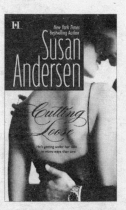

New York Times Bestselling Author

BRENDA JOYCE

"Steeped in action and
sensuality...superlative."
—*Publishers Weekly*, starred
review, on *Dark Seduction*

THE MASTERS OF TIME

DARK EMBRACE

Dear Reader,

Come with me into a dark, dangerous and passionate new world, where you will meet medieval Highlanders with extraordinary powers—and extraordinary desires.

Meet the Masters of Time: Highland warriors sworn to protect innocence through the ages. They do not choose their destiny; it chooses them. Once chosen, these medieval knights walk the world through the centuries in absolute secrecy, serving the Code, the unnamed Brotherhood and mankind. Nearly immortal, they are dangerous, powerful and gorgeous.

Now meet the women who are fated to love them. They are smart, courageous and unsinkable modern women who can't help but fall in love and fight for that love, no matter how daunting their heroes seem. And so the classic clash of man and woman begins: independent modern woman meets macho medieval man. Need I say more?

Welcome to the MASTERS OF TIME!

Brenda Joyce

PROLOGUE

Loch Awe, Scotland, 1436

"A HIGHLANDER WITH NO CLAN, no father but Satan's spawn and ye still war for land? 'Tis not the land ye need, Lismore," Argyll spat. "Ye need a father and a soul."

Aidan of Awe trembled with rage, the glen behind him filled with the dead and the dying. His Campbell rival sawed on his steed's reins and smiled savagely, clearly aware he had delivered the final blow that day, and galloped off toward his departing army.

Aidan breathed hard, blue eyes flashing. His breath was warm in the cold winter air, hanging there like the smoke from the camp's fires. He could not know if Argyll had chosen his words with care or not. It was not a secret that he was a bastard, born in rape and shame. Still, when his father was alive, he had been the king's favorite and the Defender of the Realm. Aidan realized he could turn over Argyll's meaning a hundred times and never decide if the man knew the entire black truth about the Earl of

Moray. But in these dark and bloody times, only the most foolish of men would be oblivious to the war between good and evil that raged across the world, and the Campbell was no fool. Perhaps he knew of the matters secretly spoken of betwixt the Masters and the gods.

He turned now to stare at the last of the warring men, his leine soaking wet and clinging to his muscular body. His men were all Highlanders and they'd fought mostly on foot, with long and broad swords, with daggers and pikes. They were dirty, tired, bloody—and loyal to him. Men had died for him that day. The snow was red with their blood, and that of the Campbells.

Aidan took up his stallion's reins. His men were returning from the glen, trudging tiredly toward him, their larger weapons heaved over shoulders, the wounded being helped by their comrades. Still, every man smiled and nodded at him as they passed. He spoke or nodded to each in turn, to let each man know he was grateful for their arms and valor.

Tents were raised and cook fires started. Aidan handed his stallion off to a young, hopeful Highland lad, when he felt a frisson of alarm. The emotion came from afar, but the vibration went entirely through him.

In that instant, he knew that the fear he sensed came from his son, who was safely at home.

Or so he had thought.

With his seven senses, he pinpointed Ian. His son remained at Castle Awe, where he had left him.

He did not hesitate. He vanished into time.

It took a very brief moment to be flung through time and space back to Castle Awe. The leap ripped him through the forest, pine branches tearing at him, and then past the rock-strewn, snow-tipped mountaintops, through white stars and bright suns, with such terrible gut-wrenching force and speed that he wanted to scream. The velocity threatened to rip him from limb to limb, and shred him into tiny pieces of hair and skin. But he had been leaping time for years, ever since being chosen, and he had learned how to endure the torment. Now his only thought was that evil was hunting his son, and his determination overshadowed the pain.

He landed in his own north tower, going down to all fours so hard it was as if his wrists and knees had shattered. The chamber was spinning with dizzying speed while he urgently tried to become oriented and find his power and his senses.

The room had not ceased turning when he felt a huge evil presence approaching, a power so great and so dark that he dreaded looking up.

With the evil, there was Ian's fear and rage.

He raised his head, in growing horror.

A huge man stood in his chamber doorway, holding Aidan's young, struggling son.

His father was not dead. Moray had returned.

Aidan leapt to his feet, eyes wide with shock as the terrible comprehension sank in.

The Earl of Moray smiled at him, very much alive, white teeth flashing. "Hallo a Aidan."

Aidan's gaze slammed to his son. Ian did not resemble his mother, who had died in childbirth. He looked exactly like his father: fair in complexion, with vivid blue eyes, perfect and beautiful features and dark, curling hair. It took him one moment to comprehend that Ian wasn't hurt—yet. Then Aidan looked at the man who had alternately seduced, raped and tortured his mother. The deamhan who had spent a thousand years stalking innocent men, women and children all over the world.

Clad as a courtier, in long velvet robes of crimson and gold, he was blond, blue-eyed and handsome. He did not look a day older than forty years. "I decided it was time to meet my grandson," Moray murmured in flawless English.

Aidan trembled. Nine years ago, his father had been vanquished at Tor in the Orkney Islands. His half brother, Malcolm, and Malcolm's wife Claire had beheaded Moray in a great battle, but only with the help of a goddess. Evil could not live without a flesh-and-blood body, although it was rumored that the greatest demonic energy was immortal. Aidan had never really believed his father gone; he had secretly expected him to return one day. *He had been right.*

"Yes, I am alive," Moray said softly, their gazes locking. "Did you really think I could be destroyed?"

Aidan breathed hard, preparing for a terrible battle. He would die to save his son from whatever Moray intended. "Release Ian. Whatever ye wish, I'll do it."

"But you know what I want, my son. I want you."

Of course he did; nothing had changed. Moray wished to turn him into his greatest deamhan, a nearly immortal soldier of destruction and death.

"I'll do as ye wish," Aidan lied. As he spoke, he blasted Moray with his god-given power, not thinking twice.

But his father's teeth flashed in a delighted smile and he blocked the surge of energy easily. Then silver blazed from Moray's hands like lightning, and Aidan was flung across the chamber into the far wall. The impact took his breath away, but he remained on his feet.

A dagger appeared in Moray's hand, and he sliced through Ian's ear.

Aidan shouted as blood gushed all over his son's pale leine. "Cease," Aidan roared. "I'll do as ye wish!"

Ian choked on pain, holding his head. Moray grinned at him and pushed the piece of ear across the floor with the pointy tip of his shoe. "Do you wish to keep it?"

Aidan trembled in rage.

"Obey me and he will not suffer," Moray added softly.

"Let me stop the bleeding." Aidan had healing

powers. He started forward for the piece of ear. He would put it back together, make it mend.

Moray held Ian harder, causing the boy to grunt. "Not until you prove yourself to me."

Aidan halted. "I'll heal him first."

"You dare to barter with me?"

In that instant, Aidan knew that unless help arrived in the form of other Masters, they would battle to the death.

"No aid comes," Moray said with a laugh. "I have blocked your thoughts. No one knows what you suffer now."

He believed him. "Tell me what I must do to free and heal my son."

"Father, no," Ian cried, his blue eyes wide.

"Be quiet," Aidan said firmly, meeting his gaze.

Ian nodded, mouth pursed, near tears.

"The village below Awe. Destroy it."

Aidan went still.

Moray stared at him, smiling.

Aidan became aware of his heart pounding, slow and sure, sick with dread. He knew every habitant of that village. The villagers traded and bartered with the castle, with him, on a daily basis. They depended on him for their livelihoods and their lives. The castle defended the village from all attacks, and Awe was sustained by their services and goods. Most importantly, he was sworn before every god on earth to protect the Innocent.

He could not destroy an entire village of men, women and children.

Moray took the dagger and laid it against Ian's throat. Blood oozed and Ian cried out, blanching.

Aidan leapt unto time.

He landed in the castle's great hall moments earlier. The huge room spinning with shocking speed, he saw Ian there, calmly conversing with his steward. On his hands and knees, he tried to fight for his power and choke out words. "Ian. Son!" He would somehow prevent this, undo it. The rules were very clear—no Master could go back in time to change the past. But he would change the past now!

Neither his son nor the steward heard him.

Shocked, Aidan got up. "Ian, come here," he began, but Ian didn't hear him this time, either. His son walked from the hall, heading up the stairs.

They couldn't see him or hear him.

Something had happened to his powers.

He refused to believe it. He ran after Ian, rushing up the narrow, winding stairs. The moment he reached the upper landing, he saw Moray materialize in the upper corridor, surprising his son. Like Ian, Moray could not see him. Aidan tried to blast Moray with power, but nothing came from his hand or his mind. Furious, desperate, as he saw Moray move to seize Ian, Aidan tried to blast him again, but with the same results. "Ian," he screamed in near panic. "Run!"

But Ian did not hear him, and Moray caught the little boy in his powerful embrace. Ian began struggling, and Aidan almost wept as Moray started toward the north tower, dragging the nine-year-old with him.

Aidan ran after them. He launched himself at Moray, intending to assault him as an ordinary human might—but an invisible wall came between them, sending him reeling backward across the corridor.

Were the gods interfering? He was incredulous.

He cried out in fury and saw himself landing in the tower on his hands and knees. There were other rules. A Master must never encounter himself in either the past or the future. The rule was not explained. Afraid to move, he watched his younger self look up in horror.

"Hallo a Aidan," his father said to the man he had been a mere moment ago. "I decided it was time to meet my grandson."

Was this why a Master must never encounter himself in another time? Because he would lose his powers? For he could only stand there and helplessly watch as the drama unfolded—the very drama he had just lived through!

"Yes, I am alive," Moray said softly. "Did you really think I could be destroyed?"

"Release Ian," his younger self said. "Whatever ye wish, I'll do it."

"But you know what I want, my son. I want you."

Aidan watched as his other self tried to blast Moray—and as Moray's own power sent Aidan flying across the tower and into the far wall. He breathed hard, tensing, knowing what was to come. Before Moray lifted his dagger, he launched himself at him again.

Aidan crashed into the invisible wall and bounced off it, choking on rage and anguish. The dagger sliced off the lower lobe of Ian's ear. Ian choked on a scream, and Aidan heard his other self roar in rage—as he did.

And as the other Aidan tried to barter with his demonic father to heal his son, a huge force began dragging him inexorably toward the trio. Aidan tried to halt, but he simply couldn't. He was rapidly being swept toward his younger self.

Aidan braced for an impact, uncertain of what to expect when his body came into contact with his younger self.

"The village below Awe. Destroy it."

But there was no impact. Briefly there was an odd, sickening sensation, and then he was staring at Moray and Moray was staring back at him. He was no longer a spectator to the terrible drama. He had gone back in time to prevent this moment—to change it—but now he was facing Moray. He had come full circle to the precise moment where he had leapt.

He could not destroy an entire village of men, women and children.

Moray took the dagger and laid it against Ian's throat. Blood oozed, and Ian cried out, blanching.

Aidan's mind raced and he shielded his thoughts

so Moray could not lurk. He did not have the power to change this moment.

He was sick now, sick in his soul. "Release my son and I will destroy the village," he said tersely.

"Papa, no!" Ian cried.

Aidan didn't look at him.

Moray grinned. "You will have the boy when you have proven you are *my* son."

"Papa," Ian panted in protest.

Aidan looked at him and wanted to cry. "I won't be long."

"I'll die for them!" Ian cried, struggling furiously now.

Moray jerked him, his expression one of anger and disgust. "He will be useless to me," he spat.

"You won't need him. You will have me," Aidan said, meaning it. He left the tower, feeling as if his soul had already left his body. His movements felt mechanical, except for the wild pounding of his heart and the lurching of his stomach. For the first time in his life, he felt raw fear.

He went swiftly downstairs, awaking the five armed men who slept in the hall. They fell silently into step beside him.

Outside, the moon was full, the sky a deathly black, stars glittering obscenely. He roused another two dozen men. As their mounts were saddled, the men gathered torches. One of the men came up to him, his face set and grim. "What passes, Aidan?"

He looked at Angus, refusing to answer. A steed was brought forward and he vaulted into the saddle, signaling his men to follow.

The troops rode through the gatehouse and over the icy bridge that spanned gleaming waters. When they reached the village on the loch's shores, Aidan pulled up. He did not look at Angus as he spoke. "Burn it. Leave no one—not even a dog—alive."

He did not have to look at Angus to feel the man's absolute shock.

He stared ahead at the village, not bothering to repeat himself.

A moment later, his men were galloping through the thatched cottages, torching the straw roofs, which instantly became infernos. Men, women and children fled their burning homes, crying in fright, and his men chased them down, one after one, swiftly ending each life with one thrust of a blade. Screams of terror filled the night. Aidan sat his restless mount, not allowing it to move. He knew his face was wet, but he refused to wipe the tears. He kept Ian's image close in his mind until the night was silent, except for the hissing of flames and a single woman's sobs.

Her weeping abruptly ended.

His men filed past him, no one looking at him now.

When he was alone, he choked and slid from the mount. He began vomiting helplessly and uncontrollably in the snow.

When he was done, he stayed there, breathing

hard. The screams echoed in his mind. He kept reminding himself that at least he had saved Ian. And he knew he would never forget what he had just witnessed, what he had just done.

He heard a movement behind him.

Aidan slowly got up and turned.

A woman stood by some trees, weeping soundlessly, clutching the hand of a small, terrified child. She was staring at him. His heart lurched in absolute dread. He unsheathed his sword and started toward them.

She didn't run. She hugged her child and shrank against the huge fir tree, eyes wide. "Why, my lord? *Why?*"

The hilt of his sword was sticky in his hand. He meant to raise it. He said hoarsely, "Run. Run now."

She and the child fled into the woods.

He tossed the sword at the ground and leaned his face on his arms, against the tree. *Ian…he had to free Ian from Moray.*

And then he felt the shocking, evil presence behind him. Tensing, Aidan whirled. Moray stood there, Ian in his grasp. He saw the blade Moray held flash silver.

"Give me my son!"

Ian made an odd, strangled sound.

Horrified, Aidan saw the dagger embedded in Ian's chest. "No!"

Moray smiled—and Ian's eyes rolled back in his head lifelessly. Aidan screamed, rushing forward as Ian became limp. But when he reached them, they were gone.

For one instant, Aidan stood in shock and disbelief. *Moray had murdered Ian.*

Anguish began, and with it, more rage than he had ever felt. He howled, holding his head, and furiously, he leapt back in time. *He would not let Ian die.*

He returned to that moment at Awe when he had found Ian in the great hall with his steward, but once again he had no power, and no one could see or hear him. He tried to assault Moray, but an invisible wall came between them and the past repeated itself, exactly. This time, he was a sick spectator as his younger self sat on his steed and watched his men destroying an entire innocent village.

And this time, when he saw himself discover the woman and child, he rushed forward. "Do it," he shouted at his younger self. "You must do it!'

But the man he had been a moment ago did not lift his sword. "Run. Run now!"

The woman and child fled into the forest. He watched as his younger self turned to face Moray, who held Ian tightly to his chest.

And that huge, unnatural force began pulling him inexorably toward the trio. Aidan screamed in warning at Ian, at himself, but no one heard him. He saw the silver dagger flash.

The anguish was even greater now, but so was the rage.

He fell to his knees, howling and maddened, and then he leapt back in time again.

And again.

And again.

And each and every time, it was the same. An entire village destroyed by his command, one small woman and child fleeing and Moray still murdering Ian before his very eyes, only to vanish with his dead child.

And finally he gave up.

He roared and roared, blinded by the grief. He cursed evil; he cursed the gods. He was below Awe's curtain walls, although he did not recall returning from the village. And then, finally, the tower roof above his head collapsed. The entire wing of the castle started to crumble. He wept, openly and brokenly, as the stone walls rained down upon him. And when he was buried beneath his own castle walls, he became still and silent.

Aidan waited to die.

CHAPTER ONE

The Present
September, 2008, New York City

THE ROAR OF HUMAN PAIN AWOKE HER.

Brianna Rose sat bolt upright, awoken from a deep sleep, horrified by the sound. It was filled with rage and anguish and disbelief. And then the pain cut through her.

She doubled over in her bed, clutching herself as if someone had actually slid a butcher's knife through her chest. For one moment, she could not breathe. She had never experienced that kind of anguish in her twenty-six years. Panting hard, she prayed for the pain to end. Then, suddenly, it did.

But as the torment vanished abruptly, a man's handsome image flared in her mind.

A new, terrible tension began. Carefully, Brie sat upright, shaken and stunned. Her loft was silent, except for the sounds of the cars and cabs driving by outside on the street, and the accompaniment of blaring horns. She trembled, glancing at her bedside clock. It was ten after one in the morning. What had just happened?

All the Rose women were empathic to one degree or another. Their empathy was supposed to be a gift, but too often it was a curse, like now. She had been consumed with another human being's pain. Something terrible had just happened, and she could not shake the dark, handsome image she'd just seen from her mind.

Brie trembled, tossing aside the covers. Was Aidan in trouble?

She became very still, her mouth dry, her heart thundering. She'd met him exactly a year ago, perhaps for two whole minutes. Her best friend, Allie, had been missing for weeks and she'd returned briefly to New York—from the Middle Ages—with Aidan's help.

He was the most beautiful man she had ever seen. Allie had explained about the secret Brotherhood and the men belonging to it, men who called themselves the Masters of Time. All sworn before God to defend mankind from the evil in the night. Brie hadn't been surprised—there had been rumors of such warriors for as long as she could remember. In fact, like Allie, she and her cousins, Tabby and Sam, had been thrilled that the whispers were reality.

Brianna had no personal delusions. He was absolutely unforgettable, but she knew a man like that would never look at a woman like her twice—or think about her twice, either. She didn't blame him. She didn't even mind.

She was really good at wearing baggy clothes to hide her curves, and she never wore her contacts. Her eyeglasses were downright ugly. She knew that if she had her dark hair cut and styled properly, if she dressed fashionably and wore makeup, she'd probably look exactly like her mother, Anna Rose.

Brie had no desire to resemble her beautiful, passionate and rebellious mother in any way. Anna had been that rare Rose woman who had not been handed down any gifts. She had been destructive, not constructive; her touch and beauty damaged instead of helped others. In the end, she had hurt those she loved the most, and she had destroyed not only her own family, but herself. Brie didn't want to recall finding her mother dead on the kitchen floor, shot by her jealous boyfriend, with her father weeping over Anna's body. Being a retiring nerd was way better than following in Anna's footsteps.

But Brie had other gifts, making her a lot less nerdy than she appeared. She had been gifted with the Sight. It was the greatest gift a Rose woman could have, handed down from grandmother to grandchild. Brie had been terrified of her visions at first, but Grandma Sarah had explained that the Sight was a precious gift, one meant to be cherished. It was a great resource, meant to help people, which the Rose women were destined to do—and had been doing for hundreds of years. Grandma Sarah had taught her almost everything she knew about good, evil and life.

By now Brie was almost accustomed to the wiles of Fate. Life wasn't easy and it wasn't fair, and the good died young every single day. She didn't blame Anna for the woman's uncontrollable passions. She knew Anna hadn't been able to help herself. She'd resented her sisters for having their gifts and their lives, and her own simple marriage hadn't been enough for her. She'd been an unhappy woman. She had been selfish, but not cruel—and certainly not evil. She hadn't deserved an early death.

It was all ancient history. Dad had remarried—the best thing that ever could have happened to him. Anna was dead and buried, but not forgotten. Brie was determined to be as solid, dependable and trustworthy as her mother was not. Her life was helping others, giving selflessly—perhaps to make up for all the hurt Anna had inflicted. She was thrilled to be employed by the Center for Demonic Activity, a secret government agency dedicated to the war on evil. There, she fought dark forces throughout the ages from the basement, at a computer.

Her cousins claimed she was doing her best to hide from men. They were right. The last thing she wanted was for a man to notice her. She would probably die a virgin, and it didn't matter.

Aidan hadn't noticed her, she was certain, but she had taken one look at him and had fallen hard. She was hopelessly infatuated. She thought about him every day, dreamed about him at night and had even spent hours on the Web, reading about the medieval Highlands. The Rose women came from the northern Highlands originally, so she'd always been fascinated with Scotland's history, but now she foolishly hoped to learn more about him. When he'd brought Allie back to the city from 1430, he'd appeared to be about twenty-five years old. Allie had returned to her lover, Black Royce, at Carrick Castle in Morvern. Brie wished she'd asked her friend about Aidan, but their visit had been too brief. So she kept returning to Carrick's history, yearning for a mention of a man named Aidan, but that was like looking for a needle in a haystack. Still, there were many references to the powerful Earl of Morvern and his fair Lady of Carrick. Brie was thrilled. Even across time, she knew Allie and Royce were fulfilling their destinies together.

She would probably never learn anything about Aidan, and she was sensible enough to realize it, but that didn't stop her crush. A fantasy was harmless. She hadn't even tried to talk herself out of it. If she was going to fall head over heels in love and never act on it, why not do so with someone absolutely unattainable? Aidan, a medieval Highlander with the power to time travel and a mandate to protect Innocence, was a really, really safe bet.

Brie was feeling sick now. It was one thing to have visions and empathy, but she had just *heard*

Aidan roaring in anguish, as if he'd been in the same room with her. How close by was he?

What had happened to him?

Afraid he was in the city, and hurt, Brie got up. She was clad in a simple pink tank top and briefs. It was Indian summer, and even at night it was warm and humid. She hurried across her large, shadowy loft, hitting lights as she went. She'd half expected Aidan to be present, maybe unconscious in the shadows and sprawled out on her floor, but the loft was empty.

At her front door, which was triple locked and had multiple alarms, she peered through the peephole into the hall. It was lit and empty, too.

Even though her loft was thoroughly fortified with Tabby's spells and prayers; even though she wore a Celtic cross and never took it off; even though a small page from the Book handed down through generations of Rose women was framed and nailed to her door to keep evil out; Brie said a silent prayer to the long-ago gods.

She could feel evil, very close by, drifting about the streets, preying upon anyone foolish enough to defy Bloomberg's voluntary curfew. But she didn't want to think about the city's problems now. She had to somehow find Aidan and make sure he was okay. Maybe Tabby and Sam could make heads or tails out of this. The other person who would probably have a clue was her boss, Nick Forrester, but she was hesitant to call him. She kept a very low profile at

CDA. He knew nothing about her gifts—or her cousins and their extracurricular activities.

Brie grabbed the phone as she went to her computer and began logging onto HCU's immense database. The Historical Crimes Unit was a part of CDA. She spent her days—and even her nights—looking through two centuries of case files, searching for historic coincidences. Her job was to find matches between their current targets and demons operating in the past. It was amazing how many demons terrorizing the country today came from past centuries.

Because searching for coincidences involved comparisons with active cases, she had access to current criminal investigations, including federal, state and local NYPD records. Multitasking, Brie began to search for the most recent reported criminal activities as she dialed her cousins' number. She pictured Aidan lying hurt on a dark, slick city street, but she knew it was only her imagination responding to her worst fears.

Tabby answered, sounding as if she'd been deeply asleep. She'd divorced well over a year ago. It had taken her a long time to recover from her husband's infidelity, and she had just begun dating again. But she was very conservative, and Brie had expected her to be alone and asleep.

"I really need your help," Brie said swiftly.

"Brie, what is it?" Tabby was instantly awake.

"Aidan is in trouble—and I think he's nearby."

Tabby paused and Brie felt her trying to recall just who Aidan was. "You don't mean the Highlander who brought Allie back last year?"

"I do," Brie whispered.

"Can this wait until morning?" Tabby asked.

It wasn't safe for anyone to tool around the city after dark. "I don't think so," Brie said grimly. "It wasn't a vision, Tabby. I felt his pain. He's in trouble—right now."

Tabby was silent, and Brie heard Sam in the background, asking what was wrong. The sisters shared a loft just a few blocks away. "We'll be right over," Tabby said.

Brie hung up, slipped on her jeans and sat down to seriously go over the cases she'd pulled. She was immersed in files when the doorbell rang twenty minutes later. She'd found nothing, and she supposed that was a relief. What she didn't want to find was a dead victim with Aidan's description. For all she knew, though, he was immortal. She hoped so.

Maybe the worst was over, she thought as she went to let the girls in. Maybe he'd gone back in time, where he belonged.

Tabby entered first, a willowy blonde in slacks and a silk tank top who always looked as if she were on her way to or from the country club. No one would ever guess from looking at her that Tabby was an earth mother. Sam followed, shockingly gorgeous even with her short-cropped platinum hair—but then, she had a Lara Croft from *Tomb Raider* body. Brie admired her immensely because she was so fearless and so open about her sexuality. She happened to know that Sam's messenger bag was loaded with weapons, and she carried a stiletto strapped to her thigh beneath the denim miniskirt she wore. On anybody else it might be corny, but on Sam it was darned serious.

Tabby took one look at Brie and rushed to hug her. "You are so worried!"

Sam closed and locked the door. "Did you find anything?" she asked, nodding at the computer.

"He's probably gone back to his time," Brie said. She wet her lips, aware of an absurd disappointment.

"Don't look so happy about it," Sam said wryly, striding across the loft to the computer and peering at the screen. "I don't think a man like that is easily hurt."

"I think he was tortured. I have never felt so much pain," Brie said.

Sam didn't look up from the screen, scrolling through files she had no right to view.

Tabby put her arm around Brie. "You're so pale. Are you all right?"

"I'll survive," Brie said, forcing a smile.

"Are you sure it was Aidan?" Tabby asked, rather unnecessarily, as Sam sat down at the desk. Tabby glanced at the poster from the movie *The Highlander,* which Brie had framed and hung on her living-room wall, her hazel gaze narrowing.

"One hundred percent. I saw him as clear as day. It wasn't a vision, but it wasn't my imagination, either. I can't empathize across time. I certainly can't hear someone cry out from far away. He was here, close by. He was hurt. Really, really hurt." Brie trembled, feeling sick again.

"If he's hurt and in the city, we'll find him," Sam said firmly.

Brie felt reassured. Sam always got what she wanted.

"When did you put that poster up?" Tabby asked.

Brie blinked at her. "I don't remember," she lied, flushing.

Tabby stared. Then she moved toward the living area. "Well, this looks to be an all-nighter," she said cheerfully. "It's almost three in the morning, and I don't think any of us will make it back to bed." She began laying out her mother's crystals on the coffee table.

And the roar of anguish began again, deafening Brie. She gasped, stunned by the bellow of rage. Her hands flew automatically to her ears. His pain sent her down to the floor, where she doubled over, crushed by it, consumed by it…imprisoned by it. This time, the sensation was unbearable.

Oh my God, what's happening to Aidan? Is he being tortured?

"Brie!" Tabby screamed.

Vaguely, she was aware of Tabby holding her, but it didn't matter.

Brie knew they were ripping his heart out now. They were ripping *her* heart out. She wept in Tabby's arms, her world spinning with shocking force and then going black.

Aidan, she somehow thought. He was dying from the torture, and she was dying, too.

NICK FORRESTER sat at his computer in his night-darkened living room, clad only in his jeans. He'd completely forgotten about the leggy blonde who lay asleep in his bed. In fact, he couldn't recall her name. He'd picked her up outside the Korean grocery, and maybe he hadn't ever known the name. It was late, but he didn't need more than a few hours of sleep—especially not after a long round of sex, which he found energizing. Sex always empowered him.

He was working again. The "witch" burnings in the city were on the rise. His latest intelligence debriefing had indicated that Bloomberg was seriously consider-ing calling in the National Guard, and he thought it was about time. Pleasure crimes still dominated the murder rate, but those random demonic acts were almost un-preventable—like suicide bombers. The "witch" burnings were another matter. He knew in his gut that the gang leader of these medieval crimes was a great demon from the past. His gut was always dead-on.

Now he was immersed in medieval history, looking for any references to such burnings in past times. HCU had software to look for coincidental data, but he didn't trust the damn programs and he never would. The program wasn't that sophisticated, only matching words and phrases. A single isolated burning of a heretic, a traitor or a witch didn't interest him, nor did the burning of a thirteenth-century peasant's home or a baron's castle. He was looking for a series of the violent crimes, probably committed by a group of adolescents but run by a single, very clever entity.

His cell buzzed.

Nick picked up at the first ring. A woman he did not know spoke. "Brie Rose needs medical attention, ASAP!"

"Who the hell is this?" he demanded, alert but annoyed at her commanding tone. He was wary, too. She could be a crank or even something else.

"Her cousin Sam Rose, and if you don't want her going to Emergency, you need to send your people in. Hurry—she may be dying." The phone went dead.

Nick was already speed-dialing his own medevac people while pulling up Brie Rose's file on his HCU screen. In thirty seconds, he had sent his medical team to her loft and was pulling on a T-shirt, seizing his Beretta, car keys and shoes. He ignored the sleeping blonde as he left his condo, stepping into his shoes in the elevator. A minute later he was peeling out of the building's underground garage in his black Expedition; eight minutes later he was leaping out of the vehicle, an ambulance marked Cornell Presbyterian already in front of Brie's building. The ambulance belonged to CDA, and was deliberately mismarked.

He went up with the paramedics, growing aware of Brie's struggle. He could feel her fighting for her life, and her fear of dying. Alarmed, he searched the perimeter but did not sense evil nearby. He couldn't discern what had put her on the brink of death.

A beautiful blonde who looked like a rock star met him at the door. He felt her power and instantly knew she was a vigilante warrior. Glancing past her, he saw Brie, unconscious on the floor, in another beautiful woman's arms. That one had power, too, but it was not that of a Slayer's. He didn't have time to try to identify it.

Although he knew the gossips nailed him as cold and uncaring, it wasn't true. He'd hand-selected every single employee at HCU and considered them all his personal responsibility, especially mousy Brie. He was even a bit fond of her—and not because she was brilliant. He felt sorry for her. She was a recluse, with no life outside of work. He had sensed her powers before he'd hired her. It had taken him a moment to decide what they were but he could read minds whenever he chose and he was fairly conscienceless about it if it was in the line of duty. He didn't expect her to come clean. He knew that her unusual perceptions were often used on the cases he sent to her and that worked fine for him.

As the medics went to take her vitals, he said grimly, "What happened?"

The woman holding Brie in her arms looked up at him. He felt his interest quicken. She was elegance and beauty personified. She said hoarsely, "She's empathic, and someone we know was being tortured. She felt everything they did to him. She's hurt."

"No kidding." He was wary. These women were outsiders. How much did they know? And vigilantes always messed up his investigations. He looked at his watch. It was 3:24 a.m. "When did it start?"

"Eight minutes ago," the blonde with the body said. From her voice, he knew she was Sam Rose.

"Frank?" he asked.

"Her pulse is weak and her blood pressure is low," the medic said, administering oxygen.

Brie's eyes fluttered. Nick knelt beside her, smiling. "Hey, kiddo. We'll take care of you. Tell me about your friend."

She gasped weakly, "I think they're slowly killing him, Nick." Tears fell. "Please help him. He's one of us."

He stared at her, lurking. His eyes widened; Brie had met one of the Highland warriors? He was her *friend?* His agents had been hoping to bring in a Master for a long, long time.

"She had an episode earlier," Sam said tersely. "That was when she called us."

Nick absorbed that. "What do you know about the Highlander?"

Sam Rose was good, he had to hand it to her. Her

eyes didn't even widen, not a drop. "I'm worried," she said. "If this person is being tortured, Brie might go through this again when they start in on him."

"She won't make it," the other blonde cried. "I've never seen her like this."

"Take her to Five," Nick said. Because the agency was covert, CDA had its own medical facilities known simply as Five. But as Brie was loaded onto a stretcher, he pulled Frank aside. "Can an extreme empathic reaction kill her?"

"I don't know."

"Is it a safer bet to keep her sedated until we can remove the source of the empathic reaction?" When Frank nodded, Nick said, "Do it."

The *Town & Country* blonde said, "I'm staying with her."

Nick seized her shoulder, staring as coldly as he could. It wasn't hard to do; he was getting pissed. How much did these women know?

"Lady, you are not cleared to stay with her. You and your friend are coming with me, now, to my office."

She stared at him, close to tears. "After we tell you what we know, I beg you to let me stay with her."

"I'll think about it." He looked at the warrior, Sam; and because he didn't like the look in her eyes, he read her mind. "You're coming with me, but I'll put all my agents in the field. If your *friend* is in the city, we'll find him."

Sam stared at him, clearly unhappy with his

decision. He was aware she wanted to hunt. "Yeah, well, I hope you find him alive," she mocked.

BRIE STRUGGLED TO SWIM THROUGH the thick, heavy darkness. She heard voices, but they seemed impossibly far away; still, she wanted to reach them. Some of the darkness shifted...lifted. Her mind flickered. She needed to think. There was something happening, something she had to do. She didn't know where she was, but she sensed Tabby and Sam were nearby, and there was relief in the comprehension.

"Brie? It's me, Tabby. Can you hear me?"

Tabby sounded closer now. Why was she so heavy, so groggy? Brie fought to swim to her cousin. Light began shining against her closed lids, and she somehow opened her eyes. Instantly, she blinked against the sterile white light of an office or a hospital room.

Tabby held her hand. "Welcome back."

Brie met her concerned amber eyes. Without her glasses, she couldn't see farther than her hand, but she didn't have to see Tabby clearly to know it was her. Her mind remained sluggish, but she knew there was something urgent she had to remember. And suddenly she gripped Tabby's hand hard in return. "Aidan!" There was total recall now. "Did you find him?" As she spoke, she saw the blur that was Sam, standing next to Tabby. Dear God, her boss was behind them. He was entirely out of focus, but it didn't matter, she still felt his hard, unwavering stare.

"No, we didn't." Tabby slipped her eyeglasses on for her. "Is that better?"

So much fear for him began. Without a doubt, Brie knew that he was being tortured by great evil. He could still be alive and in torment—or he could be dead.

"How do you feel?" Nick asked.

Brie was almost afraid to look at him now that she could see. He was a macho-looking man of about thirty—muscular, tall and really good-looking; women were always trying to pick him up. Nick was a cool player, but he was all work and no play when it came to HCU.

"Am I drugged?" She finally looked at him, and sure enough, he had that steely, take-no-prisoners look in his eyes.

"Pretty heavily, but we're taking you down so we can chat." Nick smiled, as if encouraging her to be candid, but that smile never reached his blue eyes.

"It's been twenty-four hours, Brie," Tabby said softly, squeezing her hand. Her gaze was filled with worry.

Brie stared at her, almost reading her mind. Now she remembered fighting the pain, in this very room. "He's still being tortured," she gasped.

"Every other time we brought you down, within an hour or so you started having extreme empathic reactions to your friend," Nick said flatly.

Brie blinked at him. He'd stressed the word "friend." How much had she said? Nick was pissed; she could feel it, even as messed up as she was.

"Maybe you can tell Nick something to help his people find Aidan," Tabby murmured.

"It's hard to think," she whispered. Had Tabby told Nick about the Masters of Time? As groggy as she was, she was certain Nick wouldn't be surprised that the rumors floating around the agency about a race of evil-fighting warriors were true. Sometimes Nick seemed to know *everything*.

Nick said to the physician, "Take her down a bit more."

As the sedation was further decreased, Brie recognized that she was ill with exhaustion. She felt nauseous, and she began to realize how utterly sore her body was. Every muscle throbbed, as if she was the one who'd been mercilessly tortured. But her mind leapt to life as the sedation was reduced. What had they done to him? Was he alive? "How can I help?" she asked Nick, trembling.

He dismissed the doctor and turned to Tabby and Sam. "Goodbye, ladies."

Tabby was alarmed. "I can't leave her."

Nick gestured toward the door. "You can, and you will. It will only be for a few moments."

Brie didn't want to be alone with him and she knew Tabby knew it. Sam gave Nick a cool glance. "Don't bully her," she said.

When they were gone, he said, "I need you to come clean, kid. If you want to help your friend, you need to clarify exactly who we're looking for."

Brie wished she could think more clearly. "His name is Aidan—and he's not from our century." She stopped. "He's from the past, Nick."

He leaned close, his face expressionless. "When did you meet the Highlander, Brie?"

He was really mad. "I met him a year ago," Brie breathed, hoping she was doing the right thing by telling Nick the truth. Their eyes locked. "You're not surprised."

Nick folded his muscular arms across his chest. "Tell me more about him."

Brie tried to think clearly. The Brotherhood was secret—Allie had stressed that—but so was CDA and every unit within. "When I met him, he'd come from 1430, from Carrick Castle," she said. "He has powers, Nick—special powers, just like the demons do."

Nick searched her gaze and Brie had the uncanny feeling he was searching her mind. He said softly, "Does the name Aidan of Awe ring any bells?"

Oddly, the name resonated with her.

"Take her up," Nick snapped.

Brie felt the last bit of fogginess dissipate. Nick became completely clear, his eyes blue steel. He knew all about the Masters, she realized.

"Yeah," he said, "and I've wanted to bring one in for a long, long time."

But he hadn't even finished when she heard Aidan. His roar of pain was filled with despair and protest. This time, it was the roar of grief.

Brie went still.

He's lost everything. Before she could assimilate that, a huge weight fell on her, crushing her. She cried out in alarm and fear as more stones fell, rapidly burying her in darkness.

Brie wanted to panic and scream; she wanted to fight the rocks, try to push up against them. But instead she lay very still, absolutely calm, aware that she was entombed.

"Brie, what is it?" she heard Tabby cry from far away.

Brie's eyes widened. She was looking up at black stone; it was as if she was buried alive. She tried to move her arms, her legs, but stone pressed in on her from all sides.

Aidan has been buried alive.

And he was utterly calm, utterly resigned, a man without hope.

She reached out to him.

She felt him start.

She tried to focus entirely upon him. He was physically trapped, unmoving. Like her, he had no difficulty breathing. He was staring at the blackness. She felt him more acutely now. The stones were painful, their weight crushing, but he didn't care. They weren't crushing him to death. It was the heartache that was killing him.

And she felt his acceptance of death.

He was waiting to die.

"Brie, honey, it's okay. You're here with us, on Five."

Aidan, Brie tried. *You can't die!*

If she had reached him, he was now gone. He had slipped so far away that she couldn't feel anything at all.

"Can you hear me?" Nick asked, sounding far away.

She could, but she couldn't answer Nick now. Aidan had powers. He could break free of the rocks and stone if he wanted to. If she had reached him a moment ago, surely she could find him again. She was almost certain he had felt her, or heard her. She strained for him, calling his name. *Aidan, break free of the stone.* She waited for him to respond. A long time seemed to elapse, and he never moved, never answered.

She couldn't stand this. *Don't die!*

Nick was speaking to her again.

"Brie, it's Nick. We've given you Ativan. It's an antianxiety med, and you should be feeling pretty good right now. You're at CDA on Five and we're taking care of you. You're having an empathic reaction again. Look at me."

Brie felt her body soften. She looked at Nick. His handsome face and sexy body formed before her, coming gradually into focus. Someone had put her eyeglasses on, she recalled inanely, and she smiled.

"Good. To find the Highlander, we need you. Where is he?"

She could see Aidan so clearly now, in his grave beneath the rubble, a red castle soaring above a loch. Brie said, "There's a castle on a lake. He's in Scotland…and he's in the past." She was so surprised by her response that she faltered, but she knew she'd sensed the truth.

"Are you certain?" Nick asked. "Are you certain he's not in the city?"

"Yes." Brie had never been more certain of anything. She had been wrong earlier. He hadn't been close by. She'd try to figure that out later, she thought. "We can't let him die."

Nick turned away and said, "Her Encounter last year should have been reported. Now that I know what you two ladies are up to, any Encounters or Sightings come right to me. Failure to do so is against the law."

"I'm not aware of any such laws," Sam said bluntly.

"It's against Nick's law," Nick said swiftly. "And you really don't want to break Nick's law."

Brie was floating, feeling really wonderful now, as if she'd had three or four glasses of champagne. Sam sat down and smiled at her. "Your boss is such a jerk."

"Yeah, he is," Brie agreed, aware that Nick had walked out. No, he'd stalked out, like a hunting tiger.

Sam leaned close and whispered, "I'm calling in every favor I have. If he's here, someone's seen him. You just rest."

"He isn't here. He's far away." Her happiness was gone. "I don't want him to die. I love him, Sam."

Sam's blue eyes went wide. "Brie, I know you're high right now, but if it's Fate, you know we can't change it."

"It can't be his time," Brie whispered. She wasn't sure what happened next, but Sam was gone, and it was only her and Tabby, who sat by her bed, holding her hand. Then Brie blinked curiously. A little boy was standing at the foot of her bed, clad in a white hospital gown that was oddly belted. He started speaking urgently to her. His blue eyes were so familiar, as if she knew him, but she didn't think she did. Brie realized she was too high to hear a word. He seemed frightened. She knew he wanted to tell her something important, and she turned to Tabby. "What is he saying?"

Tabby was surprised. "Who are you talking about?"

Brie looked at the foot of her bed, but the little boy was gone. "I guess it doesn't matter," she said.

She must have been dreaming.

CHAPTER TWO

Castle Awe, Scotland—November 17, 1502

Sex no longer mattered to him.

Like the best wine drunk far too often, it could not be appreciated. Pleasure escaped him now.

But he moved harder, faster, into the woman, not seeking release, even though a release was inevitable. Instead, he used her for his own ends, taking power, euphoric, until she lay unmoving and silent beneath him.

Aidan held himself over the woman, breathing hard. He had experienced the powerful ecstasy of *La Puissance* thousands of times, a climax that combined raging power with sexual release. When he had first begun to hunt Moray after Ian's murder, he'd taken power to assure himself of victory over the deamhan he was now sworn to kill. But Moray had vanished in time, fleeing him. And Aidan had needed more power to chase him.

Power was addictive. He lusted for it now. Unfortunately, the lust for power was terribly arousing. Otherwise he would not even bother with the sexual act.

Still consumed with a sense of invincibility, he moved away from the woman. He leaned against the wall, arching back, savagely relishing the power coursing through his muscles. It even throbbed in his bones.

No one could defeat him now—not man, not beast, not deamhan and not even a god. Not even his demonic father. His father had returned to murder Ian, when a beheading would destroy most deamhanain. There were Masters who believed Moray immortal. Others said he had returned with otherworldly help. Aidan had dared to demand answers upon Iona. MacNeil had told him Moray's return was written, but that no deamhan was immortal, no matter how it might appear.

Ian's image seared his mind, as hot as a firebrand. He welcomed the pain.

"Is she alive?" The other woman gasped, kneeling half-naked beside the Innocent.

He barely glanced at the lush redhead, who was flushed with her own pleasure. He'd left the Innocent alive, although barely. "Aye. Tend her."

Anna Marie took the limp woman in her arms, but she was staring at him with glittering eyes. Most women feared his desire. Having lurked in her mind on several occasions, he knew that she both feared and desired his passion—all of it. Now, she said, "Do you want me again?"

He'd found her in Paris in the mid-eighteenth century. She was the courtesan of a prince. She enjoyed hours in his bed and understood his need to take far more than pleasure from her and others, even simultaneously. Her presence was convenient, especially because he never slept and there was one certain way for him to pass the long, dark hours of the night.

He hadn't slept in sixty-six years.

Sleeping only brought nightmares.

He bared his teeth at her. What she did not understand was that he looked at her with absolute indifference, and felt nothing when their bodies were joined except for the lust for power and revenge. He would avenge Ian, even if it took an eternity to do so.

"Nay." Naked, his body still hard and huge, he stalked from the chamber, and as he did so, he heard her moan.

He didn't care. He didn't need her or the other one now. He had enough power to destroy his father—if he could find him. For Moray had vanished into time sixty-six years ago, and Aidan had been hunting him ever since.

It was time to hunt now.

A pair of chambermaids were hurrying down the hall. A glance at the single, barred window at the hall's east end showed him that the sun was high. He'd been with the women since the previous day at dusk. The maids looked at him and froze in their tracks, terrified and mesmerized at once. Ignoring them, he was about to enter the east tower room when he felt a huge power approaching, fierce and determined and white.

He roiled with anger, instantly aware of the intruder's identity. He turned to face his half brother, Malcolm, the man who had unearthed him from Awe's rubble instead of allowing him to die.

He would never forgive him for it.

Malcolm of Dunroch came up the stairs at the hall's far end, a large, powerful man in a leine and dark-green-and-black plaid, wearing both long and short swords, his muddy boots indicating a long, hard ride. Dirt flecked his bare thighs. His face was flushed with anger. "Ye canna march on Inverness with the rebels," he said harshly, striding up the hall. He gave Aidan's naked body a quick, dismissive glance.

"Do ye nay march on Inverness with Donald Dubh an' Lachlan Maclean, yer cousin?" he mocked, knowing Malcolm was too busy saving Innocence to bother with political intrigues. Politics didn't interest him, either, but feeding and horsing his four thousand men did.

And destroying the Campbell was something he could still do for his son.

Malcolm's face hardened. "Ye'll hang with the traitors when they're defeated," he said tersely, legs braced as if to bar his way.

"Good," Aidan said softly, meaning it. He wasn't

afraid of death. He looked forward to it—as long as Ian was avenged first.

Malcolm seized his arm. "'Twas not yer fault. Ye have yer destiny to return to, Aidan."

"Yer nay welcome here. Get out," Aidan roared, shrugging him off. He whirled, entering the tower room and slamming the door closed behind him.

His damned brother was wrong. He had failed to keep his son safe. He had saved hundreds of Innocents, but not his own son; he would never forgive himself for it. He steeled himself against the anguish, but too late.

From the door's other side, he heard Malcolm's every silent thought. *I willna let ye die an' I willna give up on ye. Nor will I be leavin' Awe soon.*

Furious with his brother, hating him for refusing to lose faith, Aidan threw the bolt down on the door. Inside it was dark and cold. No fire burned in the stone hearth and every small arrow slit had long since been nailed closed with shutters, so the darkness was complete.

Eventually Malcolm would leave. He always did, as there was always a deamhan to vanquish, an Innocent to save. Malcolm served the gods as if his vows were his life, with his wife at his side. But Malcolm was not a deamhan's son. He was the son of the great Master, Brogan Mor, and a Master himself—as well as the laird of the Macleans of south Mull and Coll. They had nothing in common.

Malcolm had been raised at Dunroch by his father

and then, after Brogan Mor's death in battle, by his uncle, Black Royce, to be chief of Clan Gillean. Aidan had been sent as an infant into a nobleman's foster care, for his mother had retired to an abbey to spend the rest of her life there. Malcolm had often gone to visit Lady Margaret at the abbey, ever the dutiful son. His calls had been welcome. Aidan had met his mother but once, when he was a Master, and she had not been able to look at him. He had quickly left her to her prayers and repentance.

He had grown up an outsider; his brother had been the next great laird, a Master whose vows were his life.

Aidan had forsaken his vows the day of Ian's murder.

If Moray's return was fated, the gods, apparently, had written his son's death, as well. He hated the gods passionately and he cursed them now—as he did every single day of his life.

He felt Malcolm leaving the hall, going below, and his mind began to ease. His senses intensified impossibly.

Tonight, he thought, he would find and destroy Moray. Tonight, he would tear Moray's throat out with his teeth. Then he would feed his heart to the wolves.

And he gave into the wolf, a savage and ruthless beast he could barely control, an animal intent on mayhem and death. He lifted his face toward the moon and howled. Outside, he felt the pack gathering and begin to howl in return, lusting for blood and death. He quieted, leaving the wolves to their eerie, savage chorus. He was ready now.

He walked to the center of the circular room and sank to the floor, where he sat cross-legged on the cold, hard stone.

More than six decades had passed since his son's murder. His demonic father could be in any time, in any place. Moray clearly thought himself the victor in their privy war, but he was wrong. Their war would never end, not until one or both of them was vanquished. He didn't care which it was—as long as Moray went to the fires of hell with him.

He began sifting through the sands of time, in the future and the past, through deserts and mountains, villages and cities, searching for Moray's evil power.

Hours passed. He strained through time, evil everywhere, a long, painstaking process. The moon rose. He did not need to see it to know. The hairs on his nape prickled, like hackles rising. But the blackest power he was hunting eluded him.

He could not give up. He growled in frustration.

And through the hours of the day and then the night, Innocence wept for salvation. He heard every single cry for aid, for his senses were not just attuned to evil but to its helpless prey. Men, women and children begged him to rescue them from destruction and death.

He would not recall the last time he had protected Innocence. It was before his son had died.

He ignored their cries now.

He did not care who died.

TABBY UNLOCKED THE DOOR FOR HER, giving her a smile. "Isn't it great to be home?" she asked.

Brie didn't smile back. She stepped into her loft, wearing the clothes Tabby had brought her—an oversized sweatshirt embroidered with a blue-and-gold dragon and her comfy loose-fit jeans. She was more worried than ever about Aidan. She'd spent another full day at Five, under close observation, and she was champing at the bit. She had been taken off all sedation and the antianxiety medication, so once again she could think clearly. Aidan was no longer being tortured, and he was no longer crushed by stone. She couldn't feel anything from him at all.

God, was he even alive?

She was adept at blocking out human emotion, for it was a necessity in order to get through each and every day. But she hadn't been able to block his torment at all. His emotions had consumed her as no one's ever had before, even across centuries. What, exactly, did the fact that she felt him so powerfully across time mean?

Everything was meant to be, and every Rose woman knew it.

Brie shivered as Tabby's cell phone rang. Brie shut and locked the door, going to her work station on the far side of the loft. She sat down at her PC, which remained in sleep mode. *He could not be dead.*

Tabby came over. "That was Sam. She's talked to every contact and snitch she knows. It looks like you're right. He's not here."

Brie whirled her chair to face her. "How could I empathize across time?"

Tabby clasped her shoulder, their gazes locking. "You must really love him, Brie. It's the only explanation I can think of."

Her heart lurched. Her crush had been so safe and silly, until now. Loving him was terrifying, because he would never love her back—even if their paths crossed. "It's just a crush," Brie whispered, turning back to her PC. She was praying that there was another reason for her amazing empathy.

But now she stared at her computer's wallpaper, the ruins of a castle on Loch Awe. Nick had asked her if the name Aidan of Awe was familiar. Her heart thundered. It felt so right. She'd put up the wallpaper after meeting Aidan…and there was no such thing as coincidence.

This past year she had been tempted to go through HCU's immense historical database, looking for a mention of him, but it was against the rules to use the system for personal projects and she hadn't done so. She hit a button and CDA's site filled her screen. She began to log on, a process that required three passwords. She had something to go on now. And what did Nick know about Aidan, exactly?

If HCU had anything on him, by now, Nick was on it.

Brie was still amazed that she hadn't been fired.

"What are you going to do?" Tabby asked. "He's not here, Brie, and we can't time-travel."

Brie bit her lip and punched in a search for Aidan of Awe. As the search began, she shifted restlessly, and then she cried out, getting a hit.

Tabby peered over her shoulder.

The message on her screen was glaring. *Aidan of Awe—Level Four—Access Denied.*

"There's a file on him?" Tabby exclaimed.

"I'm only Level Three," Brie cried in frustration.

"Maybe that's not our Aidan," Tabby tried.

Brie stared at the flashing message. "It's him. I *know* it. Damn Nick," she cried.

Tabby started. "Brie, you're exhausted. You absorbed so much pain, you need to rest. Leave the search to Forrester. He's certainly on this."

"I can't," Brie said. She was afraid to ask Nick what was in that file—he was so intimidating—but she had to try.

"Can I make you something to eat?" Tabby asked.

Brie didn't care, even though Tabby was a great cook. As Tabby went into her kitchen, separated from the loft only by the kitchen counter, she went to her favorite online research library. She had part of his name to go on now. As she went to her medieval-Scotland virtual bookshelf, she dialed Nick. It went right to voicemail.

Brie pulled the first of two hundred and thirteen volumes, and as she typed in the words Aidan of Awe in the search box, she said, "Nick, it's Brie. Please call me at home. Thanks."

Her search yielded zero results, and she pulled the next volume and repeated the search. On her fourth search, a sudden nausea began, and Brie cried out. The floor tilted wildly, accompanied by a terrible feeling of dread.

And the vision began.

She gripped the arms of the desk chair tightly, no longer aware of her surroundings, entirely focused on what she was meant to see. Aidan was lying on his back. He was bare-legged, wearing high boots and clad in a leine and black cloak, the latter pinned to one shoulder and belted. His hands were folded atop the belt, which held two huge swords. The image sharpened. He was asleep, his eyes closed, his face relaxed, at peace. The necklace he wore became apparent, as if her mind's eye had zoomed in on it. A fang, capped with gold, lay against the hollow of his collarbone.

He turned into stone, becoming an effigy atop a tomb.

She sprang to her feet, crying out.

Tabby was hovering over her. "What did you see?"

Brie hardly heard her. She could not have seen what she had! Her premonitions were never wrong. She looked at Tabby, aghast. "I saw him in stone effigy, atop a medieval tomb."

Tabby took her hand. "Brie, he's from the fifteenth century," she said carefully.

"So what? Allie is still alive, isn't she? And he was alive the other day!" she cried. And her grandmother's ring began pinching her.

Brie had been wearing Sarah's garnet ring since she was thirteen. Sarah had always claimed it would protect her and enhance her gifts. She twisted it nervously, aware of desperation surging. Tabby said, "Honey, he *is* alive, somewhere, farther in the past. But we can't time-travel like they do."

Brie stared at her. She wanted him to be alive right then and there. "My visions are a tool. They're meant to help others. Why did I have that vision?" she cried.

"I don't know. Brie, would you please rest? And eat?" Tabby returned to the kitchen, then set a sizzling plate before her. Brie had been hungry earlier; now, she had no appetite.

"I'm going to go," Tabby said. "I haven't been home in three days. The neighbor's been taking care of the cats and the plants. And I really need a shower."

Brie stood to hug her. Tabby looked as if she was on her way to take tea at Buckingham Palace. "I'm fine. Thank you for everything."

When Tabby was gone, Brie—almost desperate—went on to her next search, and the words *Aidan of Awe* produced a result. She froze in sheer disbelief. Then, her heart leaping painfully in her chest, she hit the enter key. She quickly skimmed down the first page and began to read.

In December 1436, Aidan, the Wolf of Awe, a Highlander with no clan, sacked the stronghold of the Earl of Moray at Elgin, leaving no one alive.

She breathed hard and read the rest of the page.

However, Moray escaped the Wolf's wrath intact, to take up his position at court as Defender of the Realm for King James, the same position he had enjoyed ten years earlier. But when James was murdered at Perth the following February, Moray, who was known to be at court, vanished, never to be heard from again. Quite possibly, Moray was slain with his king. The Wolf of Awe proceeded to spend the next nineteen years ruthlessly destroying the families and holdings of Moray's three powerful sons, the earls of Feith, Balkirk and Dunveld. Retribution came from Argyll, and in 1458 Castle Awe was burned to the ground. Although the Wolf spent twenty years rebuilding his stronghold, he forfeited his other holdings, his title and earldom (Lismore) to King James II. He remained universally distrusted and feared until his demise. In 1502, after his mercenary role in the MacDonald uprising, he was accused of treason by the Royal Lieutenant of the North, the powerful Frasier chief. Badly wounded from an escape attempt, he was publicly hanged on December 5th at Urquhart.

Brie couldn't see the page, for her vision suddenly blurred. The terrible Wolf of Awe could not be her Aidan. Her Aidan was a Master of Time, sworn to protect Innocence through the ages, a mighty hero defending mankind from evil, upholding God. And Aidan could not hang. He would simply vanish into the future or the past.

Except he had been badly hurt.

She started to cry, but wiped the tears away. She read the next sentences.

His tomb had been carefully restored at the ruins of Castle Awe on Loch Awe. To this day, it remains a popular tourist attraction.

She was so upset she was shaking. She looked at the plate Tabby had set down before her and wanted to wretch. Picking the plate up, she carried it to the kitchen, set it down and leaned hard on the counter. What did all of this mean?

If she went to Loch Awe now, would she find the tomb and effigy she'd seen in her vision?

The Wolf of Awe had been *hanged*. He was cruel, mercenary. Surely he was not the same man.

But in her vision of him, she had seen her Aidan before he'd turned into stone. He'd worn a wolf's fang.

Good humans were possessed every single day and then they committed unspeakably evil acts.

Brie moaned. Had Aidan become the Wolf of Awe? Was it somehow possible?

Her head exploded with pain. Brie stepped behind the counter into her kitchen, opening the refrigerator to chug a glass of wine. She was shaking like a leaf. *What had happened to him?*

Brie slammed the refrigerator door closed. She had to know what was in that Level Four file. She grabbed her purse and keys and stormed from the loft. If Nick wasn't at his office, she'd wait.

HE FELT THE MOON SETTING for the third time.

Aidan slowly came back to the tower room, a dark despair clawing at him. This hunt had lasted three days and he had not found anything.

He blinked and adjusted his eyes to the dark, shuttered room. As the swirling black evil and the cries of innocence faded, he became aware of his body and his power. All sense of euphoric invincibility was gone. Most of what he had taken three nights ago was gone. The power in his body was hardly ordinary; it was that of the son of one of the greatest deamhanain ever known to Alba. He was arrogant enough to think he might, even without the extra life coursing through him, be capable of defeating a lesser god.

Still he was tired. His body and his mind begged him for rest, but it was time to think of other, worldly matters. He commanded an army of four thousand men—some soulless humans, others fierce Highlanders. He usually sold his army's services to the highest bidders, and had done so for the past sixty-six years. He didn't care about the land, the mortal power—although he needed the gold to maintain his army, but he took vast pleasure in every single battle. If he could not engage Moray, he would go to war and relish destroying his other enemies, one by one.

The MacDonalds were marching on Inverness, a royal garrison, and he was joining the rebels, as Malcolm had said. He had personally helped Donald Dubh, their imprisoned leader, escape from Innischonnail, where the Campbell had imprisoned him. Argyll had been infuriated. Had Ian lived, he would have been pleased and proud.

A cry of alarm filled the tower.

Aidan was on his feet, bewildered, unbelieving.

He had met her once in the future, perhaps seventy years ago, and had not thought of her since then.

Now he recalled a small woman with white powers, dressed in shapeless garments and ugly spectacles.

Why had he just heard Brianna Rose cry out in alarm? How had he just seen her frightened face so clearly? He had ceased hunting evil through time.

No other cries resounded, but he could feel darkness now, encircling her.

Tension riddled his body. He did not protect Innocence; he used it ruthlessly for his own means, for the attainment of power. He did not want to know what was happening to her. He simply did not care about other people's problems.

She screamed.

It was a scream of fear and pain; he knew she'd been wounded.

He did not think. He leapt.

STILL DEVASTATED BY THE IDEA that Aidan had become the Wolf of Awe, Brie hurried down the block. Dusk was approaching and she knew she had better not be caught outside. The city wasn't safe after dark and although the mayor's curfew was voluntary, very few of the city's denizens disobeyed it. Every shop on the street had already closed, except for the grocery store on the corner, and they were pulling their blinds.

She started to run. She couldn't recall ever being this upset, not even when Allie had vanished into time last year. But she had known that Allie's journey to the past was her Fate, she'd even seen the golden Highlander coming for her. This was entirely different.

The Book, handed down from generation to generation of Rose women, was very clear on the matter of Fate. It could never be defied by a mortal. Only the gods could rewrite it—and they never entirely did.

But sometimes events happened that were not in The Game Plan and the gods corrected things when they went awry. Eventually, what was meant to be would happen.

Brie prayed that the historian she'd read had gotten all his facts wrong, or that her vision was wrong. She began to think that maybe she'd better go to Scotland and check out the tomb there, but she was really afraid of what she'd find. And why was her grandmother's ring bothering her?

Grandma had given her the garnet ring, just as Grandma's mother had given it to her. The ring had been passed down through generations of Rose women, like the Book of Roses. It had always fit perfectly, but now it was pinching her.

Brie stared at the ring. "This is meant to happen, isn't it?" she murmured.

Her grandmother had passed away a decade ago, at the ripe old age of 102. She'd been in full possession of her faculties right up until she'd taken her last breath. When she passed away in her sleep, Brie had somehow known her time had come and spent the night at her grandmother's Bedford, New York, house. Sarah Rose had died smiling, and Brie often felt her presence.

She felt her now. "I mean, I could have felt all that pain and anguish last year or the year before—but I felt it now, for a reason. He needs me. I'm supposed to help him." She thought about her crush. Had she become infatuated with him so she could help him? "Why else would I feel him so strongly?"

She felt her grandmother's benevolence. If Sarah approved, Brie was on the right path, she thought. That only made her more determined to get into that Level Four file.

A shadow fell across the pavement directly in front of her.

Her heart seemed to stop with alarm. In a moment the sun would be vanishing beneath the horizon and the city would be lost in the gloom of the night. She'd never make it all the way to CDA.

A teenage boy stood in front of her, smiling maliciously.

He was pale, pimply and wore a long black cloak, marking him as a member of gangs who reputedly burned "witches" at the stake.

Brie breathed. "Get lost!" she cried, even though she was terrified. "It's light out!"

"Not for much longer." He snickered.

She tensed as three more teenage boys barred her way, all of them ghostly white, their lips nearly purple, wearing the same long black cloaks, as if they'd come from the Dark Ages.

She knew all about the ongoing investigation into these gang members at CDA. The "sub-demons," or subs, as they were often called, were human, with normal DNA and very real identities. They were missing boys and girls, belonging to distraught family members, but, robbed of their souls, they were pure evil.

Brie whirled to run, and faced two more leering teens in black hoods and cloaks. She was in big trouble. She prayed that Tabby and Sam would sense it and come to her rescue. And simultaneously, she thought about Aidan. It was instinct. If he was near, he had the power to save her.

"She's fat and ugly," one boy said. "Let's find someone else."

Brie didn't want to die, but she didn't want anyone else to die, either. She glanced back over her shoulder at the setting sun and cried out. The sky was mauve now, the sun out of sight. In another moment or so, dusk would become night and she would be killed.

Brie tried to run.

They let her. She ran as hard and fast as she could, across the empty street, aware of them laughing with malicious glee. Hope began when she didn't hear their footsteps behind her. She was going to make it. She didn't know why they'd let her go and she didn't care.

Suddenly three different boys appeared in front of

her and barred her way, grinning. She tripped, crashing into them, but was seized from behind and pulled ruthlessly up against a lean and young male body. *They had only let her go to torture her.*

She fought wildly, writhing, her mind exploding into shards of terror. Her captor jerked on her so hard that something inside her snapped. Brie screamed in pain and fear.

The boy holding her laughed. The pimply-faced blond boy held a knife and he hooked it into her jeans, jamming it through the denim. She felt blinded by her terror. The steel met the sensitive flesh of her belly. He said, "Witch. You're a real one, ain't you? You reek of witchcraft!"

"No!" Brie begged. But she didn't dare struggle now.

The boy glanced past her. His face paled and his eyes widened with alarm.

A low, long, very menacing growl sounded.

It was otherworldly.

Shaking, Brie looked behind her.

A huge wolf with blazing blue eyes crouched behind her and the boy, his hackles raised. Wolves did not exist in New York City. This one was oversize, demonic. Brie felt his huge black power.

And in that split second, before it leapt, she met eyes that were human and she suddenly comprehended.

The Wolf of Awe had heard her.

The wolf snarled and leapt—-at *her.*

She screamed, glimpsing enraged blue eyes, expecting the beast to land on her, dragging her down and mauling her to death. As her heart burst in terror, the beast somehow twisted and landed only on her captor, and she spun aside.

The wolf ripped the sub's throat out and then, with a bestial roar, turned to one of the other boys.

They had guns and they started firing at the wolf as it drove another teen to the ground, savagely ripping him apart the way dogs shred stuffed toys. Brie was frozen in horror, but only for a single breath. She turned to run.

But as she did, the wolf raised his head, bleeding from its shoulder and its chest. It looked right at Brie with its eerily human eyes. Brie backed up, terrified. It leapt at one of the other boys and she did not think twice. As the sub-demon screamed, she fled.

She ran up the block as hard and as fast as she could, acutely aware of the snarling wolf behind her on the city street, making sounds she wished she could not hear. She somehow unlocked the front door of her building and ran inside. She didn't even think to lock that door or use the elevator. She ran up the three flights of stairs to her loft and somehow unlocked her door, her hand shaking as if with Parkinson's disease. Slamming the door closed, she speed-dialed Nick. Tears blinding her, she spoke before he could even answer.

"I think he's here. He's shot. He needs medical help, Nick!" She wept into the phone.

"Don't fucking move," Nick said, and the line went dead.

She dropped the phone, images of the vicious wolf as it destroyed the boys filling her mind. Subs or not, they were once human. Sometimes, souls could be reclaimed when evil was exorcized.

Instead of calling Tabby and Sam, she silently begged them to hurry to her. And then she went still, paralyzed.

A huge power filled her loft behind her.

Brie began to shake uncontrollably. Slowly, she turned.

Aidan of Awe stood there.

HQN™

We *are* romance™

HAPPY READING!

As part of our special sizzling summer reads offer, you can now **SAVE $1.00** on the purchase of **DARK EMBRACE** by *New York Times* bestselling author **Brenda Joyce**,

available in September wherever books are sold, including most bookstores, supermarkets, drugstores, department and discount stores.

NEW YORK TIMES BESTSELLING AUTHOR

CHRISTINA SKYE

TO CATCH A THIEF

*A new adventure
begins at Draycott Abbey.*

Dear Reader,

Some characters you never forget.

Some stories grip you from the first word, locked deep in the heart. For me, that love struck with a great gray cat, a brooding English abbey and its aristocratic guardian ghost, Adrian Draycott.

I've walked through eight books and two novellas set at the abbey now. Each story brings more secrets and the heady scent of rich heritage roses climbing up tower and parapet.

Dangerous magic.

White-hot passion.

Undying love.

How could any writer resist?

And just to keep the tension hot, I've brought a rugged navy SEAL from my CODE NAME series to the abbey, locked in pursuit of a vicious enemy.

I hope you'll enjoy the adventure.

See you at the abbey.

Christina

PROLOGUE

Draycott Abbey
England
Summer 1785

THE WALL WAS EMPTY. Plaster spilled from a gaping hole, wood beams broken crudely. Blood stained the silk wallpaper where the thief—or thieves—had worked in painful haste. Boot tracks crossed the white snow of fallen plaster, vanishing at the far window, where the curtains fanned out like searching hands.

Adrian Draycott scowled at the hole on the wall. He cursed as he saw the broken recess, the hiding place of his family's da Vinci masterpiece. Now only a carved and gilt frame remained, its pieces discarded on the marble floor.

The thief had come by night, moving straight to this room while Adrian was in London on estate matters. No one had heard the furtive steps. No one had seen the knife that slit the wall and dug to find the hiding place of Leonardo's chalk study of the *Mona Lisa*.

Now the elegant smiling face, accursed in its glory, had vanished. The eighth viscount Draycott closed his eyes, breathing hard in the shock of the theft. Yet even then he felt something close to relief.

Maledetto a mano e a lingua.

The words drifted, twisting like smoke.

Cursed by hand and tongue. Cursed to dream and want.

The still-hidden notebook had recorded Leonardo's curse long centuries before. Both sketch and notebook had been stolen from Leonardo's studio by a charming servant ever alert to the chance for profit. For his crime the servant had earned the artist's curse. So had all others who came in contact with the stolen possessions.

Adrian Draycott ran a hand across his eyes. Well did he know the bitter pains of great loss, of trust betrayed. That pain he kept well hidden beneath a cold, languid facade. He cared for no one and nothing—only his beloved home.

The great gray cat pressed at his boots, tail raised, eyes alert. The viscount bent low, smoothing the warm fur. "So here ends both the tale and the curse, my friend. The art is gone, and though I should feel fury, I do not. I am…relieved. Let another poor fool carry the curse's weight. The *Mona Lisa*'s smile is too cold and enigmatic for my taste."

At his foot the cat meowed, brushing against the viscount's boot. "I almost wish they had taken the notebook too. In truth, I care not for this curse it carries."

The cat's eyes moved, keen in the spring night. Slowly Adrian turned, facing the open window that marked the thief's retreat.

The drops of blood still stained the broken sill.

Maledetto.

Cursed.

"No matter," the viscount muttered, trying to believe his words. "The curse cannot hold power here. Not after so many years. It is done. Over."

Adrian Draycott prayed it was so. But the cold wind through the tall windows and the prickle at his neck argued otherwise.

CHAPTER ONE

The Isle of Skye
Scotland

SHE WAS COLD and tired and hungry. Her blistered feet ached and right now all Nell MacInnes wanted was a hot bath and a steaming cup of Earl Grey tea, followed by a warm bed to rest her weary body.

She closed her eyes, listening to the buzz of quiet pub conversation around her. The little inn nestled up against a pristine loch with towering mountains on three sides. The locals were far too polite to intrude on Nell's reverie, and when she dumped her mountain gear and backpack on the floor, sinking into a worn wooden chair, no one raised an eyebrow.

It was heaven to be warm and dry after six days of climbing the nearby peaks, battling rain and wind on every ascent. If not for her climbing partner, Nell might have curtailed the trip three days sooner, but Eric's enthusiasm was hard to resist. No doubt he would jog down from his room upstairs within the hour, after taping his badly sprained ankle.

Warmth began to seep into her bones, as gentle as the low burr of the Scottish voices around her. Scotland was truly heaven, she thought.

"And I'm telling you it was no such thing as my imagination, Angus McCrae. A grand fish it was—bigger than two arm spans, I'll tell you this."

Over the muted, good-natured argument about a lost fish, Nell heard the pub's front door open. Cold wind snapped through the room as two men entered, scraping booted feet. "Where is the American man, Angus? We need the climber called MacInnes."

Nell stiffened at the flawed description. Who wanted her now, when all she craved was one precious night's rest? No one from San Francisco even knew she was in Scotland.

The man at the door wore a well used parka and broken-in boots. A satphone was gripped at his chest. "We've bad weather up on the hill and I need the American—assuming the man's as good as I'm told."

Nell took a short, wistful look at her half-eaten shepherd's pie and the cup of tea, but a request for help was never refused. Climbers stuck together.

She gulped the rest of the tea and stood up. "I'm the American named MacInnes."

"You—a woman?" The man looked startled.

Nell nodded, used to the surprised glances after twelve years of climbing on four continents. "How can I help you?"

"A team of young climbers has gone missing on

Blaven, and there's bad weather already, with more due through the night."

Blaven.

Nell recognized the name of the lowering and dark peaks that girded the valley on three sides. "They're on the peak now?"

"Aye. They were expected down three hours ago and no sign of them yet. We have just now received word that they're stranded." He raised the satphone, his eyes grim. "A German climber saw them scattered out over the south slope like lost sheep. They did not answer his hails, and at least two had the look of being hurt." His voice fell. "Badly hurt."

Nell thrust her arms into her waterproof jacket, already making mental notes. "How many are in the group and what level of climbing experience? I'll need to know the exact coordinates where they were last seen, too." Even in a blizzard, the GPS would help Nell track those missing.

"I'm assembling that information now."

Nell unzipped her pack, assessing her resources. "I'll need drinking water and dried high-energy food, along with a more extensive first-aid kit."

"I will have it prepared for you, Ms. MacInnes, and our thanks to you for your help. My SAR team is understaffed, all but myself sent over to assist in the recovery of plane crash victims on Uist. A terrible thing, that. I only wish I had two more people here and I'd climb up myself."

"No, you're right to stay here. Someone experienced needs to be available to coordinate resources and guide the authorities. Besides, I'm familiar with Blaven." She smiled crookedly. "I worked SAR here myself nine years ago during my summer vacation."

The man looked pleasantly surprised—and a little relieved. "So you know the Cuillin, do you now? I'm glad to hear it. There are some who take our Cuillin lightly. Some of them do not live to learn their error, I'm afraid."

"I won't make that mistake, rest assured." Nell's voice was firm. She had seen enough dazed climbers and shattered bodies during her rescue summer to know just how fast the weather could change up on the nearby peaks. Within minutes an exhilarating climb could turn into a zero-visibility nightmare given the vagaries of the weather. "What's the weather prediction up there?"

"Northerly gale force eight. Snow already falling on the summit. Temperatures dropping to minus nine Celsius."

Nell made the conversion to Fahrenheit quickly, taking the bottles of water and zippered food bags that the local SAR coordinator handed her. "One more thing." Ruefully, she looked down at her feet. "I'm afraid I'll need dry socks. These are fairly well soaked after walking down through the rain all day."

Without a word, every man in the now silent pub bent down and began to unlace shoes or unzip boots, hearing her quiet words.

In seconds hand-knit socks appeared on every table.

Nell felt warmth block her throat at this instant generosity.

She cleared her throat. "I appreciate your help. What I meant is, I have special climbing socks up in my room. I'll do better with my own gear, you understand."

"Of course." The local SAR man said a few words of explanation in Gaelic. The men around Nell nodded. The socks vanished back on hidden feet.

She started toward the stairs to her room, calculating exactly how much she could cram into her pack and what injuries the lost climbers might have incurred. There was only so much possibility for medical intervention on the top of a mountain with limited supplies.

"One word, miss. Your partner—he will be going with you, will he?"

Nell shook her head. "Not with a sprained ankle, he won't. But Eric will stay in contact. He can help you down here with backup arrangements. I'll tell him the situation."

Nell knew her friend would insist on joining her, sprained ankle or not, but he'd be no help with an injury that had kept him limping for most of the day. She'd have to make the climb alone. She didn't need any amateurs slowing her down.

"I'll be down in two minutes. If someone can drive me up to the trailhead at the end of the loch, it will save twenty minutes."

"A Land Rover is already waiting for you, miss." The local rescue coordinator ran a hand through his hair. "I'd much prefer to go up the hill with you, truth be told. It's a fair nasty stretch across the south slope in weather like this."

"I'll be fine." Nell was calm, with years of climbing experience, focused on planning her route. She was used to facing the worst. Climbing a rugged peak in nasty weather wasn't half as bad as the other shocks that life had thrown her.

HE WATCHED her shoulder the heavy pack and then adjust both padded straps, working with the intense focus of someone used to carrying heavy weight well into the pain zone.

The woman clearly knew what she was doing, Dakota thought, slouched out of sight inside a dusty delivery truck parked up the road from the inn. The bug in her backpack was working perfectly, allowing him clear access to every word she said. So far she'd made no slips. Her conversation with her climbing partner had been full of good-natured bantering and reminiscences of earlier climbs.

No talk of art theft or organized terrorist activities, the Navy SEAL thought cynically.

His orders were absolutely clear. Close surveillance and assessment of all contacts made by Nell MacInnes. She'd done something to land on the government's highest priority watch list.

Better than anyone, Dakota Smith knew that SEALs didn't get called up for aimless threats. Nell MacInnes was up to her slender neck in trouble.

With or without her father's help, she was suspected of participating in the theft of one of the most valuable pieces of art ever to enter the National Gallery. Dakota's job was to find out who she was working with and locate the stolen Renaissance masterpiece before it vanished forever, traded through a shadow network of international criminals, sold to finance the activities of an elusive terrorist group active on American soil.

The SEAL's eyes narrowed on the woman's back as she climbed into a battered Land Rover, accompanied by the head of the local search-and-rescue volunteer team. Dakota wondered what made her tick, what drove her back out into a pounding storm after six days of strenuous climbing. He doubted it was simple selflessness. No, he figured that Nell MacInnes enjoyed walking on the edge, tasting danger. She looked like a classic thrill seeker, which would also explain her involvement in a complicated, high-stakes robbery.

Not greed. She didn't drive a late-model Maserati or own a string of houses. Her apartment back in San Francisco was neat but small, and her only hobby appeared to be climbing. Yet appearances could be the most unreliable thing in the world, Dakota knew.

Still, he wondered about that brief note of resignation he'd heard in Nell's voice back at the pub. The confidence had faded, along with the high energy, and she had sounded tired and worried, as if she genuinely cared about the missing climbers.

Forget about the target's emotions, a voice warned flatly as Dakota pulled onto the road, following the Land Rover at a careful distance. He'd track her up the brooding slopes of Blaven and make certain she came down in one piece. But he'd break his cover to save the other climbers only if it was absolutely necessary, obeying his orders to stay well under the radar until all Nell MacInnes's shadowy contacts were bagged and tagged. The mission came first.

Always.

After parking down the slope from the small trailhead, Dakota pulled on an all-weather parka and a fully stocked backpack, then fingered his shortwave radio. His contact would be waiting for an update. "Teague, are you there?"

"Yo." Izzy Teague's voice was clear, despite an edge of static. "I've got the topo map on the screen in front of me. I checked with SAR and got the coordinates. You'll have a straight ascent for an hour, followed by a fairly strenuous climb through shifting rock when you near the south face. A chopper is on its way over from the mainland, but the weather may prevent a landing until tomorrow."

"So I'm on my own," Dakota said calmly. "Fine with me. I don't need anyone slowing me down or asking questions."

"Watch out for yetis up there," Izzy said wryly. "I'll keep a bottle of Glenlivet on ice for you."

"You do that. Alpha out."

The dark face of Blaven was veiled in clouds as Nell set off up the rocky trail. The Land Rover headed down to the inn. The first wet flakes of gale-driven snow lashed at Dakota's face as he started up toward Blaven's brooding darkness, Nell already out of sight before him.

FOR SOME REASON she couldn't shake the sense that she was being followed. For the third time Nell stopped, peering through fingers of clouds, looking for other climbers behind her.

Only rocky slopes met her sharp scrutiny.

Of course you're alone, idiot. Any climbers with good sense are inside huddled before a roaring fire right now.

But a climber didn't turn away in an emergency. Rules of the road.

Rules of life, too.

Turning back into the cutting wind, Nell nursed her aching right knee and chose each step, careful not to trigger a slide in the loose rock. Her face was cold, wet from the wind driving up from the sea. She estimated she'd reach the missing climbers' last coordinates in another twenty minutes. If the weather didn't shift, she could begin guiding them down off the peak immediately.

But Nell was prepared for a dozen unknown variables from shattered morale to shattered ankles. Any one of them could hamper a fast descent.

No point tilting at windmills, MacInnes. Every rescue was different, so she'd tackle each obstacle as it appeared. She eased her pack lower on her shoulders, trying to stay loose.

Once again she was struck by the twitchy feeling that someone was down the slope in shadow.

Watching her.

Blaven face.
One hour before sunset.

WIND STRUCK Dakota's face.

Icy rain howled over the cliff overlooking the dark face of the Sea of Hebrides.

Visibility was down to zero and already the storm was driving intermittent gusts of nearly sixty miles per hour.

Over the slope Nell MacInnes had made contact with the frightened climbers. Thanks to the howl of the wind, Dakota could only pick up one word in three, but from what he heard, Nell was dealing with the rescue quickly and by the book.

She assessed injuries, boosted morale and passed out dry trail rations and chocolate, then radioed down to the SAR leader to have transport with a medical team waiting at the foot of the mountain. The climbers were teenagers from an international school in London, and their leader, a burly ex-naval officer from Brighton, was clearly out of his element. Why he had tried the ascent was still unclear, but Dakota knew the speed of weather changes on Skye could take anyone by surprise.

Dakota fingered his transmitter. "Alpha to Teague."

Instantly static crackled. "Pizza to go. What can I get you, Alpha?"

"I figure a large cheese with double pepperoni is out," Dakota said dryly. "So I'll settle for backup medical response at the lower trailhead. One girl up here has full-blown asthma with signs of respiratory distress. One of the boys has a broken arm."

"Roger that. I'll wander on by to help and make sure it looks like a coincidence. What about the other climbers?"

"There are six in all, plus their leader, Ian Westlake. He might have had a heart attack. He's holding on, but he's no help to anyone. Nell's going to try guiding the able ones down and I'm going to meet her on the slope to help out."

"Copy that. Better get the lead out, Alpha. That storm is picking up speed."

Bad news, Dakota thought. "Roger. I'll check back in ten. Alpha out."

The SEAL stared across the slope. To his right a steep cliff fell away in a vertical drop straight down to the loch. To his left a lower ridge vanished into the notched teeth of the Cuillin range.

There would be no climbing down tonight.

They were on their own. No rescue chopper could land in this wind, even if any were available in this remote corner of Skye. Dakota had to help Nell hold the kids together, dig in on the ledge for the night and wait out the storm.

In exactly eight minutes he rounded a turn and saw the little group, huddled beneath a ledge. Nell was snapping out crisp orders to a gangly teenager in a brand new parka.

"Hamilton, get your pack lashed over that boulder. Then I want you and Meyerson inside your tent in sixty seconds."

"Yes, sir. I mean ma'am."

Once the boy's pack was secure, he joined his terrified partner in the tent that had been pitched and tethered around stones in the lee of the wind.

What lee there was.

Another icy gust pounded over the ridge.

"Wu, secure your tent. Hernandez, get that lantern ready to help him."

Dakota watched Nell work beside the kids, making temporary shelter. She was using their last names, which created distance and the comfort of hierarchy, making orders easier to give and follow.

He noted that two other boys were working to

secure another tent to nearby boulders, with packs tied down near the tent entrance.

"Good job," Nell called. "Now all of you get inside."

So where were the wounded kids? Dakota wondered.

A tent flap opened. A slim girl crawled out, looking for Nell. "I found that radio you asked about, ma'am. "It's—"

"Wilson, go back inside and take cover. This wind is—"

The rest of Nell's order was swept away in an icy gust that screamed over the ridge, caught two unsecured backpacks and threw them into the teenage girl, knocking her into a spine of sharp granite. As her scream was swallowed by the wind, Dakota dove forward and caught her waist, pulling her away from the cliff edge. She moaned brokenly as he lifted her into his arms. Blood streamed over his fingers from a gash down the side of her forehead. Dakota noted her erratic pulse and diminished pupil response.

Neck wound and probable concussion. Internal injuries were also possible.

"Who the heck are you?" Nell blocked his way, looking angry and wary and relieved, all at the same time.

"I was climbing over on the far side of Blaven when I picked up a distress alert from the local SAR. I changed route, circled the corrie and came up to see if you needed help."

Nell bit her lip, studying him intently. "You're American."

"Navy." Dakota gave a wry smile. "This was supposed to be a little holiday until I'm redeployed out of Coronado. I wasn't counting on the weather going all to hell."

Nell seemed to relax slightly. "It does that a lot here on Skye. So you're a good climber? Can you help me get these kids down?"

"I'll do whatever I can. Say the word." Dakota frowned. "You're up here alone?"

"Yeah, I am. Look—it's a long story and I don't have time to fill in the gaps. I'm Nell MacInnes."

"Lieutenant Dakota Smith."

"Well, Lieutenant Smith. You can put Amanda Wilson inside this tent." As she pointed to her right, wet sheeting snow cut off every sign of the terrain. "All of you stay in your tents and keep your backs to the rock. No one moves. Hammond, get that flap closed."

Dakota checked his watch as the teens obeyed Nell's terse commands. She had chosen the camp site well, bunkered down under a ledge in the narrow rift between two cliff faces.

The teenagers looked cold and confused as Nell went from tent to tent, giving calm orders. "Remember, you are fit and you are smart. We *will* survive this. Lieutenant Smith out there is going to help us."

"But what about Amanda?" A younger girl cut in,

her voice shrill with panic. "She hit her head. Is she going to be ok?"

"She'll pull through." Dakota's voice was firm as he set the girl carefully in the tent Nell had pointed out. Despite his assurances, he knew the girl was far from safe. If she had internal injuries, she might not last the night without medical intervention.

Briefly, he considered packing the wounded girl into an improvised travois and pulling her down as soon as visibility returned. But that would leave Nell alone in deteriorating conditions—and protecting Nell was his mission priority.

FUBAR.

As he rose from the tent, the wind howled over the ridge. Nell staggered, tossed sideways, and Dakota caught her quickly, his arms locked around her waist.

He felt the strength of her slim body as she fought the wind, trying to stand. "Thanks," she rasped. "We'd better get inside."

Beneath her safety helmet her eyes were calm and dark, the color of racing gray water through the mountains near his home back in northern California. As the two squeezed inside the tent next to the girl named Amanda, Dakota pulled a silver thermal blanket out of his backpack. "Looks like you could use this. The girl's shivering. She doesn't seem to be breathing very well either."

"Asthma." Nell spread the blanket over the girl's body and tucked it in. "Thanks again, Lieutenant—"

"Dakota will do fine."

"Don't suppose you've got a few other seasoned climbers with you who could help guide these kids down?"

"Afraid not. I'm traveling alone."

Nell glanced at him intently. "Not many people I know climb alone." She raised an eyebrow, waiting for his answer.

"If I wanted noise and crowds, I would have stayed in London," he said easily. "I prefer climbing alone."

She nodded. "I can understand that." She unclipped a rope from her belt and wrapped it in neat coils, every movement smooth and precise.

She was definitely a professional, Dakota thought. He gave a small nod toward the motionless girl and her friend at the other side of the tent. "She needs care. The sooner the better."

"Tell me something I don't know," Nell muttered. She turned to the other frightened teen, made a little light banter, then leaned back toward Dakota. She studied his shoulders, his high-tech boots and climbing gear. "How good are you, Lieutenant?"

"Good enough." There was no empty boasting, just cool truth in the words.

"Then you can help me rope a safety line?"

Dakota shook his head. "Maybe you haven't looked outside. This storm is gaining steam. I heard that sixty-mile-an-hour gusts were clocked near Portee. With windchill factored in, we—"

"We're screwed," Nell said quietly. "I got that much already. Right now as I see it, our only choice is to get these kids down as soon as possible. They're not dressed for a night of wet, freezing conditions." Short copper hair tumbled around her flushed cheeks as she leaned down to check Amanda Wilson's pulse.

Dakota had seen that hair before. He'd seen her excited and tired. But he'd never seen her so focused or so worried, as if these kids really mattered to her. Somehow it didn't fit with the thrill-seeker image captured in her file.

But what she was suggesting was one step short of crazy.

"You can't get them down in a whiteout. One wrong step and they plunge into freefall, and you'll go over with them." Dakota kept his voice low so the other girls wouldn't hear. "We'll have to stay put."

Nell looked down at the girl named Amanda, whose breathing was growing more labored. "I know a way. This ridge leads down to a back route. If you help me, I can set a safety line in fifteen minutes. I can get them down one at a time after that."

"How?"

"I'll clip each one into a harness, secure them into the safety line and work back down to the mid-peak."

"You've got only an hour of light left, and that will be pushing it."

Dakota stared out the tent flap at the gray slope.

He didn't like the risks—not for Nell or the stranded kids. "Have you ever handled a rescue like this?"

"At least a dozen times. A lot of climbers get cocky and forget that the weather up here can change on a dime. But I can get four of these kids down to the SAR meeting point. Trust me, I know this area pretty well." Her mouth curved in a sudden smile, and Dakota blinked at the force of the determination. Did *anyone* say no to Nell MacInnes?

The danger didn't seem to bother her, and her choices seemed logical. A good leader took controlled risks as necessary.

Dakota couldn't help but admire her courage and her skill.

"I've got a radio for contact. I've also got this." Nell pulled a silver whistle from inside her parka. "The SAR people will be expecting an alert once I'm close to the bottom of the safety line. I'll hand off each teenager and then head back up." She smiled gamely and gave an experimental whistle. "But if we're going to do this, it has to be now."

Dakota had to admit that her plan made sense, especially since staying put offered a risk of exposure and hypothermia.

But habit was habit. A SEAL never trusted any plan he hadn't tested himself. Watching on the sidelines wasn't in a SEAL's job description.

He had to keep Nell safe.

But he couldn't let any of these kids die in the process.

He watched Nell slide her climbing rope through her fingers, testing each coil. The fibers were smooth with no frays, clearly well tended.

She tugged on fingerless climbing gloves, looking impatient. "Look, Lieutenant—"

"Dakota."

"We have to move, Dakota. In twenty minutes we really will be boxed in here. Do you want to save these kids or not?"

"I want to see *all* of you get down safely."

"Don't worry about me. Last year I took third at Chamonix. That's an open climb with professionals—both men and women."

"But you were probably climbing in good weather, fully roped and hydrated." He glanced back and lowered his voice. "These kids are frightened and near the end of their endurance."

"I'll get them down the ridge. My safety line will hold, trust me." Nell leaned closer, her voice falling. "Otherwise we could lose them up here in the cold."

Dakota listened to the howl of the wind beyond their narrow, protected ridge. It was a perilous point of safety, one that would vanish as the temperature fell and the poorly dressed group of kids faced hypothermia. With gale-force winds in a whiteout, the disoriented teens could crack at any minute, driven by panic to do something stupid.

He was trained to be flexible, and he did that now, assessing the choices and the risks. As wind roared over the ridge, Dakota made his decision.

He zipped up his parka. "Show me where you want to set this safety line."

CHAPTER TWO

NELL SHIVERED IN THE biting wind, painfully aware that every second they were losing light.

So far she had managed to guide three of the teens down, turning them over to the Scottish SAR people at the waist of the mountain. The fourth one was clipped in and ready to escort down.

But conditions were getting risky. In a few minutes all light would be gone.

She rechecked all the carabiners and anchors, then gave a reassuring smile to the gangly boy who was watching her in abject adoration. "You'll be fine, Jess. Just keep breathing and count your steps the way I told you. Stay cool and stay focused. I'll be on the rope right in front of you, so don't crowd me. Can you do all that?"

"I—yes." He tried to hide his fear. "Let's go."

Nell touched his face and held his gaze with the force of her own. "You're going to survive this, Jess. The other three are down and you're next. Just do what I told you and you'll be fine."

"You—you're amazing." The boy gripped the

safety line with both hands, but his gaze was locked on Nell. "I thought we were all dead, but you walked out of the rain like some kind of angel."

"I'm glad I was around to help."

"What about Amanda? Is she going to make it through this?"

He was a nice kid, Nell thought. They all were. None of them were going to die, she vowed. Not while she had hands to knot a rope and lungs to breathe in icy air.

She checked that all the carabiner gates were fully closed and secure, then gave the boy a jaunty smile. "No offense taken. Now get yourself down to the inn and warm up. They'll have a fire and dry clothes ready. Drinks tonight in the pub are on me. Cokes, of course."

He smiled crookedly. "I'll be waiting. You couldn't keep me away."

Nell looked down into the swirling blanket of clouds and gave two short bursts on her whistle. Seconds later she heard the faint answering notes from the SAR people waiting at the end of the safety line, followed by the answering whistle from her climbing partner lower down the slope.

Then a gust of wind slammed over the cliff face and she forgot everything but keeping her footing as darkness closed in around them.

WHAT THE HELL was taking her so long?

Dakota stood at the top of the safety line and

checked the luminous dial of his watch. Nell had been gone almost twenty minutes.

He fought an urge to go in search of her, but he needed to go back to keep an eye on Amanda, who had roused once, asked for water, then slipped back into unconsciousness, struggling for breath.

Asthma and possible internal bleeding, with hypothermia a distinct risk. In addition, the British tour leader had nausea, sweating and crushing chest pains that radiated down his left arm, clear indicators of a heart attack. Dakota had given him a small aspirin to chew, followed by sublingual nitro, but the man didn't look good.

He couldn't afford to lose Nell in the storm, the SEAL thought grimly.

He stared down at the safety line, thinking about the night two weeks earlier when a Renaissance masterpiece worth thirty million dollars had disappeared from a locked vault....

Washington, DC
South Conservation Workroom of the National Gallery
Two weeks earlier

THE SECURITY LIGHTS BLINKED, a nonstop race of green against a high-tech control panel. The night guard, fresh from six years at the Metropolitan Museum in New York, reached for his log sheet to verify a completed security cycle.

Even then his eyes didn't leave the sleek security panel, where half a dozen cameras picked up deserted hallways and an empty loading dock. Two floors above, Rogers walked the offices, checking every door. At the end of the hall he used his passkey to call the elevator, then continued on his rounds.

The night was quiet and uneventful. Even the streets were calm, with no sirens for several hours. But the museum was on special security measures due to a new piece of art entered for appraisal. Only five people on the staff knew that the work was judged to be from the hand of Leonardo da Vinci, a Renaissance masterpiece that would command millions when it eventually went up for auction.

The air-conditioning clicked. The head guard, Everett Jonell, checked the control panel. Lights flickered briefly. The locked room with the new da Vinci blurred to gray.

Everett's hand went to the alarm.

Then the power came back on, with the hum of the HVAC restored. The row of monitors showed empty corridors. The door to the vault in south storeroom #3-A was locked as before.

Everett Jonell relaxed, leaning back in his chair. He felt sweat bead his forehead and shook his head. He'd be relieved when the art in storeroom #3-A was on its way and things settled back to normal. Until then, people would be edgy, under orders to report anything that seemed unusual.

On the black-and-white monitor, Jonell watched Rogers cross the big atrium and move toward the new sculpture wing. There was something off about the man. Two nights earlier Jonell had stopped at a small jazz club for a drink after work and he'd noticed Rogers getting out of a parked car across the street. The sleek black Mercedes M-Class sedan had seemed way above Rogers's pay grade, so Jonell had made a point of checking out the driver and noting the license plate.

He'd been surprised to see one of the senior curators emerge, a slender workaholic from Harvard who never went anywhere without her cell phone headset in place. There were no explicit rules forbidding social contact between security and academic staff, but you didn't see it happen just the same. Different worlds, different goals, Jónell thought. But the way the curator had plastered herself all over Rogers as they'd kissed long and intimately in the shadows across the street had Jonell scratching his head.

Maybe you never knew what made people tick. After twelve years in the Marines he'd seen a lot of things and figured he was a good judge of people. Rogers seemed like an okay guy, but it wasn't up to Jonell to judge.

He'd report what he'd seen to the head of museum personnel, just in case. Until the da Vinci in storeroom #3-A left the premises safely, they would all be under extra scrutiny and Jonell wasn't risking his job and a nice pension for anything. Not with a new grandbaby on the way and three more years until Medicare kicked in.

He frowned as he saw Rogers reach into his pocket and pull out a cell phone.

A personal call? What was the man doing? He knew that personal cell phone use was forbidden during work hours for security. Now Jonell would have to write the man up, which involved reports in triplicate and copies to both union representatives.

Blast the man. Didn't he know that the video cameras would pick him up?

The monitors flickered again and the HVAC clicked off. Lightning crackled high overhead, the sound muffled by the museum's thick walls.

Jonell sat forward as all the monitors went dark. Cursing, he lunged for the security phone, but the line was dead. He grabbed the battery-powered walkie-talkie to put in a radio alert to the general switchboard, standard procedure, even though a backup generator would kick in shortly.

The movement came from his left and he dropped the walkie-talkie as a leather strap locked him to the chair, his hands caught behind his back. He struggled against cool fingers that gripped his neck.

"No, you can't—"

The needle prick came quickly, burning against the inside of his nose, which made no sense at all. The room blurred and he tried to speak as he heard the sound of the security panel door being unlocked. Someone was removing the surveillance board timer, he realized. Blurring fingers ejected the surveillance disk.

It had all been planned to the second, Jonell thought dimly. Planned by someone on the inside.

Was it Rogers? Another one of the new guards they had hired in the past month?

He moaned, caught by crushing pain at his chest. As his body went slack, Everett Jonell realized that he'd never see the new grandbaby or his wife or his proud daughter again. The sorrow was the last thing he felt.

Six minutes, fifteen seconds to go.

The figure at the security command post inserted a new time stamp digitally at the security panel, typing in a string of computer code. Then he pocketed the old surveillance disk and inserted a new one, already formatted and complete with museum images calibrated to the current time stamp. Nothing had been left to chance.

Nudging his boss's lifeless body onto the floor, the figure finished his disk exchange and then checked the black-and-white images that appeared on the row of monitors.

All good to go.

He opened his cell phone, dialed a number and hung up after one ring.

Though the far monitor showed no activity, he knew that someone was carefully easing open the door of storeroom #3-A at that very moment.

He closed his eyes, savoring his memory of the exquisite chalk sketch of the most famous woman on the planet.

Thanks to his discreet program override, the monitor display would loop back with preset images and movements timed to coincide with normal museum patterns. After the thorough infrared assessments that had just been completed, no new tests on the art were scheduled for thirty-six hours. Only at that point would the theft be discovered.

By then, da Vinci's preparatory ink and chalk study for the *Mona Lisa* would be safely locked in a vault, ready for covert transport out of the U.S.

He checked his watch.

Three minutes, twenty-two seconds to go. Calmly he lifted Jonell's fallen walkie-talkie and studied its face. Everything appeared to be in working order, he was happy to see.

His cell phone buzzed quietly, one burst and then no more.

All clear.

Target acquired and clues in place. Ready to exit the building. Everything was moving nicely ahead of schedule.

He thought briefly about the funds that would be wired to four of his offshore accounts by this time tomorrow. Maybe he'd buy that island in the Seychelles after all. It was remote enough and there was a fresh water source as well as a sizable bungalow with upgraded docks.

He shoved away the thought. There was still risky work to be done. In two minutes he would phone in an emergency call notifying the switchboard of Everett Jonell's collapse, sounding suitably shocked and upset. Once his regular shift was complete, he would drive to the short-term apartment that he leased in northern Maryland under one of his many other names. Once there he would collect the carefully wrapped piece of art. After the transfer was done, he would follow his normal schedule with no deviation.

He'd even attend Everett Jonell's funeral and offer deep and sincere condolences to his wife.

He'd stay in place after the theft was discovered, monitoring progress on the investigation inside the museum. In six months he would resign quietly, pleading health problems, and then vanish completely.

He glanced at his watch.

Showtime.

He took a deep breath, schooling his features to a frown. When he triggered the walkie-talkie alert, the alarm in his voice was deeply convincing.

"Command post one. Guard down. I repeat— *guard down!* Backup needed immediately."

He was kneeling over Jonell's lifeless body, looking pale and agitated, when the first security patrol car screamed up the museum's back service drive.

CHAPTER THREE

DAKOTA WATCHED A SMALL shape appear out of the windblown snow. Relief kicked in when he saw Nell wave one hand in a brief thumbs-up gesture.

She looked like hell, he thought. Her hair was flecked with frozen snow. She had mud on her gloves and a welt across one cheek.

"Amanda's stable," Dakota said, catching the anxious glance Nell sent to the first tent. "The group leader needs hospital care, but he's finally calm, which won't create such an oxygen debt. Go inside. You need to rest."

Nell looked exhausted as she crawled into the second tent, snow swirling up behind her. She pulled off her climbing gloves and flexed her hands. Her teeth began to chatter. "There's more snow on its way. I can feel the moisture. In icy conditions—"

Without a word Dakota unzipped his parka and pulled it around her shoulders.

She stiffened and tried to push away his hands. "What are you doing? I can't take this. What about *you*?"

"I'll be fine. I've got excellent cold tolerance. You need this more than I do right now."

She started to protest, but Dakota cut her off.

"How did it go?" He held out a canteen with water, taken from his pack.

Nell took a drink, then handed back the canteen. "They'll be fine. A doctor was waiting at the inn." Her voice tightened. "The last trips down were pretty bad. The wind—" She closed her eyes, hunching over to cough sharply.

"Let it go, Nell," Dakota leaned over and zipped his parka around her trembling body. "You've done all you can. Once the weather clears, a chopper will be dispatched for Amanda and the group leader."

Nell nodded slowly, but her body remained tense. She didn't seem to notice when Dakota pulled a second thermal blanket around her and tucked it into the rope wrapped around her waist.

"How do you let it go?" She shivered, ran a hand across her cheek and stared at a line of dried blood covering her palm. "The last boy, Jess, panicked and he was going to let go of the rope. If he had, I would have lost him. No doubt about it. And it was so *close*."

Dakota heard the horror that she had tried to hide beneath anger. "Nell, you did everything right. Let it go."

"I *can't*."

Dakota was acutely aware of her scent and the sounds of her breathing as he pulled her slowly toward his chest. He told himself the gesture was entirely impersonal, meant to drive off her panic and uncertainty.

She'd just completed one of the riskiest rescues he'd ever encountered, but even strong people had limits, and Nell MacInnes was at her own personal boundary. Dakota didn't wait for more arguments, didn't try to reason or explain. He pulled her against his chest, sliding her thighs around his waist. His hands moved under her jacket, massaging her back and shoulders for warmth and circulation.

He was keenly aware of her hair, pressed against his cheek. In different circumstances he might have turned his head to taste the smooth line of her throat and test the full curve of her mouth with his lips.

Very bad idea. Here and now there was no place for emotion or desire. She was his mission.

Their eyes met. She shivered and studied his face as if she'd seen something there that she couldn't understand.

She looked down and seemed to realize how her legs were wrapped around his waist.

With a low gasp, she tried to pull away.

Dakota held her right where she was. "Don't fight me, Nell. We need to stay warm. Now close your eyes and rest. I'll keep an eye on things."

"Why should I trust you?" she whispered.

"Because right here, right now, I'm all you've got," Dakota said gruffly. As he wrapped the thermal foil blanket around them, the wind howled out in the darkness.

OKAY, THE MAN was tough and he thought on his feet. Calm under pressure, he had a way of moving in and taking charge before you realized what was happening.

But Nell wasn't a skittish child and she didn't take orders from strangers.

She yawned. Even as she struggled to keep her eyes open, she couldn't ignore the hard lines of Dakota Smith's thighs. The man had a great body, and the warm strength of his arms was like a dangerous drug.

She felt the hammer of his heart beneath her cheek, felt the rise and fall of his broad chest. Even his scent teased her, a blend of salty air, sweat and heather.

As he stretched slightly, Nell felt his thighs tighten against her, and his arms shifted to hold her steady. Though they were thigh to thigh, chest to chest, he didn't brush her breasts or make suggestive comments.

Life seemed small and very fragile as they waited out the storm's fury. Idly Nell rubbed her elbow, which had begun to ache. Might as well try to sleep until the storm ended, since they were going nowhere.

She closed her eyes, feeling her hips slide over his thigh. The man had excellent thighs, too.

Maybe sleep wasn't going to be so easy.

"So what do you do when you're not on a climbing vacation?" she muttered. Anything to distract her from the feel of his lean, sculpted muscles.

"My job keeps me busy."

"Before we went down, Jess told me that you're a SEAL. I've never seen a kid in such an advanced state of hero worship. This is probably a walk in the park for you, Lieutenant."

"I never take any threat for granted," he said roughly. "That includes weather and people."

Was there an edge in his voice? Nell opened one eye, but in the darkness she couldn't read his expression.

His arm cradled her head. His chest was warm and he seemed calm, but absolutely distant.

Probably she'd been wrong about the edge in his voice.

Quietly, he slid free. "Time to check on Amanda."

He was gone before Nell could offer to go with him.

"How is she?" Nell was feeling a little blurry. Actually a *lot* blurry. A wave of dizziness hit her. She had forgotten the adrenaline spikes of rescue work—and the inevitable crash.

"Her pulse is stronger. Right now I'll take small favors. The cardiac patient is holding on, too." With economical movements, Dakota sat down and drew her against him, covering them both.

Nell tried to focus, but the growl of the wind was distracting. "So what made you decide to be a hero, Lieutenant?"

"I just happened to be around when you needed me. It's nothing heroic."

Nell studied his face as he switched on a small

penlight. "When did you start your climb? I never saw you before today." She angled her head, trying to read the expression in his eyes. The man didn't reveal anything, she thought irritably.

"I arrived yesterday. I've been on the move."

It made sense. As he pulled her closer, the soothing warmth of his body made her relax.

The man would make a fantastic climbing partner, she decided.

The penlight flashed off. Rough fingers opened on her hair. "What are you thinking about?"

"I figure you have great deltoids," Nell said sleepily. "That's always the first thing I look for in a man."

"You look for his deltoids?" He sounded amused.

"Absolute first thing." Nell yawned. "Always look for the deltoids. Best way to judge climbing strength. How long can you hang, hands only, unassisted?"

"Seventy-one minutes." His breath was warm against her ear. "More or less."

Even in a growing haze of cold and exhaustion, Nell was impressed. "*No way*. Not for over an hour." Nobody could do that. At least nobody that *she* knew.

"I could be lying," he said calmly.

Nell didn't think so. He didn't strike her as the type for casual boasts. In fact, *nothing* about the man seemed casual. "What exactly do you *do* in the navy?"

"This and that. Nothing you'd be interested in." His hands slid slowly into her hair. Nell felt the strands spill over his fingers.

At every movement, she was stunned to feel little

jolts of desire. The heat grew where their bodies were joined.

Crazy. They were camped out on the edge of a cliff and he was a complete stranger.

But the heat didn't go away. His hands kept moving, slow and thoughtful, until Nell thought she'd scream.

Or curl up against his chest and sigh in noisy pleasure.

She frowned. She knew better than to relax or trust a stranger even if the gentle motion of his hands *was* hypnotic. "The tents are taking a beating. I need to go check to see if they—"

"Already done. The lines you rigged are solid. Nice work."

"Two of my best ropes are out there," she said sleepily. "I've got trail mix and three protein bars in my left pocket," she added. "Take them if you need to."

"I'll be fine. Go to sleep, Nell."

She wasn't used to being taken care of. It had been years since her father—

Don't go there.

The past was a sinkhole filled with bad memories. And this man was still a stranger. She wiggled, trying to find a position that wasn't starkly intimate, with their shoulders touching and their thighs locked together for warmth. Finally she gave up.

It was just one night, after all. She'd never see this man and his gorgeous, powerful body again. There was no chance for mingled laughter or shared secrets.

And that was *exactly* the way Nell wanted it.

She twisted her body, shoving away his hands as she closed her eyes. "Just don't get any ideas while I'm asleep," she said huskily. "That cliff wall is only a few feet away. You wouldn't like the drop."

She thought she heard his quiet laugh before she drifted off with the howl of the wind in her ears.

NELL FELT the wind in her hair.

Hands sweaty, she was chalking up before her last climb of the day. The sun lay hot and heavy on her shoulders in a band of liquid gold. Body straining, muscles in the flow while Yosemite spread out like a Technicolor postcard.

Beautiful.

Then the sudden hiss of falling rope. A violent jerk as a cam broke free, slamming her into a wall of granite, breaking her nose and cheekbone, blood gushing onto her neck.

The sound of her own scream jerked her upright in the icy darkness.

"Nell, wake up."

Lines broken. Carabiners blown. Falling, falling...

"Hey, wake up." Hard hands locked around her shoulders.

She fought blindly, her nails raking warm skin.

Panic. Falling...

"Stop fighting, Nell. It's Dakota. You're just dreaming. Something about Yosemite, but it's over now. Calm down and breathe."

Breathe.

Nell forced her muscles to loosen.

Just another dream. Always about falling, somewhere alone in the darkness...

She took a deep breath and shoved a damp clump of hair from her eyes. "Okay, back among the living—more or less. Thanks for the wake-up call. What time is it anyway?"

"Almost five. Should be light soon. You okay now?"

Nell straightened the small light clipped to her belt. "Great," she said through clenched teeth.

"You keep that light with you all the time?"

"When I'm next to a three-thousand-foot drop, I do. In case you didn't notice, that first step can be really unpleasant." Nell slanted her small light through the tent. "How is she?"

"No change. Stable and warm."

"Westlake, our fearless tour leader?"

"Asleep, last time I checked."

Nell frowned. "What about you? Don't *you* ever rest?"

"I closed my eyes for a few minutes. It's all I need." His hands smoothed the thermal blanket around her shoulders. "Do you always ask this many questions?"

"Yeah, I do. Call it terminal curiosity."

Amanda Wilson tossed in her sleep, and Dakota leaned down to check her pulse.

At his touch the teenager twisted, muttering hoarsely. "Mummy, you left the window open again.

It's so c-cold…" Then her eyes opened and she coughed, staring blankly up at Dakota. "My arm hurts." She craned her head anxiously from side to side. "Where are the others?"

"Back at the hotel. We'll get you there shortly." Dakota raised the tube of her hydration pack. "How about you drink a little water?"

"How long have we been up here?"

"Most of the night." After Dakota helped Amanda drink, he pulled the silver blanket back in place around her. "But the weather looks to be clearing. Just think of it this way. You're going to have a great story to tell all your friends."

The girl's lip quavered. "I want to g-go home."

"We'll get you there," Nell said firmly. "We're going to watch the wall and make it through this."

Amanda took a labored breath. "Is that what you do?"

"Sometimes life gets messy and complicated, but I don't look down and I don't look back." Nell's voice was flat.

She sensed that Dakota was studying her. "Something wrong?"

"I didn't say anything."

"You were *thinking* plenty loud, Navy."

Across the tent Amanda giggled. "She's got you there. You do seem kind of—intense. I guess that's a navy thing."

Dakota moved to help her drink some more water.

"What, can't a man enjoy the company of two gorgeous women in peace?"

The teenager wheezed out a laugh. "Very funny."

Over the howl of the wind, motors droned closer. Nell could see the dim pattern of light around the flap of the tent. "They'll have to land below the ridge. Someone needs to guide the rescue team up." Nell pushed to her knees and grabbed her climbing gear.

"Sure you're up to it?" Dakota asked quietly.

Nell shoved a coiled rope over her shoulder. "No offense, Navy, but I think I'm the best guy for the job."

His expression was unreadable as he reached out and brushed one finger along the corner of her lips. It was almost as if he was memorizing her smile, Nell thought.

Then his expression hardened. "I hate to admit that you're right. Watch your six out there. The wind's still stiff."

"SHE'S REALLY great, isn't she?" Amanda was watching the spot where Nell had disappeared. "I don't think anything in the world frightens her. I wish I was that way."

Dakota listened to the chopper approach. "You never can tell what makes people tick. I think Nell enjoys the thrill of being in danger. Besides, you're pretty brave yourself. You took a real beating."

The teenager shrugged. "Not like you two. So why don't you *like* her? I mean, you smile at her, but it never quite reaches your eyes."

The girl was a little too observant, Dakota thought irritably. "Nothing wrong with Nell MacInnes. I like her fine." He just didn't *trust* her.

"How's Ian doing? Is he…" Her voice trailed away.

"He's still alive." Barely, Dakota thought. "That's a helicopter coming in out there. With luck, you'll be down at the hotel in ten minutes. How do you feel?"

The girl swallowed hard. "Like I might throw up."

"I'll let you in on a secret." Dakota slanted her a quick smile. "Happens to the best of us."

The tent flap rose and Nell appeared, snow on her cheeks. "A team is headed up to hitch you into a sling, Amanda. Ready to go?"

"I guess so. You'll both go down with me, right?"

Dakota zipped up his pack. "You bet."

"Do you need any help in here?" Nell's climbing helmet was hanging over her shoulder and she was half-turned to the light, looking relieved that the ordeal was nearly over.

"Not a bit. I'll help Amanda outside and then go see if I can help them with Westlake."

Nell stuck out one hand. "Nice to meet you, Navy. You can climb with me anytime."

Dakota gripped her hand and studied her face, looking for traces of cunning or arrogance, but there was only excitement and a hint of a smile.

"I hear the girls are placing bets down at the inn."

"What kind of bets?"

"Whether or not your butt is as incredible as they

all think it is." She gave a wicked smile. "I'm guessing it is."

Dakota's brow rose. "I thought you were into deltoids."

Amanda gave up trying to hide her laughter. "Where *are* the deltoids?"

"Right here." Nell reached out and tapped Dakota's upper arms. "Something tells me these are pretty spectacular. Too bad I'm never going to find out."

"I'll show you mine, if you show me yours. Just name the time and the place," Dakota said huskily.

Nell's smiled faded. "I don't think so. Something tells me it would cost a lot more than I'm prepared to pay."

"How much are you prepared to pay?"

She studied him a long time. "I'm not sure. Whatever it is, you'd probably cost more. Watch yourself on the big walls, Lieutenant." She tossed a coiled rope over her shoulder and headed out into the cold gray light of dawn.

Dakota was still watching her as the snow swirled up and the rescue team appeared on the ridge below them.

CHAPTER FOUR

THIRTY MINUTES LATER the storm clouds had moved inland and Amanda Wilson and Ian Westlake had been transferred to a medical flight bound for Edinburgh. Now the rescue team was relaxing, glad that there had been a successful end to their dawn ascent.

Meanwhile, Dakota's Foxfire contact was waiting in a military helicopter on the far side of the loch. Izzy Teague was roughly six foot five and could have passed for Denzel Washington on Oscar night, but his grave eyes made him look older than his years. One of the government's finest security operatives, the man could assess photographs or triangulate cell phone positions faster than most people could breathe.

The chopper was quiet. Restless, Dakota drummed on the window, waiting for the pilot to return.

"Something wrong?" Teague opened his medical bag and pulled out a small metal case.

"Not a thing."

"Yeah? Then why are you scowling?"

Dakota shrugged.

"How's your hand?"

"Fine." Dakota didn't look up, intent on stowing his gear. He especially refused to look around in hopes of seeing Nell.

Teague glared at him. "Fine? You've got two lacerations that need sutures."

"Nothing that can't wait."

Izzy stared at him thoughtfully, then glanced down and made quick notes on the sleek laptop that was never far away. "How did that climbing gear work out?"

"The shoes get high marks. Solid traction and balance. The gloves were useless. No possible way to handle a weapon in them."

"I'll pass the word to Ryker and his science boys." Izzy gave a cocky smile. "Back to the drawing board on the gear." When Dakota didn't answer, Izzy raised an eyebrow. "Something eating you, Smith?"

"I'd like to get moving, that's all. Has my surveillance mission changed?" he asked quietly.

"First things first." Izzy's eyes narrowed as he held out a digital keypad. When he triggered a button, a row of lights flashed red-orange. "Before we leave, Ryker wants a medical update. Log in for *Madonna* and record your response times."

Madonna, as both men knew, was the code name for Dakota's unique visual skills, part of the biomedical program based at a top-secret government lab in New Mexico. Thanks to his extensive training and ongoing enhancements, the SEAL could see far beyond the normal spectrum into infrared, ultraviolet and thermal ranges. His skills offered unique applications for military surveillance in high-risk, fast-extraction situations.

But excellent was never enough for the head of the Foxfire program. A cold, untrusting bureaucrat, Lloyd Ryker demanded constant updates on all his assets.

"*Madonna* is doing just fine." Coolly Dakota logged onto the handheld unit and ripped through the tests, shifting easily from light source to light source. Like every man handpicked for the elite Foxfire team, Dakota liked difficult challenges, and he always played to win.

Izzy watched the lights flash, scoring Dakota's speed. "Want to tell me about Nell MacInnes?"

"Not much to tell. She saved those kids, no doubt about it." Dakota started to add a character assessment but decided against it. Saying more would amount to empty speculation.

"Did she say anything useful? Any comments about her father or her future plans?"

"We didn't get around to trading life stories," Dakota said flatly. "There was a gale up on the summit, if you recall. And now maybe you'll let me concentrate here."

For some reason the questions about Nell irritated Dakota. When he was done with the test, he handed the unit back to Izzy.

Across the snowy field, Nell was talking animatedly to a man in a bright green parka and high tech climbing gloves. "Is that her partner?"

Izzy nodded. "He helped coordinate the rescue ascent. I understand he's climbed with Nell for almost twelve years."

Dakota watched the tall climber squeeze Nell's shoulder. "Are they sleeping together?"

"He's married with two kids."

"Which means nothing," Dakota said curtly. "Married men can screw around as much as single men."

Nell laughed at something her partner said, and for some reason that irritated Dakota, too.

"My research says no. The relationship is strictly about climbing."

"Any sign that he's involved in the theft?"

"I've got him on the radar in case of anything out of the expected. He's had no large bank deposits that would indicate unusual payments." Izzy closed the digital unit and stowed it in a case.

"Neither did Nell." Dakota rubbed his shoulder idly. "Maybe he's being careful."

"I'll handle him. Right now I want you to calm down and rest."

"I'm not—"

"Of course you are. You've been wound up tight ever since you got down. I checked out Amanda

Wilson and gave her one of the field hydration lines before she was flown out. You could use one too."

"I'm fine, Teague."

"Can it." Izzy slipped a syringe expertly into Dakota's arm. "There's a serious nutrient boost in that line. Shut up and let it take effect." Dakota muttered something gruff that made Izzy laugh. "I doubt that's physically possible, my friend, and I don't intend to find out."

As the liquid dripped into his arm, Dakota's gaze slid restlessly over the lower glen. He couldn't seem to stop thinking about Nell. What made her tick and how many secrets was she hiding? Both questions were suddenly very important.

Izzy followed Dakota's gaze. "What's eating at you?"

"Nell. She doesn't add up, Izzy, and I don't like things that don't add up." He took one last look across the loch, where Nell was laughing with her partner, piling ropes in a canvas bag.

The woman had guts to spare and a quick, clever brain. If things had been different he would have enjoyed a little recreational climbing with her. They could start on a cove in Thailand near the South China Sea.

A beach where clothing was optional sounded good.

The thought of Nell in a tiny string bikini—and no top—made muscles tighten all over Dakota's body. He let the 3-D fantasy smolder.

And then he put the thought away.

Never gonna happen, pal. She's the target and you're too smart to forget that.

Staying focused on the moment was the best way to stay alive.

Dakota's rules.

He glanced down at the sealed security file Izzy was holding out. "New developments?"

"An international terrorist group just took credit for the Smithsonian theft via the Internet. Ryker wants you fully briefed within the hour. The mission just got elevated to a level-four priority."

Dakota watched the loch glitter silver beneath them as the chopper pilot returned, squinting into the wind. "What group?"

"The October Twelfth Brigade. They've been on our watch list for almost two years now."

"That's the same group who claimed credit for the theft of the Rembrandt last year?"

"One and the same. The painting never resurfaced, and we assume it was sold clandestinely." Izzy's eyes hardened. "I don't need to tell you the money will be used in very unpleasant ways."

"How much money?"

"The da Vinci could bring somewhere in the area of thirty million dollars."

Dakota said something low and vicious.

"My sentiments exactly. Meanwhile, no more surveillance. Our new orders are to locate that piece of art and make certain it does not leave U.S. soil at any cost." He pointed to the file in Dakota's hand. "Read it. We have new information from a prison source that Jordan MacInnes is involved. You're to use Nell to locate the painting. Use her in any way that's necessary," Izzy said coldly. "Is that clear?"

"I TOLD YOU already. I'm fine."

Despite Nell's protests, a young med tech was scrubbing her hands with Betadine. When he pushed up her sleeve, she was surprised to see cuts and bruises covering her wrists. In all the chaos, she hadn't noticed.

"Bad night up there, I'm thinking. Nasty patch of weather you had." The tech glanced out at the remaining clouds that drifted across the dark summit of Blaven. "At least no one was killed."

"The cold was the worst part." Nell's teeth chattered a little. She was feeling dizzy, which irritated her. Fighting exhaustion, she rubbed her face with her free hand. "Where did my partner go?"

"He's helping to sort out the last kids. They're phoning their parents now."

"I should go help—"

"You'll stay right where you are. Your friend is managing fine."

Nell had trained with Eric and climbed with him

on three continents. They had shared dangerous conditions, then traded stories when they came down. And after that Eric went home to his beautiful, understanding wife and two kids back in Idaho.

End of story.

There was no other man in Nell's life.

Nell looked up as she heard the roar of a motor.

"One of the choppers is pulling out." The med tech glanced through the ambulance's rear window. "They seemed in quite a rush to leave, according to my crew. Your American climber was aboard."

Nell shifted, trying to look out the window, seeing Dakota's outline inside the helicopter. So he was gone. No farewells or an exchange of phone numbers, just a swift, silent departure.

Which was for the best, wasn't it? There had been something too physical and intense about Dakota Smith.

"Did you need to speak with him? You look upset."

Nell stared out at the dark peaks trapped in heavy clouds. "No. He's just someone I met up on the mountain."

Nell felt an odd punch at her chest as the dark chopper lifted off.

He could have said goodbye.

He could have found time for that.

Well, she didn't care one way or another.

"I hear you've climbed at Chamonix."

Nell nodded, trying to ignore the chopper as it droned past. She didn't let men into her life, not ever.

No trust.

No leaning.

MacInnes rules.

"I thought I recognized your name. You took third prize, didn't you?"

Nell nodded, barely listening. In the gray light the chopper's black body grew smaller.

"It makes you feel alive," the tech said quietly. "Nothing can touch you up there. You'd know that feeling, I guess."

Nell knew exactly what he meant. Her art restoration work kept her busy, but her climbing kept her sane. She had to admit that Dakota Smith would have made one heck of a climbing partner. Maybe he could have been something more.

Instantly she forced away the thought.

"By the way, did you get the messages?"

"Messages?"

"Your father has been trying to reach you. The manager of the inn asked us to tell you that he had called the hotel six times. He said it was urgent that you phone him as soon as you returned."

"Did he say *why*?"

"I'm afraid not. But I'm almost done here. Then I'll drive you down to the inn."

Nell felt an odd prickle at her neck. Her father

wouldn't have phoned her here unless it was something very serious. "You're sure he called six times?"

"That's what I was told."

Out over the Sea of Hebrides the big black helicopter thundered south and was swallowed up by the fog.

✦HQN™

We *are* romance™

HAPPY READING!

As part of our special sizzling summer reads offer, you can now **SAVE $1.00** on the purchase of **TO CATCH A THIEF** by *New York Times* bestselling author **Christina Skye,**

available in September wherever books are sold, including most bookstores, supermarkets, drugstores, department and discount stores.

If you've enjoyed this sizzling excerpt,
purchase the complete book

TO CATCH A THIEF

Available in September

by *New York Times* bestselling author

CHRISTINA SKYE

at Borders and **SAVE $1.⁰⁰**
on your purchase!

BORDERS.

PHCSBORDERSBPA